Children of the Forge

Book One of
The Chronicles of Avinol

MIKE ATCHLEY

Copyright © 2024 by Mike Atchley

All rights reserved. No part of this publication may be reproduced, distributed, or transmitted in any form or by any means, including photocopying, recording, or other electronic or mechanical methods, without the prior written permission of the publisher, except in the case of brief quotations embodied in critical reviews and certain other noncommercial uses permitted by copyright law.

Children of the Forge

BODA

SKA

STRATH

SIENNA

KUR

BLOODWO

THE MINE
OALLENAKAN

BELI

THE WINDMILL

PORT LTOR

TORMUNO
FIRST PORT

EMERALD ATOLL

To my family.

For putting up with a son, husband, and father always with his mind in clouds and daydreams.

May you now find joy in those same clouds and dream the same dreams.

Based on the Award Winning Podcast **"Dice Tower Theatre presents Dawn of Dragons"**

Written by Mike Atchley

"Avinol Poem" *by Daniel Nichols*
Cover Art *by Matthew "Little Bird" Baker*
Interior Art *by Storm S. Cone*
Editing *by Chelsey Hunninghake and Susan Thomas*

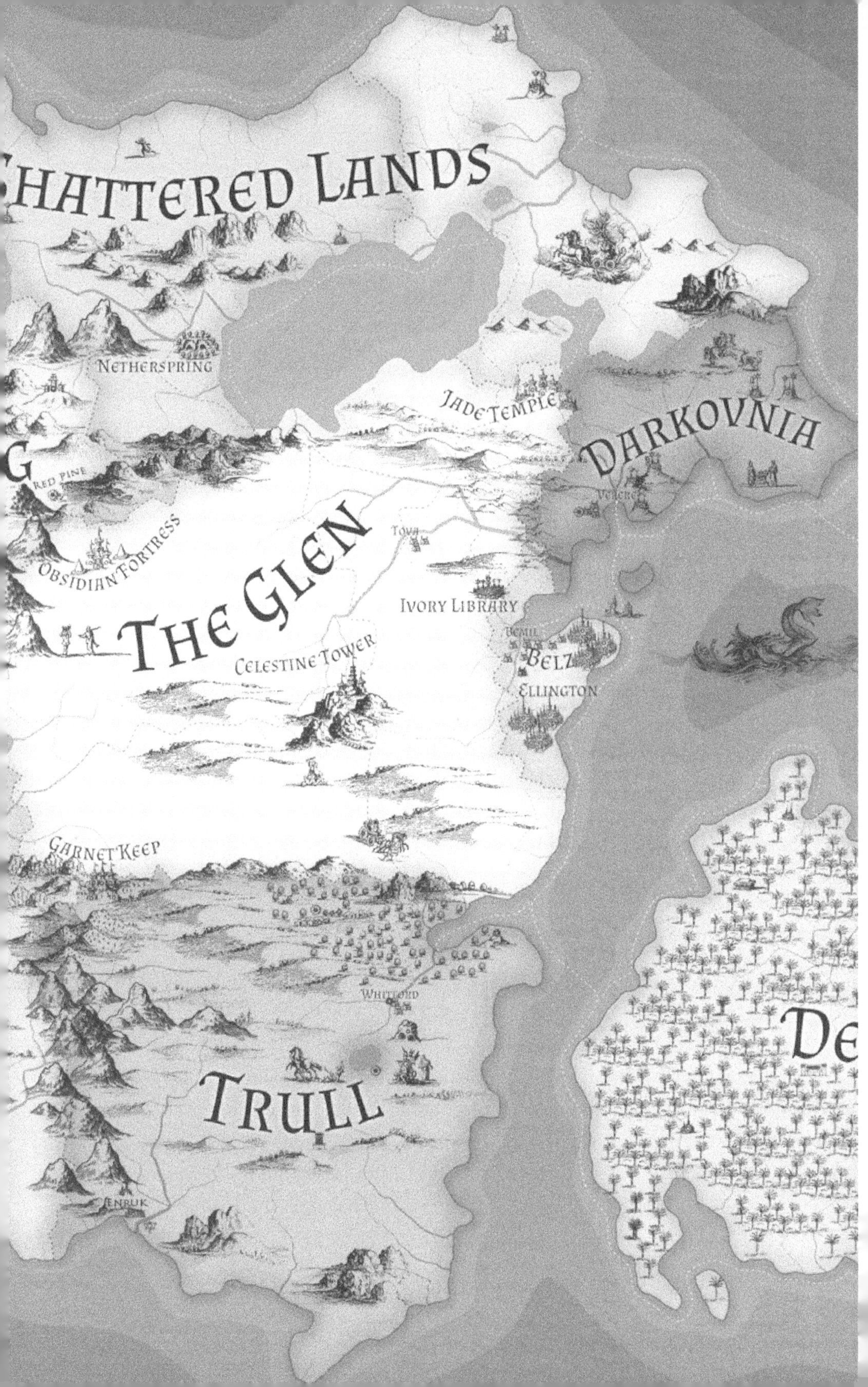
HATTERED LANDS
NETHERSPRING
JADE TEMPLE
DARKOVNIA
RED PINE
OBSIDIAN FORTRESS
THE GLEN
IVORY LIBRARY
CELESTINE TOWER
BELZ
ELLINGTON
GARNET KEEP
TRULL

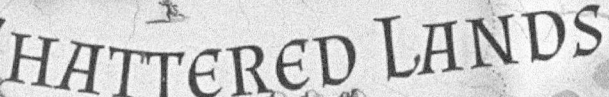

CONTENTS

PART 1 — 12

Chapter 1 – Fire and Forge ... 13
Chapter 2 – The Mine ... 25
Chapter 3 – The Crucible ... 37

PART 2 — 52

Chapter 1 – The Dawn ... 53
Chapter 2 – A Night to Remember ... 61
Chapter 3 – A Dark Reunion ... 73
Chapter 4 – Forest of Memories ... 83
Chapter 5 – To Find a Passage ... 93
Chapter 6 – An Unlikely Conversation ... 103
Chapter 7 – The Ivory Library ... 111
Chapter 8 – The Long Night ... 129
Epilogue ... 139

PART 3 140

   Chapter 1 – The Games 141

   Chapter 2 – The Baron 155

   Chapter 3 – The Deep 165

   Chapter 4 – Chains of Darkness 175

   Chapter 5 – City of the Great Forge 187

   Chapter 6 – The Prisoner in Ruby 197

   Chapter 7 – The Song in the Dream 211

   Chapter 8 – The Deep King 221

   Chapter 9 – The Promise 233

   Chapter 10 – The Six Winds 241

   Epilogue 251

Acknowledgements 253

About the Author 259

About the Podcast 261

"This way."

His voice was deep and resonant, reverberating from inside the powerfully built blackened chest plate. Charcoal gauze snaked up his arms, covering his skin as he pulled back the emerald and olive vines from the ancient carved stone entryway. An entryway that led to a forgotten temple, but one he knew. Stone carved from an ancient time when gods and man walked this place; when the halls of the temple were alive with the sounds of the holy people of the world leading others in worship of the four elements. He could smell incense in his mind but he knew it was only a trick, or possibly an echo of the past. No one had been here to worship in almost two millennia, he supposed, but he had found his own peace here.

He was shunned once, pushed from his tribe. An abomination.

He paused for a moment and listened to the soft wind in the jungle canopy mix with the distant howls of monkeys and birds calling to each other. In the days following his banishment, this dense and humid jungle was the familiar peace he called home away from their eyes and judgment. Isolation was harsh, but looking back seemed welcome when compared to the fiery hate that now passed through his heart.

He was a freak. He snickered at that thought. A monster. Behind the blackened steel helmet framing his glowing red eyes, he smiled. The twin forward-pointing horns of his helmet turned upward with his gaze, pointing at mist settling in the swamp as he looked above. The sun was getting low. They must hurry.

"Come, Maldros…you will bring me my freedom and, of course, you will have your revenge."

The raspy voice hissed in his mind. It was a mix of sound like gas escaping a tea kettle, but deep and hollow. His hand went to the sachet at his throat which he had carried from those dark times in isolation…a satchel he had found here, along with the voice.

"We are so close."

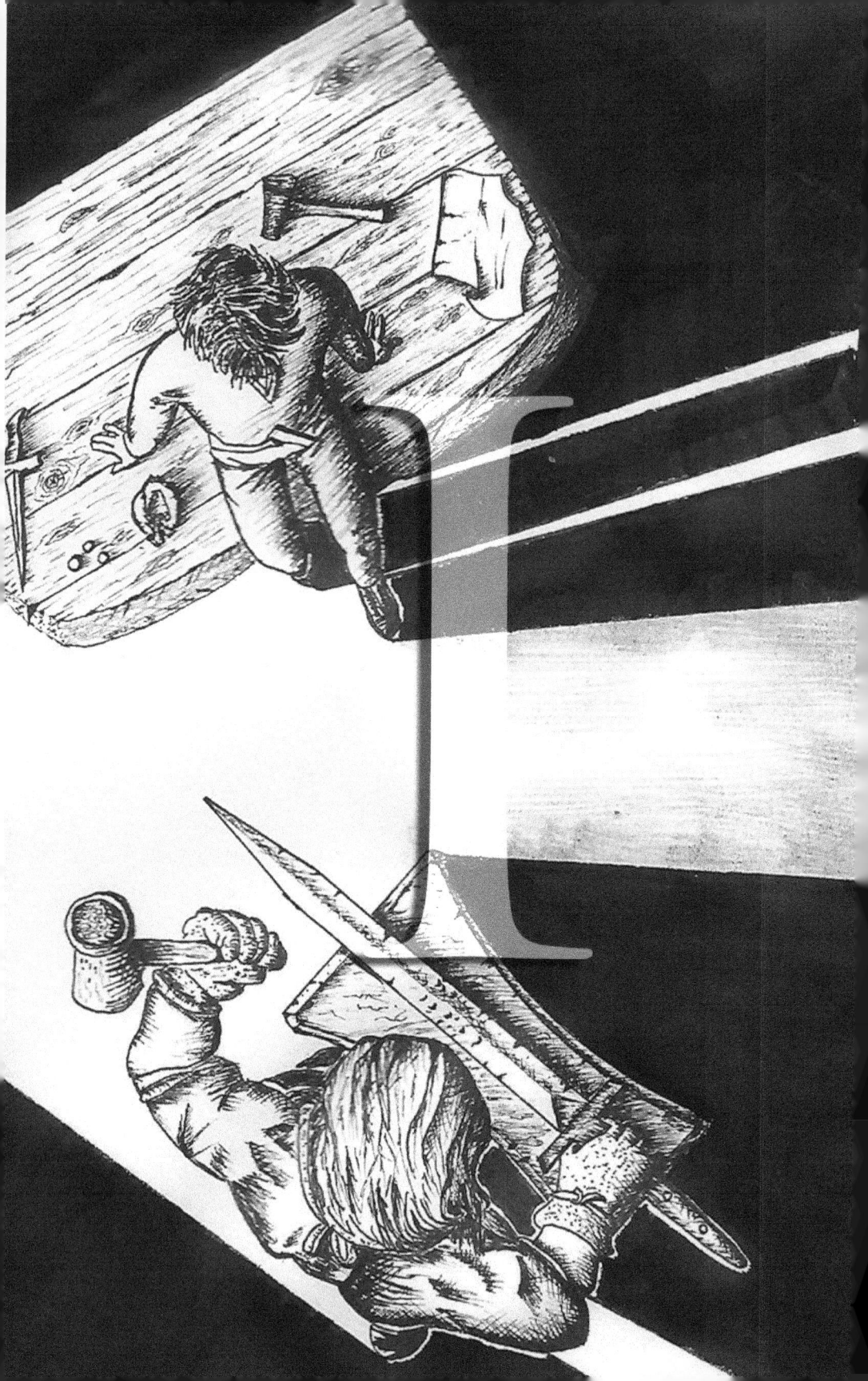

CHAPTER 1

FIRE AND FORGE

The sun slowly traveled in a thin beam across the far wall of the Blacksmith shop, the light bursting through a gap in the dry and blackened oak doors. Heaving great bellows pumped the coals of the forge with life-giving air.

A young boy, barely 11 years old, pumped the worn, hand-smoothed arm. A few beads of sweat dotted his brow just below his black mop of short, thick but well-trimmed hair. It was a respectable hairstyle for a boy of his age. Respect was a gate to honor, he noted from one of his books on etiquette and though he seldomly found a reason to practice it directly, he found it to be a place of comfort. He smiled at his work as he squinted into the change of the coals.

Benedict remarked how they changed from a deep cherry to a yellow much like that beam on the whitewashed wall. The booming voice of Erebus Shieldheart rang out in that room like the ring of the anvil in the dull smoky air.

"There, boy! You've stoked the fire good and hot now. Keep it going, and I'll get the steel."

Together, they rolled the bar in the inferno of the forge, heat dancing across their arms as they worked near the fire.

Benedict looked back at the crafting table where a silver dragon turtle sat. He was impressed by the detail of the sculpture and silverwork. Mithril was rare, but even more so was the heat required to bend it to the form required.

Dragon turtles were legendary sea monsters. Common enough to be known, encounters with them were so rare that there was still a mystery around them. According to sailors, they looked like giant snapping turtles with shells as big as an island. Its red eyes, two deep garnets, seemed to stare back at him. He couldn't shake that uneasy feeling around it. Like it called to him.

"Ow!"

An ember singed his arm, making him wince and return his gaze back to the steel he was turning in the fire. Erebus chuckled from behind, his blue eyes smiling and ever-watchful. Benedict was safe here, safe to explore the craft of smithing within the guidance that Erebus provided.

Soon, Erebus nodded in approval of the yellow-white glow and called for him to bring it to the anvil. Hefting the heavy forge hammer in his massive hands, Erebus delivered great blows to the glowing steel. Benedict marveled at his adoptive father's arms. They were scarred from the years before Benedict, and strong from driving that hammer for as many as he could remember. Benedict saw the glow of the steel in Erebus's kind, deep blue eyes, which were surrounded by lines that told a story of hardship that never escaped the lips hidden behind his long mustache.

Erebus eventually stopped and motioned for Benedict to lift the steel so that he could inspect the rough shape of the sword. Benedict struggled to lift the blade of the greatsword, thinking to himself how strong someone must be to actually wield it. Erebus smiled slightly as he hooked the crook of the hammer under the other end to brace it. Benedict felt himself relax slightly.

"Good. This is good. Send her back into the fire, Benedict."

For hours this cycle continued. All things in the room moved in rhythm with the pace of the blacksmith and his young apprentice. The door to the shop opened and a woman with dark hair tied back in a neat bun stepped into the bright daylight pouring onto the floor.

She swung a hip to brace the door, her hands carrying a tray covered with a draped white cloth. Behind the woman, a girl a few years younger than Benedict skipped into the room, careful to keep distance from the fiery metal the two men held and the forge that birthed it. Her innocent brown eyes looked upon the fire with wonder, awe and, ultimately, respect.

"Lora! What have ye brought us, love?" Erebus smiled and lowered the steel, picking up a towel. As he began to wipe off his hands, he nodded with pride for Benedict to step away from the bellows for a much-needed break.

The woman pulled back the soft handwoven cloth and the smell hit them before words could be said or eyes could see. The sweet smell of the fresh bread mixed with the smoked fish made Benedict's pasty, dry mouth begin to water. When his eyes fell to the pitcher of cool water, though, he could imagine how that first drink was going to feel. That became his priority.

As he began to pour a glass, his young cousin Cordelia wrapped her arms around him in a big hug from the side, barely missing his elbow as he poured. Lora kissed Erebus on his black sooted cheek, laughing when she saw the small clean spot she left. Erebus smiled as she brushed the soot from a corner of her scarlet lips.

He thought of the years they had been together, how she was still so beautiful. Her raven-black hair was showing some gray now and her eyes had fine lines, but her brown eyes themselves still shone with that fire he had always seen. She knew more than

Erebus, he had thought on more than one occasion, and she had proven it on many more than that.

He glanced at their children, who were sitting now. Benedict had a fistful of broken bread with a decent portion of the smoked trout hastily shoved in one side. He was greedily eating it while Cordelia talked excitedly about meeting up with her friend Sophie later.

As he watched both of his children share a meal, Erebus briefly reflected on his adopted son.

"His father would be proud, Lora. He's going to be a great Blacksmith," he beamed, with a whisper in her ear. Her kept hair felt like silk across his cheek and smelled of the lilies in the front planters she was tending earlier.

"He's a good boy." She looked into his eyes with purpose as she wore a wry grin. "As is Zane."

Erebus rolled his eyes slightly and chuckled.

"Yes. I suppose," he said as he turned away.

He reached for a bit of bread and fish before Benedict could completely eliminate the meal by himself.

He thought of Zane, Benedict's older brother. Calling him a free spirit was the kindest thing Erebus could say about the boy. He was undisciplined and unfocused, nothing like his brother. Zane was like Elona, the sworn sister of Erebus and mother of both boys.

ZORIN WALKED DOWN THE DIRTY alleyway with his hands in his pockets, deep in thought. He was not looking where the ground passed lazily, pebble by pebble, but he heard the window above creak closed and a cat's steps on the gutter by the rooftop. He listened to the wind pick up slightly, and could feel the dry arid draft against his cheek pull a little moisture as it went by. He could smell the rotting trash and stale beer behind the Tavern as he approached the rear entrance to the kitchen.

There was one thing he didn't notice, though.

"Psst! Zorin!" A familiar hiss slithered out from the stack of barrels. In response, Zorin looked around before darting behind them.

"You ready?" The face was gleaming with mischievous excitement. In the dark shadows Zorin could make out the somewhat obscured face of his best friend. The boy's blonde hair hung to his shoulders, unkempt and free in a way that mirrored his devil-may-care attitude. Zorin admired the boy's courage and will. Being the son of the local justice made him wary about taking risks, but when he was with Zane he felt free.

The boys spent their days dreaming about moving to Port L'For one day and becoming pirates, sailing the seas with no one to answer to but themselves and completely free of the day-to-day repetition of OallEnAkhan. The town was nothing more than a small village that relied on trading basic commodities with traveling merchants and the nomads from the surrounding dry, high plains.

The only tavern in OallEnAkhan was the Howling Mountain Inn, a convenient place for travelers and locals alike to stop and tell stories over a pint. The boys loved to sneak in and hear the stories being told. To them, these stories were more exciting than anything else in town.

Zorin looked at Zane and nervously nodded with a smile.

They snuck around the barrel stack in the shadow immediately to the left of the door. Zane tested the handle gently. It was locked. He looked at Zorin and nodded. Zorin took a deep breath and produced the lockpick Zane had given him as a learning tool.

"How are we gonna open buried treasure if the chest is locked? Don't wanna break the chest and have gold falling all about, right?"

Zorin nodded. Just the idea of picking up a mess like that made his head swim. He felt and listened to the lock. He could feel a grit of sand that had blown into the tumbler at some point, at least since the last time they were there. Brushing it to the side, he slowly pressed and turned, successfully disengaging the lock and freeing the door.

Zane eagerly pushed the door open slightly and peered in. The kitchen was unoccupied except for the large cauldron of rich stew slowly cooking on the fire. The smell was savory, and if it weren't molten he would stuff it in his pocket. He smiled slightly to himself at the silly thought of even trying.

Outside of the door, Zorin could see his friend's fingerless glove pressing against the wood, the horrible scar on his forearm also clearly visible. Zane had no trouble talking about how he got the scar, and often told the story with pride. "Saved Benedict from the fire," he always said. The fire that had taken Benedict and Zane's parents.

Zane's smile peeked back from the doorway. "Let's go."

They snuck into the kitchen, ducking behind the stacks of flour in the baker's pantry. Zane bounded up the stack until he could reach the rafters. Zorin quickly followed. As they crossed the beams Zane looked back at his best friend.

Zorin and Zane had met shortly after Zane's arrival in OallEnAkan, when they were nearly seven years old. He remembered the mopey kid watching him unpack until he could sneak away and ask him his name. "Ariackan," the kid said.

Zane remembered laughing, saying, "Way too big. How about 'Zorin'? It's got a 'Z' in it like mine! I'm Zane."

They both started laughing before running off to play, playing in the dreams of children with no cares for the world around them.

A hand grabbed Zane's leg as he drifted off the rafter, snapping him to reality. Correcting quickly, Zane looked back in time to see Zorin silently chuckling at the almost-mishap. Zane mouthed out a thank you before looking down at the twelve-foot drop to the table below. They had made it from the kitchen to the front of the store and the dining room.

They worked their way to the large bookcase rows in the back where they could descend to the floor and find their prize. Below them, only two tables were occupied. At the first table was Elloveve Hawklight, a local elven ranger who periodically came into town. At the second table a well known group of Hill Dwarf Miners sat tensely.

One was the Chieftain Ricaver Bearcharger, recognizable for his exceptional ugliness. His crooked nose perched below two sets of bushy eyebrows. His bald head reflected a bit of the sunlight that came in from the dusty nearby window. Around the table, his usual council of Whitacin and Olacul were listening intently to his speech.

"I dunna care if it's bad luck. The Mine stays open! We've found worse than an old hallway anyhow," he bellowed.

"Chief, it's not the discovery itself, it's the fear of what could be in there. The boys said it seemed to call to them in the darkness. Bad signs, Chief. Bad signs."

Whitacin's white braided beard whipped slightly from his chin as he spoke in an almost pleading tone. Olacul continued to stare into his mug, hoping there would be an answer. Zane always viewed him as the thoughtful one. He never spoke much but would smile at the boys when they passed in the street.

Zane looked at Zorin, who was snatching a bit of stale cake from a shelf. He grabbed a piece for himself. The boys knew that if they stayed too long it could mean trouble. Looking back at the rafters they began their ascent out of the Howling Mountain Inn. Zane bit into the Cake with a devilish grin, noting the spiced currants that popped in his mouth. The brushed icing melted against his tongue but nothing could turn his curiosity from the discovery in the old mine.

SOPHIE WAS WIPING DOWN THE small table where she'd eaten lunch a few moments earlier. She had taken her plate and silverware to the bucket of soft flowery-smelling suds and was purposefully wiping it clean. The house was so silent now.

She took a deep breath in as she looked at the front door, waiting for something. Or, maybe, someone. Sophie looked back and began to dry the dish with a dry white towel. She smiled, remembering the towel as a gift from Lorahana Shieldheart. She was a talented weaver and seamstress, after all.

Her best friend was Cordelia and it wasn't a secret that Cordelia's cousin Zane and Sophie had feelings for each other. They were both a little reckless and enjoyed each other's spontaneity. Zane's little brother Benedict would always encourage them to not do anything on the edge, but with Sophie's sister and guardian off earning money and not at the house currently, it was hard to stay on the right path.

Sophie sighed and thought of her guardian and older sister, Kartilaan. She had been away for almost a month now. Old Ricaver Bearcharger would check in periodically on Sophie and make sure she was ok, dropping off some flour or some meat as a care package. The dwarves treated the two girls like family. Although Sophie didn't remember their parents, Kartilaan did and would often speak of the love they had for each other. A fairy tale love, the town would say. No one would say much more than that, just smiles and pleasantries.

Her sister was a talented Swordmaster with a longsword, and when she was here taught Sophie as much as she could learn.

"Men are not to be trusted further than the end of your sword, Sophie." She remembered her words of wisdom. She also remembered holding that sword at Zane's chest and how he smiled back at her. She saw no malice, and something inside disarmed her. Months later he was her first kiss, and she was his.

Sophie smiled as she stood up and put the dish back in the cupboard neatly. She would go find him soon, her chores were almost done. She pulled up the pan she had used to fry a little salted meat and scrambled eggs, double-checking that it was clean before putting it away under the tall dark wood cupboard. She thought of Zorin and wondered if his day was better than the previous days. She could see the marks on his cheeks. It worried her that when confronted he would look away and change the subject hastily. Her sister had those marks when she would come back from a job sometimes.

A shudder ran up Sophie's back when she thought of his father, Pallus. Tall, dark-eyed, with long black hair that hit his broad muscular shoulders, he was the local justice for the town. He had a deep booming voice that commanded respect and allegiance. Unwavering allegiance. He stayed in his house when he wasn't traveling. Zorin had mentioned that today he was in another town for a meeting. Hopefully, that meant he would get a break for a little while.

She cared about him like a brother. In fact, she thought of her friends as a family. Even the town thought of Sophie, Cordelia, Benedict, Zane and Zorin as such. Snapping back from her thoughts, Sophie pulled her blonde hair back from her face hastily with a small bit of purple cord and took one last look at the empty house before running out to join Cordelia.

SOPHIE AND CORDELIA WERE AT the stables talking to a tall chestnut horse named Buttercup as they brushed the cockleburrs out of his thick mane. They were laughing at a joke when Zane and Zorin appeared, laughing.

Sophie smiled. "There you are, what's so funny?"

Zane wickedly smiled as he grabbed her hand. "Milady, my First Mate and I were just saying how we will sail out of L'For within a fortnight!"

Zorin tossed him a grin. "I thought I was the Captain!" he jested as he mocked a gut punch on his friend. Sophie and Cordelia laughed.

Zane apologized and began talking of the waves and their freedom again. Sophie smiled. It sounded great. Zorin held onto his dreams as truth, letting them give him hope and trying to ignore the thought that they may never come true. He had to. Cordelia loved his stories and loved her cousins very much. They were her oldest friends and Zane, for good or bad, was the oldest and therefore the de facto leader. Though he never seemed to want it.

Suddenly, as Zane was talking about pirates and treasure, he saw Benedict turn the corner.

"Hey Benedict!" Zane smiled at his brother. "You ready for some fun?" Benedict was intrigued, but was wary. Zane rarely had ideas of fun that were legal. At the very best they were questionable.

"There's something in the old mine that the Dwarves found. An old hallway or something."

Benedict shook his head and began to protest. Zane poured on the charm. Cordelia soon joined, as did Sophie. Zorin smiled at Benedict and slightly pleadingly said, "Come on. It's not everyday something like this comes up. Besides, today my Father is gone and some fun sure sounds great."

Benedict groaned, knowing he had lost the battle. Begrudgingly, he followed the group as they walked north out of town towards the mouth of the old mine.

CHAPTER 2

THE MINE

The children stood silently at the mouth of the mine. The hot dust blew across the dirt road, whipping up in small clouds that stung their eyes and cheeks. The arid smell of dry, cracked leather came from the various tools in the cart that had been hastily placed there by the Dwarves. They would be back, but only after the miners held their council and deemed it "safe". Dwarves were not known for living such long lives by making hasty decisions.

Benedict was nervously fidgeting with his hands while his eyes darted behind them, looking for followers only to find nothing but the winding trail back to the village of OallEnAkhan and his friends. Leading them was Sophie, tall with her long blonde hair blowing in the wind away from her beautiful and strong face. Next was his cousin Cordelia, who was more like a sister. Her white dress was a bit dirt-stained at the bottom from the two miles of dirt trail they had traversed from town. It didn't seem to bother her though. He did note her normal joyful banter had ceased, her dark hair tossing in the wind as she looked at the gaping maw of the mine.

This mine had been open for at least the last 100 years with rich veins of iron ore and hematite. It was rumored that the dwarves opened the mine on what was once the site of an ancient temple that had been forgotten and swallowed by the drifting sand of the desert it bordered to the north. The path snaked from the mine to the northbound merchants trail through the desert to the city of Sienna.

This trail connected the southern city of Kur in Port L'For to the northern trade route during the winter months when the northern seas were much too dangerous to cross for trade, leaving the giant lands isolated from the rest of the world with no alternative route by land. Benedict sighed. Sailing on the vast ocean was something that seemed like a fun exercise or vacation but he didn't have the same desire to be a sailor, let alone a thieving pirate like his brother and Zorin wanted to. At this rate one of them was going to end up in a dungeon somewhere or, worse yet, killed.

With a heavy sigh Benedict looked back to Zorin who was taking inventory of his various picks and a small knife he had on his side. He paused for a moment before looking at Benedict.

Zorin could sense Benedict's judgment, but what he was more aware of was his apprehension and fear. He shook his head and smiled at the boy, his dark eyes reassuring. The boys loved each other even if they had very different goals. Benedict instinctively looked to his older brother Zane Shieldheart, secretly hoping he would find something and call the whole thing off.

Zane stood at the front, chewing the end of a small piece of grass while squinting at the cave. He listened intently, focusing his sight into the darkness for any unseen lurker. He smelled past the earthy sweetgrass in his mouth, past the dust, making sure his senses didn't betray him.

He turned to Zorin and nodded in approval. Benedict's heart sank.

THE SUN WAS DIPPING LOW behind the woman as she and her companion moved to the east. The nearly two dozen foot soldiers cast shadows upon the back of the covered cart in front of theirs. Sighing, she stood up slightly, her short cropped dark brown hair brushing a pale cheek as she braced her weight on the rail of the driver's perch and the powerful black armored shoulder of the driver himself. He turned his helmeted head to her. She could see the gray eyes behind the iron visor as he nodded to her. With a slight shove she stepped back into the covered wagon.

The sun baked a dusty smell in the wagon that mixed with the various jars of arcane components in a few loose boxes. Lounging on a pile of thinly woven red and black blankets was an old man. Clad in dark, tight-fitting robes he was thin like a scarecrow and his health seemed to teeter on the edge of wasting away into death. Thin wisps of stark white hair cascaded from his head and fell across his gaunt face. He turned to her and smiled. His cold icy blue eyes betrayed his age, ancient beyond comprehension. A strength that flowed like an eternal spring lay beyond those twin orbs of ice.

The man possessed a power that struck her with fear as well as respect. He was her mentor. She was ready to learn his lessons about all that her dark craft could be.

He sat there with another dark robed man, thick-necked and bald. His face was pockmarked, with sores and lesions all over his neck and head. Some areas of his face were freshly scabbed from raking his claws across his dry skin in the dusty air. Mortas was his name, a cleric of an ancient dark goddess, one forgotten by time.

The woman looked at the flowing arcane script tattooed across the back of her hands and smiled. Her craft was necromancy. The art of sculpting flesh and bone with magic. These symbols protected her from the risks of such dark magic.

"Ash..." the old man hissed. His voice cracked and wheezed like wind in hollow reeds. "Come... won't you join us? We were just talking about what can be done with quicksilver, gum arabic and a wisp of smoke..."

Ash thought for a moment, "... sounds like a transformation spell... but these components... Would make it very powerful."

"Yes, powerful indeed... but what if we add... this?"

She looked at what was clutched in the old man's talon-like hand. A jar containing a dry, rubbery object the size of a medium sized melon. It was familiar to her but to anyone else would seem like a chunk of old flesh.

"A hyena's liver? Lord Dekkion, I... I have no idea what that would do."

"Oh but I do, my sweet apprentice. And soon, on this journey, you will too... "

He offered her a hand as she sat down next to him. She noted the dark mace he had stowed at his feet. She knew that the old man was powerful and preferred to wield the brutal clublike weapon to those with blades. He claimed there was something more primal and pure about a bludgeoning weapon than blades. He smiled, noticing her gaze, and instinctively placed the papery thin palm of one hand over the upturned leather-wrapped handle of the weapon. The heavy head began to glow with a blue ghost light, serpents of wispy mist weaving their way in a hypnotic pattern.

"We will do such great things, you and I... but first our lord must collect his things."

THE CHILDREN HAD MADE THEIR way into the dark stone archway of the mine and now found themselves on the edge of absolute darkness. Cordelia reached up and took down a beaten and dented tin lantern, checking it for oil. The vapor burned her freckled nose slightly and made her eyes water. She struck the flint starter and the wick burned to life. Her mouth pulled back in a slight grin. The blue flame sputtered to a bright yellow as she adjusted the length, illuminating and framing her face. She held it out to Benedict, who held a hand up and smiled.

Benedict was afraid of breaking his word or command, she chuckled. Not of the dark.

Cordelia had memories of them listening to Erebus tell stories of great knights and cruel orc war parties in the lands across the ocean in the new world. Stories about the savage barbarians of Wolfling, and ogres and kobolds in the lands of Trull. But her favorite stories were the ones about dragons. She loved to dream about what they must have looked like in ancient times, gleaming like precious metals in the sun or in rainbow hues under a moonlit sky. Cordelia smiled at the thought, lost in her own mind for a moment. Looking up from the flame, she saw her friends motioning her to the front with Zane and Zorin to scout the freshly lit cavernous hallway.

Dwarves rarely did anything small. Whether it was in the craftsmanship or in the size itself, everything was grand. This huge chamber was no exception. Monumental rock beams ten feet around climbed thirty feet into the air, bracing the ceiling at the top. The skillfully hewn reliefs of dwarven runes and a bearded face were carved into several of them, surrounded by an ancient angular design.

No one knew how long the dwarves had been working this mine, but it was obvious they didn't plan to stop anytime soon.

Walking into the chamber, Cordelia saw a pocket in the wall with the rune for "light" in it. Placing the lantern in the pocket set off a chain reaction with the rock network of crystal naturally inlayed in the walls. The chamber magnified that light and cast it evenly throughout the room.

Sophie shielded her eyes as the dark wall she was investigating blinded her slightly with its radiance. Squinting, she felt along the wall and soon found where it had collapsed slightly, revealing another hallway behind it.

"Hey, I think I found something! Over here!" Her voice bounced off the cool stones in perfect time as it faded into the darkness. Her friends made their way over to her. Zorin peered inside before looking back at Zane.

"This has got to be it," Zorin said to Zane, as they both nodded in agreement. Cordelia and Sophie found other lanterns nearby and repeated the lighting ritual with other alcoves. Once the room was lit, the children made their way into the relatively narrow hallway. This area was much older than the rest of the cavern. They could see etchings on the wall of a huge tower in the middle of an ancient city.

"This must have been before the knights left," Benedict remarked.

His voice was slightly mournful. He dreamed of the golden age when knights guarded the lands with righteous justice. Over time, in the wake of several centuries of widespread peace, the military had fallen out of favor. Five centuries ago they were largely replaced with the trade barons of Darkovnia. Reliance on the knights dwindled as did their numbers. According to Erebus, they still existed in the great Celestine Tower and in pockets throughout the world, but were not the same force they once had been. Still, Benedict dreamed of joining their ranks one day.

Zorin and Zane began their work on the ancient lock. The rough iron squeaked until a loud clack set the tumbler in place. Zorin smiled at his friend, who nodded approvingly. Slowly, the door groaned open. Ancient stale air rolled out of the dark opening. Cordelia covered her mouth, trying not to gag at the slightly musty and rotten sweet smell in that initial rush of air.

"What was that smell?" Zane looked back with a grin. He fanned his hand at his behind as he darted into the darkness with a snicker. Sophie covered her face as she began to laugh. Cordelia laughed quietly as well. Everything was a joke to him. Why was he the oldest? She looked at Benedict, who looked slightly disgusted and maybe a little bit embarrassed. Zorin shook his head and motioned everyone to follow him.

The hall here was nearly identical to the one before, but the walls were bare with no murals. Tattered threads of what could have been banners clung to the walls. The once brilliant hues now faded to an off white and tan mottled design in places. One of the banners may have once had the image of a dragon, but now all that remained was a horn and part of an eye. The rest were lost to time.

The lighting in the hall began to dim slightly as they progressed. Reaching up, Zorin pulled down a torch from its sconce and lit it from the lantern Benedict was carrying. The ancient fibers sprang to life in a yellow orange light. As he placed the torch back in its iron work on the wall, it flared violently for a moment. The sound of stone grinding behind them startled the children.

Across from the torch, the wall was sliding back to reveal a room. Zane and Cordelia peeked in cautiously. In the center of the room was a bench with three ancient scrolls. A deep blue glow emanating from the papers seemed to be the only thing keeping the scrolls from disintegrating and becoming lost to time. Cordelia approached the bench, the blue light casting a shine on her face. She knew this was magic. Maybe something more powerful than the small tricks her mother had shown her. Something better than simply breaking bread or wiping up some spilled broth with no hands.

The three scrolls had three different symbols: a tree, a shield, and a torch. Cordelia reached for the torch scroll; it called to her in a way that overpowered her interest in the other two. To her surprise it held its form perfectly, not a single crack in the parchment. The other two scrolls disintegrated into dust with an ancient sigh, as if relieved to have fulfilled their long awaited duty. The dust passed off the table and into the cracks of the floor to rest.

Faintly, from down the hall, the sound of a stone gate beginning to open broke the silence, but the children were so engrossed by the remaining scroll that it went unnoticed.

When Cordelia opened the scroll, she saw lettering she was unfamiliar with. Angular letters, highlighted with squared dotted marks in a language foreign to her. Sighing, she knew it would take some study to decipher the script. She tucked it in her belt for now. The children smiled at the treasure they found, though. Zane clasped her shoulder, nodding happily with a wide grin. "I can't wait to find out what it says. I know you can figure it out, Cordelia."

She smiled, a little embarrassed at the praise. They continued down the hall and found a room where scratches lined the floor from the recent stone door sliding out of the way.

The room had a table flanked on either side by two ancient sets of armor. Benedict and Sophie moved into the room. Sophie saw the dusty armor's fine steel and construction beneath the leather bindings, which were corroded and brittle; she thought the suits would still be fine to use. Benedict noted the crown and sword carved into the breastplate. Knight's armor! He looked on the table and saw a small silver amulet and an ancient crown. The amulet was a simple etching of a sword and crown symbol in the center of a six-pointed star. A symbol for knighthood.

A groaning came from the darkness behind him. Two man-sized shapes shambled into the lantern's red glow. The decayed faces of two ghouls lurched into the light. Their blue-tinged flesh fell like tattered rags from their bones. Their yellow eyes were clouded and pupil-less and they clawed at the air slowly with rotten and taloned hands. They came directly to Benedict. The other children, horrified, stepped away to the side from the shambling creatures.

Benedict reached for that symbol and, clutching the cold silver to his chest, began to chant a prayer... just as he had heard in those stories of old. Eyes closed, he concentrated. Stars appeared from his eyes being pulled so tight. He felt woozy, and all went black.

AS HIS EYES AWAKENED, HE found himself alone in an ancient room. Torches lit the walls, casting dancing embers as they sputtered in the syrupy haze of his vision. Noises delayed and reverberated as leather and twill ground the gravel on the stone floor. The sound of dragging. A heavy object was being dragged closer and closer on the floor. Benedict could smell the musty room but it was dusty and clean, he noted.

He saw the shadowy silhouette of a tall man step into the room, dragging a form behind him. A body. He let go of the man-sized leg and let it hit the floor. Chuckling under his breath, the large man stood up and stretched with a slight groan. Benedict could only make out the black outline of powerful muscles as the man set the crown and amulet on the table.

"We can wait," the dark voice cooed. "I will claim you again, but for now we will wait. I've brought you a friend to... guard you."

The man chuckled as he picked up some pieces of heavy armor and knelt to the body on the floor. Grunting, he began dressing the body. A breastplate, spaulders, pauldrons, greaves, gauntlets and, finally, a helmet encased what Benedict assumed was a man. Could be an elf, but too tall to be a dwarf. With a slight groan, the powerful man stood the body up against the wall, the helmet lolling to one side. He stepped back, holding the ragdoll form with one strong hand on its throat.

"Rog avhiuk evin shal deaavh!"

The body straightened up immediately from the magical incantation to lock at attention in eternal service to its new master.

"Hey! Who's back there?"

The man spun his head back towards the hall. Benedict could sense a tinge of panic within this otherwise powerful figure.

"Torsten? Hello? I'm back here, my friend... I've got to show you something."

The man reached down and picked up a pickaxe from the floor. Testing the weight against his other hand, he menacingly left the room towards the other voice.

BENEDICT FELT A HAND ON his shoulder and realized Zane had him draped across his leg.

"He's ok!" Zane exclaimed, and a sigh of relief was felt by all in the room.

Benedict rose up. "How long have I been out?"

"Not long," Zane replied. "You went to the table and the next thing we saw, you passed out."

"You didn't see the ghouls?"

"No..."

Everyone looked at each other uneasily. then looked at the two statuesque knights.

Noticing their response, Benedict looked at them puzzled. "What?"

Sophie looked at him. "These aren't just suits of armor, Benedict." She motioned at them. "There are actually knights inside them."

Benedict was appalled. Dead? Inside? They were at perfect attention guarding that table. Then he remembered the crown.

Zane was approaching the table and reached out to claim it. "We could go anywhere with just one of the gems alone, I think." He smiled greedily, reaching for it.

The twisted pattern on the crown revealed many serpentine and dragon heads twisted together. Five gemstones worked their way around the crown itself: ruby, emerald, sapphire, diamond, and jet. Zane picked it up and the dragons seemed to come to life. Twisting. Turning. He placed it on his head.

"What are you doing?" Benedict said.

Zane saw his little brother's greedy face lunge for the crown. He dodged to the side, pushing him to the ground. He looked at his friends. Friends who now wanted his crown. He saw their greedy, beady little soulless eyes. Their black mouths pulled back in cynical grins, dark lips curled away from inky blue-black fangs.

"No!"

Zane pulled the crown off and it clanged to the ground, lifeless again. His friends looked at him in awe. Benedict was steadying Zane with his hands, looking into his eyes.

"Are you ok, Zane?" he asked honestly. "You became very angry all of a sudden before throwing this down to the floor."

Zane nodded. "No one should put that on. We should go."

As the children left, Zane reached down and picked up the crown. Shrugging, he looped it into his belt, taking the treasure with him. Dangerous or not, it may be worth something to somebody and if they were going to strike out on their own this was a great step towards 'financial independence'. He chuckled to himself.

As they returned to the great hall, a sense of dread rolled over their hearts. There was the sound of a crowd faintly screaming in the distance. Zane picked up the pace. Sophie could smell something and she joined him as all the children found themselves bolting to the entrance. Their fears were then realized. In the dusky distance, OallEnAkhan was on fire.

CHAPTER 3

THE CRUCIBLE

The screams echoed from deeper within the town as the children scrambled to hide behind the old mine cart. It sat near the edge of the road, peeking down the dark dusky alleyway illuminated with a distant dull red glow. Smoke was in the air, and the snapping of timber and the smell of oak mixed with iron hung heavy. The metallic taste brought horrible thoughts to their minds. Cordelia was whimpering about getting home while Zane froze in thought. Worse, it was a memory. Where would they go from here?

Benedict put his hand on Zane's shoulder.

"Follow me," he said to his older brother.

Everyone looked surprised and they gazed wide-eyed at Zane's reaction. No one had ever dared to command Zane. He was the de facto leader, after all. Zane smiled and glanced back at the group. He placed a hand on Sophie's shoulder and they both smiled.

"Time to go," he said to the others.

Then he nodded his head towards his brother, his long dirty blonde hair bouncing from his cheek.

"Follow Benedict, he knows the way."

As they darted down the alley they heard two deep, growling voices laughing from around the corner. Ducking behind a pile of wet-smelling rubbish outside of the tailor's back door, they soon saw two hulking forms turn the corner.

They had deep-set, dark eyes and green skin that looked like thick pond scum. Two tusks protruded from their lower jaw over their upper lips and as one spoke the other curled one lip back, nodding in approval. The children had never seen such monsters before.

Zane held a finger up to his lips as his eyes grew wide in recognition. Orcs. These were just like the orcs that helped the bandits raid their home so many years ago. He remembered his mother reaching towards him with one hand, her chin-length blonde hair pasted to her cheek in small patches with sweat and blood. Her gold and silver armor glinted in the raging fire. She saw him as she swung her great Glaive in an arc behind her, through an orc much like those before them. "Run!" she mouthed, a silent scream as she turned to disappear in the fiery battle before her.

He never saw her again.

A battle cry roared out from the adjacent doorway as a figure in dull, battle-worn silver armor charged the two orcs. His Greatsword cleaved through one before his shoulder drove the other into the wall behind them. The grind of metal against brick made Zorin's skin crawl.

He pressed himself to the shadows, peering through the gap between the wall and the overturned barrels they hid behind.

"Die, Scum!"

The orc roared from his bloodied maw as he drove the crude cleaver-like axe down at the warrior. It froze in midair, held by a single hand. His face now in the firelight, Zorin could see that it was the powerful hand of Erebus Shieldheart.

"Not... yet!" He retorted, spinning the blade back towards its owner's gut, using the orc's own force unwittingly to drive it to its own demise.

The orc fell to the ground in a heap.

"Father!" Cordelia, sensing the end of the danger, jumped from behind the pile before anyone could stop her.

The smile Erebus had for his daughter quickly faded when the door behind Cordelia suddenly burst open. An orc, frothing at the mouth, reached for Cordelia's running form. Luckily for her, it only grasped a tattered ribbon and yanked it free from her waist. Her eyes turned to horror as she screamed.

The orc shrieked and reached for his shoulder, turning to look down the dark alley behind him. He squinted into the darkness just beyond the children. Stumbling backward, another feathered shaft ran through his throat with a gurgle. Zane felt a third whisk by as it found home in the orc's dark heart.

Cordelia jumped into her father's waiting arms. He looked behind the children.

"Elloveve! Good to see you, old friend!"

From the shadows came a slender Elven ranger, the dark earthen hues of her leather armor seeming to dampen the light around her graceful movements. Her long, flame-red hair flowing behind her, she pulled her hood back as she stepped out of the shadows into the smokey light of the alley. She smiled at Erebus and then looked at Zorin.

Elloveve winked at him as she extended her hand to him, motioning for all the children to follow her.

"Erebus. Where is Lora ?"

Erebus nodded, "Lora is at the shop gathering supplies and will meet us to the south of town by the old tree." He put Cordelia down. "I need you to get the children there. You know where we must go."

Elloveve nodded as Erebus turned to Benedict and placed a hand on the awe-struck boy's shoulder. His foster father was wearing intricately carved plate armor. He was able to make out the same crown and sword that the knights in the old mine were wearing. Erebus stood before him with the same kindness in his eyes he had always known, but now he also saw him as a defender of the people. A true knight.

"They are all we have," Erebus said over his shoulder before looking at Zorin, Zane, and Sophie, smiling in grim understanding. "They are everything. But you know that."

"I know the vow, Erebus." Elloveve chuckled. "But … stop. You need to go. Get Lora, and let's leave this place."

He nodded, smiled at the children, and darted down the alley into the darkness.

THE ROUGH SPUN WOOL OF her charcoal robes rustled gently against boots of midnight. Her pace was steady as she looked up with dark eyes from behind a low-drawn hood. A thin line of runes wove itself in muted inks across her face and over the bridge of her nose. A crooked grin split one corner of her mouth as she realized they were getting closer and she was sure of it.

She heard their footsteps echo in the ancient hallway, noting the musty smell but, more importantly, the recently lit oil that illuminated the halls. She could sense his loathsome body walking next to hers. Laboriously his breath heaved, she noticed, as slowly the chokehold of fatigue caught up to him while she marched on. The pace of the tall woman's steps increased as he dropped slowly behind her. Years of eating and drinking were now taking its toll on the round man.

The large room they entered was definitely dwarven, but this hall was different. Ancient. A hall from ancient time, likely with a purpose other than that of a random hallway from a simple iron mine. The woman ran a tattooed hand over the threadbare tapestry as she drifted by quickly.

Now she could hear his panting behind her. She pictured him trying to keep up, his bald head and swollen neck dripping sweat over his numerous sores. Smirking, she chuckled and, as if in response, the man croaked out.

"Dekkion said.."

She loved nothing less than when she was questioned. She was far from a child and this round buffoon of a priest was grating at best. She hated the way he begged to stay in favor with their dark master. Dekkion would just sneer and give him small tasks. Things a child could do, with no real challenge.

"I know what he said, Mortas. Whether or not you believe me is of no concern, but rest assured... I was paying attention."

The man shook his flabby jowls briefly before clearing his throat.

"...I meant no disrespect, my lady. I was just reminding myself, um. Not to touch the damned thing that is."

This was unexpected. She could sense fear in the round man now. It mixed with the smell of a dwindling torch now appearing in the hall that seemed to have been recently lit.

""What is this, Mortas? Is a rat loose?"

She reached for a torch that hung from an iron sconce and inspected it. Mortas saw Ash's face glint in the torchlight as she passed it over in her hands. She was tall, standing just over six foot, her thin black robes held at the waist by a leather waist cincher tooled in intricate designs depicting death. Her hood drooped across her brow and he noted how she always smelled of clove. Other spell components to be sure, but clove was always present.

Slabs of thick black leather hung from her waist to the knee where menacing, tall black boots met the slate floor.

"Someone's been here. Come, we must hurry."

She passed by a room, the open door revealing a table covered in dust. Her heart sank.

"Someone has made the choice. Fools!"

Mortas ran a hand on the dust on the table. He noted the faint blue and green pigments that could still be seen.

"The flame. They chose the flame, didn't they? We should never have locked the door with fey magic."

Ash spun her head, snarling.

"You do not know or need to know why our lord does what he does!"

She paused, taking a deep breath to calm herself.

"Come, let us see if the crown is still here."

THE CHILDREN HUDDLED CLOSER TO the elf's cloak. The smell of wet wool along with elderflowers and honey seemed to cut through the night's smell of smoke and decay. The heavy wetness hanging in the air slowly became a heavy drizzle, sinking deeper into their clothes as they walked. The rain was likely brought on from the smoke, Sophie thought to herself, as her eyes fluttered slightly looking to the dark sky.

The rooftops glowed, the air hung low and the distant shouts seemed to dim as they walked. Realization was settling in. Where was her sister now? Would she find her? Sophie shook her head.

"Keep your head in the game," she whispered to herself, a small chill shaking the words from her lips.

They stopped, and Elloveve looked concerned. Her eyes darted back and forth before she ushered the children off the road and down the small field to the stables. They could hear the horses frantically crying out as the building caught fire, spreading quickly. Cordelia saw Buttercup tied up and braying in terror. Elloveve placed a hand on her muzzle to calm her while she worked to release her from her halter, but she was still wide-eyed and tense. Then a small hand touched her cheek. Buttercup froze, her ears pricking forward in relief as she saw her little friend Cordelia smile at her with that known kindness. Elloveve was able to undo the knot, turning her over to Cordelia who led her to her tack calmly and set about preparing her for a ride.

The sound of Elloveve's blade striking rope and wood, cutting a horse free, startled her.

"Shh, it's ok girl. I'm with you. We will leave together. It's ok, I'm here." Cordelia said soothingly.

As the other five horses set out into the darkness, their severed tethers dancing at their necks, Buttercup calmly nuzzled Cordelia. Sophie gently placed the well-crafted bridle in the horse's mouth and over her alert and calm ears. They began to lead her towards the outskirts of town.

The screams of terrified villagers began to fade into the night as they moved away from town, but the roar of the numerous fires never seemed to cease. The smell of burning tar and grass clawed nauseatingly at their noses until it was gradually replaced by the dry wood smoke of several bonfires dotting the field.

The children neared the old tree and clearing to the south of the blacksmith's shop, where they could see the bonfires.

"Stick close, children. This can't be good," Elloveve said in a hushed tone. Looking down the road towards the edge of town, they kept their urgent but quiet pace. She was sure the invaders wouldn't be focused on this old mill road, a road that had been overgrown with high grasses now from the lack of use. Thinking of Lorahana and Erebus, Elloveve bowed her head. The cowl of her dark green cape and her dampened flame red hair now framed a worried face. She softly spoke to herself. "Please be there."

They led Buttercup to a small boulder just off the road and looked down to an open area in the field. A large tree was at the edge of the clearing, just outside the glow of one of the largest bonfires crackling in the night air. The rain stung their eyes and hung their clothes tight to their bodies. Sophie unrolled a few of the woolen saddle blankets and threw one over her shoulders. Seeing this, the other children each pulled one from her for comfort as well. Elloveve tensed up as she heard a familiar voice approaching the firelight and motioned for them all to hide behind the boulder.

They saw the silhouette of Erebus enter the glow of the fire, led by another in dark armor. Orcs milled about in the field laughing to each other as they searched for loot or any escapees.

Erebus's armor glinted in the firelight as he sighed.

"I did as you asked. You have the sword." Erebus said.

The dark man turned and pulled back his cowl to reveal a pasty, almost translucent, face. He was gaunt with sunken cheekbones and icy blue green eyes that held an unholy gaze. Zane drew closer to the front alongside Elloveve. She could feel him tense up, like a horse's reins drawn tight. Placing a hand on his shoulder his blue eyes met hers, pleading. She slowly shook her head side to side as Elloveve drew her bow gently to her left hand. A hoarse croaking voice cut though the cold wet air like a spear.

"Yes! Yes, you did," the dark man stated sharply as he nodded to a few orc archers. In response, they crept into the firelight with their bows trained on the knight.

Erebus bowed his head, and Elloveve's heart dropped. He had no weapon. Her right hand found the fletching of an arrow in her quiver. She sighed as she looked back at the faces of the children, eyes so wide that she wished couldn't see what she feared could come next. The dark man walked behind Erebus.

"Well done. Blacksmith," he croaked softly.

The dark man drove an elbow into the nape of Erebus's neck, dropping him to his knees with a cry of pain. In response, a banshee's cry broke through the night as the children saw fire erupting in bursts from someone running in the field towards them.

The figure ran towards Erebus, throwing bolts of fire from the palms of their hands and striking the multiple orcs stalking through the denser grasses. One by one they fell. Zorin looked on in horror, straining to see who was wielding such arcane power. Soon the woman entered the firelight, firing a bolt at the dark figure and another at a target behind the great tree. The bolts struck, sending the dark man reeling to the ground with a shriek.

Cordelia saw her mother, a determination glinting in her eyes as she ran to Erebus. Reaching down. she drew a long sword from the fallen body of an orc, smoke still rising from where her blast had taken him down just moments before. Resuming her jog to the kneeling form of her husband. She handed him the sword. A great ribbon of dark red now shone across Erebus's armored belly, a deep wound that was likely sapping his life greatly. Wearily, he drew the blade to his eye from habit, to check the edge briefly before the sound of familiar steel being drawn from behind a tree caught their attention.

Zorin's heart sank. "No, it can't be."

"This is fine work." The unmistakable voice of Zorin's father rang out. Zorin's face went white as his hands began to shake. From the shadows, his tall form stepped into the light. His long black hair cast blue highlights as light waltzed across it. Benedict noted the red scales of his armor, a five headed dragon emblazoned across the chest.

Elloveve looked back to see tears welling in Zorin's eyes. She looked down at her surrounded friends illuminated in the bonfire light. "I can't do anything," she thought sadly as she clenched the bow in her hand. "If I attack, it will draw their attention to the children. I...I have to protect the children." She brushed a tear from her eye as she tucked the bow to her back. If they needed to flee she had to be ready. "I have to keep the oath."

"Why have you done this?" Lorahana said between clenched teeth as she steadied her wounded husband. Pallus smiled cruelly as he nodded to the dark man rising from where he had fallen in the tall grass. As the dark man rose, his chapped lips split his gaunt face as his hand drew a black and copper mace to a gloved hand.

Erebus and Lora looked at each other. Erebus seemed to plead with her in that moment before she smiled knowingly at him.

Lifting the cuff of her white blouse, she revealed the sword-shaped tattoo Cordelia always admired when her mother cradled her in those cold nights. Lora reached down and, closing her eyes, mumbled some arcane words before touching that tattoo on her wrist.

A sword of pure flame erupted from her hand. She dropped into an offensive pose, her back to Erebus's. Zane now saw that Erebus held a wounded side, blood seeping through his gloved fingers. The smell of the fires was acrid and burned their dry throats. It wasn't just wood burning, he noted with fear.

Orcs came from the shadows as Lora dove at them with her flame blade. They seemed to fall before her as she danced between them without even touching them. She gently spun from one to the next, effortlessly blocking any attack and countering with her blade or an arcane blast of blue energy.

Erebus charged the dark man holding the mace. The man parried and drove the handle into Erebus's gut. Lora was startled and looked back. At that moment, time slowed for Cordelia.

She saw Erebus drop to a knee, his face twisted in pain. Her mother reeled on her heel to see her husband as a great ax struck her in the back, driving her down into the tall grass.

"No!" the voice next to her erupted, as she felt Zane leap the fence in front of them. Elloveve's hand barely missed the chance to restrain the grief-stricken child. Erebus looked up in horror as he saw Zane rushing toward them. Zane reached down and grabbed a fallen sword from an orc's body and charged towards the dark man. Stepping away from Erebus, the man growled, "Come, child, and let me show you the darkness of my queen!"

Pallus stepped forward to kick Erebus's prone body with a boot. Elloveve cloaked the children under her cape in the darkness. They had to go. Sophie looked with horror as Zane swung at the man, only to be swatted to the side like a sack of flour. Zane crumpled to the ground, unmoving.

Erebus howled with anger as he forced himself to stand. "You killed my son!" He swung a gauntleted hand into Pallus's gut. Two arrows sunk into the knight's armor from the shadows. He yelled out in anger, the pain dulled in his grief. Pallus drove a knee into his wounded side. As Erebus dropped his head he growled from his teeth, "...and my Lora!"

Pallus saw only the glint of the razor sharp steel as Erebus quickly grazed his cheek from ear to nose. He felt the warm flow of blood before any pain. Erebus smiled at him with bloodied teeth.

"My honor is my life." As he lunged at Pallus, he felt the blade pass between his ribs.

He could feel every deviation in the steel and knew what felled him was his own making. Benedict saw it too, and the glint of the silver dragon turtle's red eyes seemed to look back at him as his uncle's eyes faded, the forge's fire now forever lost to them.

Hot tears erupted down Benedict's face as Elloveve helped him onto Buttercup's back with the other children. She swung herself around them and, at a full gallop, they rode away from the town into the darkness.

Hours later, Zorin looked around in the night rain. The new smell of the salty sea air was a welcome change to the smoke and death. Cordelia had fallen asleep, exhausted by the horror and grief. Benedict glanced at him but looked away. Sophie just stared blankly into the distance where the coast's cliffs stood high above the crashing surf.

As they rode along the coastline, they were approaching the gently turning arms of the Windmill. This was the windmill that supplied the flour in the town, Zorin remembered. He remembered the stacks of flour at the inn they had bounded up. Zane and he had done that just a few hours earlier, but now it felt like another lifetime… and Zane was gone. He dropped his head to hold back the tears.

THestone base of the windmill had a small house attached. As they approached along the road, the door to the house opened up. They saw an old man, the miller, his gray mutton chops thick and soggy with rain. He waved at them and Elloveve waved back. The old man saw the fires of OallEnAkhan in the distance beyond these refugees riding by his farm. The man drew a long heavy breath and turned to the young blonde girl next to him. She was about the same age as the other children, with shoulder length golden hair and eyes to match, eyes that were like rings of gold suspended in a glacier. Though they never knew the miller and his daughter who lived in the old windmill, they were told he was a kind man who kept to himself.

Elloveve was practicing her words in her mind. She felt the need to tell him to run, to escape as they had. As if sensing this, the man smiled at her. His deep blue eyes creased gently in sad acknowledgement. With a nod he looked at his daughter and motioned her inside. Elloveve brought up a hand to speak but was interrupted by his voice.

"Bless you, be safe," he said, his eyes bright like sapphire fires as he painfully turned on his heel to walk back inside the mill. Closing the door to the area, that was the furthest the children had ever been.

Elloveve sighed as she lowered her arm back to Buttercup's oiled leather reins. Step by step, they put the windmill and their home further behind them. The distant surf crashing on the rocks below the cliffside played in concert with the breeze that gently lapped at tear-streaked faces and the wet locks of hair plastered to cheeks.

After a few moments of silence, Zorin asked, "Where are we going to go now?"

Elloveve said gently, "Port L'For." Sophie burst into wracking sobs of memory and she wrapped an arm around her. Sophie heard Zane's laughter and imagined his arms as well.

"We will start again in Port L'For."

Elloveve looked down the road. As the surf crashed below and Sophie's sobs slowed, the elven archer began to sing a song gently in harmony with the breeze. An elven tune, ancient like the forest itself. Though they did not understand the sweet language of the elves, Elloveve translated it in her head.

> *These memories of you,*
> *I will always keep.*
> *The maiden saw you were tired,*
> *And put you to sleep.*

Zorin rested his head on Benedict's shoulder and draped an arm over Cordelia and Sophie. Drawing his cheek to the backs of his chosen family, he heard her voice fade. He hoped to be swallowed into dreams, far away from this nightmare.

II

CHAPTER 1

THE DAWN

For ten years I've had nightmares of that night. I saw our home destroyed.
I watched the closest woman I had to a mother die.
I couldn't save the one who rescued me.
My greatest teacher was lost as well.
I can still hear Zorin ask,
"Where are we going to go?"

~Benedict Shieldheart

"Hard to port!" The bosun's cry was followed by the familiar and much anticipated pipe. A boy, barely 20, looked back from the rolling sea. His dark brown eyes fell to the long wooden arm he currently straddled.

The deck heaved forty feet below his bare feet as he gently swayed with the tide, the once great square sail, pulled up where he had tied it off, draped below him. He breathed with purpose into his nose and smiled.

That smell of the dockside fishery was actually a welcome sign. It always reminded him of copper and cucumbers, when it was pleasant. Today was one of those days. He could hear the busy dock, workers and laughing sailors taking to the streets, ready to spend their coin.

He felt the brown beard around his chin. "Three months." He could confirm it had been three months since he had smelled and heard Port L'For. The boy grinned as he crawled his way to the web-like network of ropes used as a ladder.

"Lads, here's your pay. Thanks for all the help."

The stout purser passed out a small bag of jingling coins to each of them in turn. His blue eyes shone from behind the ruddy face and dark orange beard. A smile broke through.

"Welcome home, Zorin ."

THE WARRIOR WALKED DOWN THE street with purpose. Her long blonde hair was pulled back from soft cheeks. Her blue eyes were like a deep ocean and her lips, which seemed to draw you closer, pulled back with a smirk as she shook her head slightly. The woman knew there were eyes on her. She just didn't care, nor did she ever care for the affections men provided. The dark scales of her armor cast a red hue at the edges, held back at the waist by a braided auburn belt from which swung a sheathed longsword capped on either end with simple brasswork. It was a sword of purpose. Not a fancy wall hanger. This was her paycheck.

The sellsword's boots fell heavily on the ground as she walked. The strength she possessed could be seen when her arms rippled as they swung in time with her steps.

The smell of sweet meadow flowers mixed with oiled steel and leather as she walked. She had returned from collecting payment for what she politely called a 'hunt.' The warrior was happy, as this was another one she was able to subdue without death. She prided herself in returning stolen goods or bringing in wrongdoers without bloodshed. The sellsword wasn't a butcher after all, though she made a living off what she was good at. That sword was as keen as her persuasive voice and her arm as strong as her startling good looks.

Strong, beautiful, and absolutely dangerous. The warrior turned to the door of the shop where a hammer rang against the steel in the next room. "Good," she smiled.

Opening the door, a wave of heat washed over her with the smell of burning coals and hot steel. She saw the young man in a dark leather apron hammering a glowing bar. His dark hair fell like raven's feathers around his face in a very traditional cut. His face was clean-shaven and glistened with sweat. She smiled at her chosen brother.

"Benedict!" she chimed, as he looked up and smiled gently.

Placing the now dimly-lit bar back in the glowing fire, he walked to her with a grin.

"Sophie." He threw his arms around her in a firm hug. "When did you get back?"

"Just now. Thought I'd stop by before going to the house."

"Thanks, great to see you. Tonight Cordelia is performing at the Pig and Turtle. Will you join us?"

"Of course!" Sophie thought of their little sister. Cordelia was amazing with both her flute and voice. This should not be missed.

"Great, I'll see you at home."

Benedict patted her armored shoulder and returned to the forge. Sophie smiled. As she left she felt a pang of regret gnaw at her heart. She remembered his brother, the only boy she ever loved. Sighing, she swung the wooden door open with a single arm, her triceps springing to a solid horseshoe shape as they flexed. Sophie paused as the sun struck her face, remembering his laugh and his cunning smile.

"I miss you," Sophie whispered to herself as she stepped into the light.

If she had not been lost in her own thoughts, she might have noticed that the hammer paused for a moment as Benedict remembered, too.

"FOUR CUPS OF FLOUR TO one cup of sugar, a sprinkle of rose water and cinnamon, beat six quail eggs."

The kitchen was alive with the sounds of pans and smells of fresh-baked bread. A woman in a dirty apron was reading from an old scrap of parchment, carefully moving each item as she confirmed the ingredients. She paused and pulled her long red hair back from her face, revealing her slender jaw, high cheekbones, and her pointed ears. There was a decorated lacy cuff of purest silver around her left ear. It was shaped like a horse's head from the intricate twisting of the knotwork.

Sitting across the oaken countertop sat her younger friend. Long black hair stood in contrast to her white blouse and corset. She was lost in thought as she commanded a small flame to dance over her knuckles. The heat wasn't enough to harm, it was just...

"Cordelia!" Elloveve barked, jarring the young girl from her concentration, causing the flame to vanish.

Elloveve chuckled. "Are you going to help me, or what? It's for your employer, after all."

Cordelia laughed. "I'm sorry, I was just thinking."

"About what?"

Cordelia was embarrassed. She wasn't sure how to respond. She hesitated, but Elloveve could read it.

"About what child? Come. You can tell me."

"It's just, tonight is my first time playing this new song. It's great that you and everyone will be there, but..." She paused and summoned some strength from deep within. "I wish my father and mother were here."

"Oh, Cordelia." Elloveve smiled and wiped her hands on a cloth. Walking over to Cordelia, Elloveve wrapped her arms around the young girl. "I do too, kiddo. I do too."

They both sighed for a moment in their embrace before returning to the kitchen. Cordelia picked up the mixing bowl and spoon as she began adding the ingredients. She smiled suddenly.

"I'm not sure why Avar likes these cookies so much." She chuckled. "I think they are a little fancy for a dockside tavern."

Elloveve looked at her with a smirk. "Well, even a dockside tavern is entitled to a little luxury now and then, I think."

She laughed, thinking of the jovial little man. He was shorter than most at about five feet even. Known for bold silks with gold and bronze accessories, the owner of the Pig and Turtle Inn was a kind and fair man. He wasn't a pushover, though. Elloveve had seen him leap onto a table in order to dress down a drunken minotaur sailor who was being aggressively rude with one of the barmaids.

Avar loved the ladies that worked for him but his true vice was sensual luxuries like soft silks, bold perfumes, gentle music, and delicate pastries. Some would whisper he was actually a half-Dwarf, given his stature and love of the finer things.

Cordelia was pulled from her thoughts when the door to the small townhouse burst open. Zorin's deep purple tunic had been fastened over his white deck shirt. He carried his canvas bag of belongings over one shoulder and a small ivory statuette in his other hand. Cordelia dropped the spoon into the bowl and ran to him, wrapping him up in a big hug.

He chuckled. "Woah there, kiddo! I missed you too, but look! I made this as we journeyed to the Southlands. One of the mates had a piece of a narwhal's horn. I beat him in a game of dice for it."

He smiled proudly but, after seeing the look of disapproval on Elloveve's face, quickly continued. "So anyway, since I was running the rigging and the journey was very calm this time, there were many hours of sitting on the yardarm or on the port side, where we had a few benches set into the deck. I'd sit there and whittle on this little guy." He proudly turned the small white dragon over in his hand.

The head was pulled back,its chin laid against its bowed throat, forming a strong S shape. Its lips were curled, showing rows of sharp teeth, and the hands and feet were one piece together. The tail coiled in the original horn's shape to form the base upon which it sat when he placed it on the counter. No matter t that Zorin thought it was crude in some areas, Cordelia was entranced.

"Oh, I love it!" she said as she crouched eye level, matching its own gaze.

"Good!" He smiled. "Because it's yours."

She threw her arms around him, "Oh, thank you!"

"Of course!" Zorin said, chuckling and turning to Elloveve. "And something for-".

Elloveve snickered. "You know how I..."

"How you hate gifts." Quickly recognizing how she hated to be interrupted as well, Zorin reached into his belt and pulled out the pouch of his earnings, a shameful apologetic smile across his worried face. Elloveve laughed as she brushed his hand holding the gold aside, giving him a hug.

"Welcome home, you dirty pirate." They all laughed.

A few hours later, Elloveve was packing the small lady finger cookies on a shiny silver baking pan. She had placed a lace napkin on it, to make it look more special. Benedict, Zorin, and Sophie were all getting caught up.

Sophie had returned with a nice bit of money, enough to

probably bring in a roast for the week. Zorin had paid the rent up to date and Benedict had brought in some fresh apples and dried smoked fish from the docks on his way home. Cordelia was absent, as she had left to go discuss with Avar the night's events he had planned and how her music would make this "a night to remember!"

Port L' For really was a decent place for them. Elloveve missed her trees, but she could periodically leave and find an afternoon hunting in the forest a few miles outside of town. She had her own memories, after all, and needed time with herself to keep those demons at bay.

Benedict looked so much like his father Lucilius, strong and proud. She smiled as she thought of how Cordelia was beginning to look just like Lorahana. Zorin was shaping up to be a great man, but humble. Unlike his father, Lord Pallus. She looked at Sophie. Sophie smiled at her friends and nodded as they told their tales, but every once in a while her eyes would look out the window, across the port of L'For into the red orange dusk beginning to settle on the town.

Elloveve sighed. She knew that look. Elloveve recognized that look in herself as she had once loved and lost, as well. But that was many years ago. Quickly brushing his memory aside, she noted the time.

"All right, are we all ready to go?"

"Yes!" Everyone excitedly rose up to go out into the bustling street, where the merchants had begun to pack up for the day. The sound of wooden shutters closing on the day shops was answered with the bustle of night vendors wheeling carts of various cooked meat and smoked fish.

Elloveve chuckled again as she glanced protectively at the tray of treats in her hands, Avar's excitement playing in her mind.

"Everyone must come! This will be a night to remember!"

CHAPTER 2

A NIGHT TO REMEMBER

The sounds of merriment were deafening outside the small oak room. The bloodwood table was smooth to the touch, a deep coat of linseed oil mixed with peppermint rubbing into Cordelia's finger gently as she stroked it. She looked at herself in the mirror and a smile crept across her face. "It feels like a full house." She looked back at the small dish of peach-colored powder and the small horsehair brush in her hand. Smiling, she dabbed at it quickly and briskly applied it to her cheeks, bringing out the soft contours of her cheekbones under her bold eyes.

There was a knock at the door.

"Come in!"

A joyful face peeked in at the door handle's height, it was Avar, the Tavern's owner. "My, don't you look splendid! We are almost ready to receive you, my shining star, though everyone will be blinded by your beauty! Only your sweet music will save us from being lost forever!" He twirled and clasped his hands together, barely able to contain his excitement. "Are you excited?"

"Yes!"

"Well this, my dear, is a magnificent evening! The ale is bold, the wine is sweet, the cookies and pastries are all lavish and not one person is in a foul mood! Ah yes! I almost forgot." He reached in his pocket. "This is for you. You look like a queen, and you need to be paid as a queen." He handed her a small bag of gold tied with a small golden dragon for a broach.

"Oh Avar, thank you."

"My dear, I should thank you. Since you've come to work for me, my place is so wonderful and cheery. What we all need in these rough times." He became a bit somber. "I know it won't last forever, but this establishment will enjoy you while you are here."

She smiled and put her hand gently on his shoulder. "Avar, I have no intention of leaving, I-"

"Hush child," he said, brushing under his eye briefly, giving her a reassuring smile. "You are young and Port L'For is not the place to build a life. We are survivors here, you and I. You are too much of a star. I want you back in the sky from which you fell." He paused, thinking of something far away as he took her hands in his. With a smile and a squeeze he said, "Wherever that is, promise me you will find it." She smiled, knowing her little friend's big giving heart wouldn't let her leave until she agreed.

"Alright, I promise."

He nodded as she rose to leave, a big grin on his face as he reached into his pocket, producing a small vial of yellow liquid. He took off the crystal topper and dropped a few drops into the palm of his hand. As he gently slapped his rosy powdered cheeks with it, the smell of pine and honey came to her nose pleasantly. He smiled at her and offered his hand with a bow.

Mustering up his pride and joviality he proclaimed to her, "Cordelia Shieldheart, muse of Port L'For, please come with me! For tonight is a-"

"A night to remember!" Cordelia and Avar laughed as they left the dressing room, hand in hand.

THE CITY WAS BEGINNING TO awaken as the sun settled and the stars began to appear. A rat scurried out of the way hastily as the boot of a fleeing man nearly crushed it. He was panting heavily as he threw one foot in front of the other. His chestnut hair spilled out from under his dark hood and he clutched a red stone dangling around his neck as he ran, reassuring himself that it was still there. She was still there.

"There!" a voice huskily panted as it reverberated against the worn brick walls. "There he is!"

A dark man appeared at the other end of the alley in front of him, with a beard under a dark hood and leather. The assassin had found him, but it didn't matter. Soon he would defeat, capture and return the assassin to Maldros, but first he had to get to the docks. The docks awaited him and, more importantly, the ruby gemstone he wore around his neck.

He planted a foot in the ground and spun deftly around, only to run headlong into the powerful chest of another man who was pursuing him closer than he expected. He felt powerful arms wrap around him instantly, the deep blue-gray skin on his captor's hands becoming apparent in the moonlight, hands he still remembered on the ground just a few days ago. He should have killed him when he had the chance. He chastised himself internally for getting so sloppy.

"Not so fast, Kehlvan." The voice came from behind the dark hood through clenched teeth. "We need to talk."

As the trembling man realized he was restrained his cowl slipped to one side, revealing his thin wiry beard and the familiar pointed ears of an elf.

THE SMELL OF SWEET SPICED wine, frothy ale, and the slight tinge of pungent pipe smoke filled the air. Elloveve noted the ladyfingers cookies had been taken almost as soon as they had set them down on the long table used for the potluck of dishes brought in for the celebration.

Tonight was the first night of the annual three day festival in Port L'For, marking the beginning of the trade season with the isolated north. Half of the year the waters only allowed trade with what the sailors called "The Southlands." Though separated by continents and cultures, the regions of Viridian and Trull actively traded year round with the region of Kur, where Port L'For resided.

Preferring to use Kur as middle-ground for trade, as they were neutral in most wars that sprouted up from time to time, the elves of Viridian and the orcs and men of Trull were always looking for the fine smithed goods of the Dwarves, whether it was golden vases with gemstones encrusting the surface, making the light dance in a room, or the dwarven-steel sword that rarely needed to be sharpened. In return, the people of Kur had to look to them for food and fineries the harsh desert couldn't provide.

Only during the warmer months did the majority of the heavy merchant ships make those trips north for other goods, making them rarer. The idea was after the ice had broken, the sea would calm and so would the creatures beneath its dark waves. Then the furs, oils, and gems of the north could be traded. The artisans of all countries looked forward to this time as many of their goods depended on this for their own trade.

The tavern was full to bursting. Shoulder to shoulder, people stood waiting in anticipation for a seat to open. A short man with bushy eyebrows looked and spied an empty seat at a table with three others. He moved through the crowd towards it and reached a leathery hand for the chair.

"Taken, friend," the young raven-haired man said..

The little man sighed and walked away, almost bumping into a tall woman with golden hair in a reddish suit of scale mail carrying four mugs in her hands.

"Woah! Excuse me!"

The woman shouted at the little man as he darted into the crowd. With a sigh, she continued to her table.

"That bar was packed. No way the barmaids can get to us right now. We are on our own."

Sophie sat down the mugs and began passing them out. "There we are, Elloveve. Wine for you and I, ale for you, Zorin, and-"

"Milk?" the raven haired man asked questioningly.

Sophie smiled, "Yes, Benedict, only the finest year of course."

He smiled and took it from her with both hands, offering a gentle nod of appreciation.

"Thank you, Sophie," Elloveve said. Glancing at the curly haired head of Zorin greedily quaffing his drink, she prompted him with an elbow to the ribs, making him spit out a bit of the drink he was hastily gulping down.

"Ack! Uh-er, indeed! Thank you!" Sophie chuckled with Zorin.

"Oi! Watch where you're goin'!" Benedict noticed the minotaur protest as two thugs pushed past to sit at a dimly lit table back in the dark corner of the bar. They had dark cloaks and hoods covering themselves, which looked to be made of rough wool. They roughly shoved a terrified man into a seat and sat to either side of him. His wide eyes seemed to dart back and forth from behind the dirty, unwashed face. What appeared to be a thin, scraggly beard framed the gaunt and wiry features of the man as he trembled. He was dressed in dark black armor that hung loosely from his body, barely finding anything to hold onto. Benedict could feel his hair stand on end.

He started to turn a hand back to the table without taking his eyes off them. "Hey, Zorin, do you see-"

He was interrupted as the stage exploded in sound. Horns, pipes and drums struck alongside a gong the size of a man. sounding like an army of musicians in the hall even though there were only six players. The room was built for performance, amplifying the sound from the stage and washing it over the enchanted crowd naturally from the shape of the curved walls.

The gong was decorated with four relief images showing four different landscapes. Lightning ripped across the sky in one. where a mountainside showed trees flowing down in a landslide. Oceans boiled, and finally volcanoes belched forth fountains of magma. Around the edge in a huge ring were symbols for the four elements. Benedict had once heard that Avar had acquired this piece from some forgotten temple in the Deadlands or the deserts of Kur, though some rumors say it was from the Jade Temple itself.

He was always curious about it, as many religious groups respected the elements in some way. This depiction of violent blends of earth, air, fire and water were jarring and seemed slightly blasphemous in contrast to the grandmotherly Hag he was accustomed to hearing about.

Avar stepped out onto the oak stage. Now towering over the crowd, he rapped a cane topped with a lion's head on oak planking that echoed through the room. The crowd grew silent.

"Ladies and Gentlemen of Port L'For! Tonight we celebrate the new season, and together may The Stone judge us to be worthy of great riches!"

The crowd erupted in cheers along with the joyous clanking of pewter and horn mugs.

He looked at the crowd and smiled, stretching out his arms and embracing the cheers, soaking the energy in.

Benedict was still staring at the motionless dark men, noting that the terrified man looked like he was about to cry.

"My friends, she is no stranger nor is she a stranger to you. Without further adieu, please welcome the Muse of Port L'For, Cordelia!"

The crowd cheered for their local favorite. Benedict noticed the smaller of the two cloaked men turn towards the stage sharply. After a moment his shrouded head turned side to side as if scanning the area, as if the name of his cousin was of interest to the shadowclad man. Benedict cracked his neck gently in anticipation. Sure, he told himself, there are many ladies with the name Cordelia but he wasn't going to take a chance.

Soon, three other musicians took the stage flanking Cordelia, each nodding and smiling before the tavern went deathly quiet. The crowd could hear her breath as she raised the ivory flute to her lips, a small carved dragon dangling from her wrist.

Her song lilted on the air gently like the breeze over the docks on a calm sunny midday, before the afternoon storms would occasionally roll in. As the other musicians set a slow wandering gait to the tune, she began to sing.

> *There were three ships*
> *In the southern sea*
> *Filled with love*
> *For you and me*
> *Silks so fine*
> *Gold and wine*

She returned to her flute, playing the opening melody again before holding a note out and drawing the song to a close.

Silence washed over their ears only momentarily before the bar erupted with cheers. Cordelia bowed her head, smiling. The other musicians grinned and applauded her as well.

Cordelia brought the flute to her lips as they launched into an upbeat melody. The room sprung to life as they began cheering and dancing. Zorin leapt up and slammed his empty mug on the table. With his practiced and usual flair, he offered a hand to Sophie. She laughed and waved him away. "Well fine, then!" He grinned and then, bowing to them, began to join a few sailors in a rowdy hornpipe dance. Sophie and Elloveve cheered.

Benedict was staring at the dark men. They were angry. He couldn't tell why, but they were both larger than the man. He saw the largest of the three men wearing some emblem he didn't recognize. A crest or shield, possibly showing they held a high rank. Military or maybe police, but not from here. Suddenly, he roughly grabbed the terrified captive with a blue-gray hand and jerked him out of his seat. The other, shorter man nodded as they made their way out of the bar. Benedict noted the sign of leadership as he turned to Elloveve and Sophie.

"Hey, I -"

He tried to get the attention of his friends, but he found it hopeless. Benedict, though someone who followed a very strong moral code of honor, wasn't a stranger to the occasional bar brawl when the cruder methods were required, and had a few scars marring his twenty-year-old's young face.

Action being imperative, he rose up and followed them outside into the street.

MOONLIGHT SPILLED ACROSS THE COBBLESTONE streets, blending with torch and brazier-borne firelight from the tavern's door as he stepped out. The market square was one hundred feet on all four sides, with a fountain of gray stone in the center of the smooth river rock cobblestones. The fountain featured a lion and a bear facing east and west, respectively.

People were still making their way to the Pig and Turtle. Cordelia had once told him this was "fashionably late," a completely unfamiliar concept to her organized and time-bound cousin. She saved her lively music for this time, knowing she could try out new material first to her more dedicated crowd of followers, who were more understanding, or forgiving at times. It was the biggest tavern and was known for the best entertainment. Other shops lined the open square, and people strolled through, making their way to various destinations.

He scanned the crowd for the three men.

A voice hissed in the darkness to his left, "Stop fighting it and just tell us. When?!"

Following the whimpering of the victim, Benedict looked to the end of the building he had just walked from. There were the two men, one gripping the collar of the small man and roughly interrogating him as the other looked on.

"You there!" Benedict started to jog to the men, his hand resting on the brass pommel of the Broadsword at his hip, letting them know he was being serious.

They jolted, startled by the outburst and the young warrior approaching. The small man broke free of the grip and ran down the dark alley, chased by the larger of the cloaked men. Benedict saw dark blue-gray hands swing outward as the tall form ran in pursuit of the smaller prisoner.

The last man, the smaller of the cloaked figures, stood up straight and shook his head in annoyance before turning and running across the market. Benedict recognized the tactic and knew him to be the one with answers, if not the leader. Sprinting through the street, the man lept over a small cart and pulled a stack of apple crates down to separate his pursuer. Benedict dodged around them deftly and continued to sprint, the broadsword clanking at his side. He noticed the man was not hindered by a sword.

The man dodged into a clothing shop and, as Benedict neared the entrance, he quickly unhooked his sword belt where it clanged to the steps just outside the door.

"Move!" he shouted at the terrified shopkeep, who dodged backward into a pile of soft linens for sale. The dark man spun around just in time to catch a fist across his right cheek and a shoulder into his chest, pressing him to the wall. Benedict could smell trail dust and the musk of a man that had been on horseback for a long time.

"Wait! You don't understand!" The voice sputtered out of breath from behind a dark veil, his blue eyes determined.

"Who are you? Why are you here?" Benedict gritted his teeth. "What were you doing with that man?"

The shrouded man grabbed Benedict's arm, his dark sleeve falling back. Benedict's eyes grew wide.

"Listen. We've traveled a long way to warn this town and don't have time to explain. Something horrible is about to happen and that man had the details as to when."

Benedict was staring at the man's arm, trembling. "It can't be…"

His captive was confused, but suddenly stopped struggling and listened to him. "What?"

Benedict nodded with a tremble, still not letting down his guard.

"Where did you get that scar?"

Roping up the man's forearm was a rippling scar, one that only the kiss of fire could bring. He sighed but, noting the time, began to protest.

"That has nothi-"

"Where!"

"I..." The man sighed and looked around, judging his options. Realizing the best one lay in front of him, he took off the dark veil, revealing a short few-weeks-old soft, blonde beard. Pulling his hood back, the sandy blonde locks fell across his cheeks. "I saved my brother from a fire many years ago."

Tears welled in Benedict's eyes. "Zane? Is it? Is it really you?"

The man's eyes welled up. Years of solitary pain and hope boiled to the surface along with his tears.

"Benedict?"

The long lost brothers embraced in that shop.

"I thought we lost you."

"I did too, honestly, and it's a story I promise to tell you soon. But we need to-"

Screams erupted from the square as flashing fire illuminated the terrified shopkeeper's face.

"We need to go!"

Bolting out the door, Benedict grabbed his sword from the ground, the red glow of erupting fire casting eerily familiar upon the dark leather scabbard. Looking up from the damp cobblestone, he saw them.

He saw the dragons.

CHAPTER 3

A DARK REUNION

Fire erupted into the tavern, billowing tendrils of amber along the ceiling like writhing snakes. The coarse acrid smoke from burning bloodwood, tar, and oak began to fill the hall.

"Cordelia!" Sophie yelled at the shocked woman on stage. "Jump!"

Cordelia looked back at Avar. The small man blew her a kiss and waved, mouthing goodbye with a smile on his face, tears welling in his eyes before he dove into the backstage stairwell. She watched as he nimbly dodged the burning debris falling from above, blocking the way for larger people than he. Avar was no stranger to a quick escape and hadn't made it this far in his life by sticking around to find out.

"Now! We don't have time!" Elloveve yelled. Snapping back, Cordelia nodded. Her eyes narrowed slightly as she jumped off the stage into Sophie's arms. Zorin was shoving a few panicked stragglers out the door.

"Move!"

One man with a short beard was still deep in his mug and unaware of the inferno beginning to form around him. His eyes tried to focus on the young sailor who grabbed his tunic roughly, trying to stand him up out of his comfortable chair.

"What's happening?"

"The world is ending, what does it matter; move, or you will too!" With a final shove, he pushed them out of the way as a fiery beam crashed to the floor where he once stood.

"Holy mother of... hey, over here!" he waved at Elloveve and his sisters. They pointed at the exit adjacent to him along the smooth stone brick wall.

The bitter smell of smoke burned his throat as Zorin made his way to the exit. Coughing, a hand grabbed him and pulled him free of the smoky room into the night air.

The air cooled his lungs immediately, but then his ears filled with screams. The roar from above sounded like a hundred lions and the huge wings that blotted out the night sky beat heavily in his ears. It passed overhead like a dark shadow as it lowered itself with its massive, batlike wings. Each beat reverberated in what was once a massive square that now seemed so small in comparison to the reptilian form. It landed with one foot on the fountain, as if simply resting its feet while stones broke and splashed into the water. The central statue remained untouched, but the pool itself now spilled into the square.

Astride his back was an orc clad in black scaled armor who yelled guttural commands at the dragon. The dragon was everything Zorin had seen in his nightmares. Its twin horns pointed forward and down its skeletal snout; green smoking acid dripped from its maw as it drooled, looking at the people running from it in the square. Its jet black color masked it in the evening marketplace, red eyes glowing with cruelty out of the obscured dark sky.

"Get down behind the barrels!" Sophie still had his arm and was roughly pulling him to join Cordelia and Elloveve behind the large casks on the side of the Pig and Turtle.

THE SCREAMS OF THE TERRIFIED people were sweet to the ears of the dragon rider flying high overhead. Chuckling to herself, she ran a deep green hand over the scaled oily skin of her mount.

"Look at them, my brother. See how they run like bugs under a rock."

"Yes… and just as filthy." The voice purred deeply in her mind. The telepathic link between them was strong. She looked up to the sky to see where her companions were. She knew she was where she was to be.

"Where are they?" She growled from behind the twin tusks gracing her mouth. Snapping her head to the right, she saw the hulking red form of the leader of this raid. She smiled cruelly. His mount was heavier and slower but also much more powerful. The red dragon descended slowly, taking the time to lazily erupt a column of red orange fire upon the roof of a large building.

She laughed at the unneeded display of power, at the same time taking pride in the destruction.

"WHERE'S BENEDICT?" ELLOVEVE LOOKED TO the group as they stooped behind the palette of barrels.

"I… I don't know." Zorin whispered, watching the roof of a burning butcher's shop collapse behind them. Fear overcame Elloveve as she realized she didn't know where the young man had gone, her own realization reflected back at her as each of them stared at each other in turn.

Elloveve looked around. She was too level with the ground. She needed a better vantage point and the children needed to get out of the area.

"Zorin, you know how to get to Viridian from here, yes?" Zorin nodded, puzzled.

"I'm going to see if I can see Benedict from above." She pointed to the long roof behind them. "If we get separated, go to Viridian, follow the coast and look for Akeshbahlol."

"Thats First Port right?"

"Yes." She smiled happily, as Zorin recognized the port city. "That's the common name for it, First Port. From there we will sail west to Belz ."

She took a deep breath, seeing their puzzled faces, and focused on Cordelia, "It is time for us to move on. We can find more answers in the Ivory Library." Cordelia's eyes grew wide.

She had heard stories of the Ivory Library and the vast knowledge contained on its endless shelves. Supposedly every bit of history, science, technology and magic was documented there and guarded by the legendary Stone Monks. The Stone Monks were not cruel or righteous, they were avid guardians of the cosmic balance.

Elloveve looked at Sophie and smiled before darting to a stack of crates, bounding effortlessly up the rough cut wooden planks to the roof. The elf never disturbed a single one, as though she were a bird's feather on a gentle breeze.

More roars rang out above, followed by the black dragon in the square. The deafening thunder from those leathery wings kicked up dust and embers from the street, causing Sophie to shield her eyes from the gusts.

Another dragon, this one with deep blue scales and a yellow, smooth underbelly, landed with a lurch as it whipped its tail into a street cart filled with vegetables. A much larger crimson scaled wyrm followed with a dark black beard of horns and scales around its chin. Two horns shot up and back from its skull as it whipped its head to the side to roar at some scurrying, terrified people.

Cordelia was frozen, horrified and entranced at the same time. Here in the flesh were dragons. Those great dragons of legend her father told her about so many years ago.

The red dragon took an uneasy step towards the stack of barrels they hid behind. Zorin ducked low with the other two and motioned a single finger in front of his lips to indicate absolute silence. As if the world was paying attention, everything froze in that moment. It was absolutely silent, save for one unnerving sound drowning out all others.

A slow, deep rumble not completely unlike a boiling underground stream was all that could be heard in the square. The dragon's head swept by the barrels with a single yellow eye of curiosity. As it approached, Zorin could smell the hot muggy breath of a rotting meal in its giant teeth. Suddenly it snapped back to attention, the black slit of an iris dilating slightly.

"Fury! Let us discuss the plan for this great city." A deep shout came from his back. The dragon swung its head back to the other dragons in the square. It was Zorin's turn to be shocked. He, wide-eyed, craned his neck over the barrels with Sophie and Cordelia.

"Is that..." Cordelia whispered, looking at Zorin.

His hands trembled as he wiped the sweat from them on his dark cotton trousers. Without looking at her he hissed, "None other."

Zorin saw the huge man drop from the back of the red dragon with a crown on his black-haired head, holding a huge sword in his hand. The pommel held a silver dragon turtle with two red eyes, glowing with power. Zorin's heart pounded deep in his stomach.

"Hello, father." He spat, restrained behind clenched angry teeth.

Lord Pallus strode to the center of the three dragons. The orc rider nimbly slid off her mount to join him, dark chains shaking like chimes as she walked. The third rider was shrouded, pale hands clutching the haft of a large, studded mace. Their eyes shone out like two orange-red glowing embers from behind the dark veil as they too dismounted and joined the other two riders.

"With this, Kur is ours along with Bloodwood and most of Viridian."

"Most, not all. Rotten elves still hold access to the dark reaches," the orc snarled.

"No matter, we are victorious. They will soon fall."

"They hold fast though, we must–"

"Silence!" The dark figure hissed, the shroud over his face falling away to show a single, sunken cheek. "This is defeatist prattle." He turned to Lord Pallus. "What now, my lord?"

"We will raze the town for supplies and set up a garrison. Then we make our assault on Viridian." He grew very cold as he thought deeply. "Our underground allies must be freed. They will be key to my ascension."

The orc leader laughed and pulled a horn from her belt. It was carved in crude symbols and wrapped with what appeared to be a copper hammer. The symbol matched one on her olive green wrist that moved like a banner in the wind as her tendons grew tight. Her lips pursed together as she began sounding it. From the shadows, a flood of orc troops in charred black armor began to flow as a single chaotic mass into the square and shops from Cordelia's right.

"Zorin?" She whispered gently.

"Hmm?" He was still intent on his father, the source of ten years of hate from that night, and a loveless relationship before then. The night he lost his best friend.

"Zorin!"

"What? Oh!"

"Move!" Sophie stood and shoved Zorin out of the way as a huge cleaver-like blade crushed the barrel they were behind. Zorin rolled and stood on his feet, his rapier deftly in his hand. He moved to Cordelia, who was cupping a small bolt of fire in her hands that slowly began to grow.

Sophie swatted the great axe to the side with a blow from her long sword as she drove a shoulder to the orc, knocking him backwards. Her eyes closed and she mumbled some arcane words before throwing it at the orc in front of Sophie. It met its mark, exploding in a shower of sparks, sending the orc back on his heels to the ground.

They darted across the courtyard towards an open alley the orcs hadn't reached yet. The red dragon roared and swung a tail at them as they scattered, barely missing the muscular tree trunk-sized limb. Zorin rolled under it, feeling the breath of wind as it sailed mere feet from his body, smashing into the store face for a bakery, sending flour dust in a plume out of the gaping wound of the wall.

"Go!" He shouted at Cordelia, who was wide-eyed next to him. Rising up he heard a shout. Standing on the rooftop was a figure. Her flame-red hair cascaded from her shoulders, keeping time with the fire now surrounding her. Elloveve calmly drew an arrow to her cheek before sending it loose. The arrow sailed across the courtyard, slamming into an orc pursuing two other figures.

Scanning the crowd quickly, Elloveve recognized the armor of one of her own. It was definitely Benedict, but the other figure was dressed in dark leathers like the orcs. They ran alongside Benedict and had two crude orcish daggers drawn. She didn't recognize this figure but they were working together, she thought. Smiling, she said softly, "Looks like Benedict found another friend."

They continued to run to the alley.

Elloveve felt the heat of the fire dancing across her back as she fired arrow after arrow, covering their escape. She was nervous, fearing that she would lose track of one of her children. Slowing her breath, she walked through each of their names, dropping those that pursued them one by one.

"Cordelia."

Arrow shot.

"Zorin."

Arrow shot.

"Sophie."

Arrow shot.

"Benedict."

Arrow shot.

She saw the figure next to Benedict running. He whipped around an orc and in the same fluid motion cut him down with those two daggers. Whoever he was, he was on their side. Therefore, she would cover him too.

Arrow shot.

The flames grew higher and hotter.

"Just a minute longer. Please. Just a minute."

She fired, the flames licking her arms. It burned, but the children were almost safe.

She fired again and again, ignoring the searing pain in her arm. The smell of smoke and burning was nauseating, making tears well in her eyes as she tracked the children. She would do this. She would do this last thing. They reached the alley.

She sighed. They had made it.

She saw the shrouded man look up at her, one arm raised in acknowledgment before, with a nod, he disappeared. She knew those eyes. At that moment something familiar washed over her, a memory at the forefront of her mind. Was it really?

"Could it be? Oh, please let it be. Run, my children!"

Tears flowed as she looked at the rising face of Fury, his face glowing with a bright red fireball in his mouth. Glowing and growing. She laughed inwardly to herself, dropping her bow to her side. She thought of all the happiness she shared in this life. It was a good day.

Elloveve saw her younger self in the arms of the one she had loved and lost. She thought of his smile and their lost friends, hoping they would meet again in the next life. She took a deep breath of the smoky air, smelling past the smoke, past the salt sea to her soft, sweet-smelling trees. She smiled wide and closed her eyes, remembering her promise.

"I held the oath, Erebus. May the Knight and Maiden watch them now."

Throwing out her arms, she embraced the white-hot fire of the dragon.

THE CHILDREN SHOT INTO THE alley, the sounds of destruction slowly dimming as they made their way in the dark musty alleys to the edge of the city.

"Wait," Zorin panted, trying to bring enough air back into his lungs after sprinting for what seemed like an eternity. His pulse raced as his heart beat in his chest, drawing in the fresher air far away from the burning dockside they had escaped from. "Wait, who are you?" He pointed at the shrouded man.

The man spoke. "We don't have time. But soon, I-"

Recognizing the voice, Sophie's eyes grew wide. "No…" She stepped forward and the man looked away quickly.

"You don't understand, I-"

Sophie reached out, "Is it?"

As her hand closed on his hood, the man's hand clasped hers gently. His eyes were pleading with her, not because of the fear of her knowing, but of him finally leaving his shroud of ten years of fear and pain. He sighed and pulled back his hood, finally releasing his tears as they streamed down towards his bearded jaw.

"I dreamed of seeing you again everyday, Sophie."

"Oh my gods, Zane!" Sophie embraced him, hot tears cutting paths in her soot-stained cheeks. Zane wept with her as Zorin, Cordelia and Benedict joined them, all together as one family again in the dark alley of Port L'For.

CHAPTER 4

FOREST OF MEMORIES

Sophie's hands broke the crystal surface of the cold forest stream. The smell of the meadow flowers mixed with aspen and birch sweetly. She smiled, thinking of her friend's stories of how the forest calmed her and set her spirit free. She blinked a tear away gently, knowing Elloveve was gone, her spirit free and hopefully back in her beloved forest.

She took a deep breath, bringing the icy water to splash gently about her face. She imagined the battle being washed away as well in her mind. She drew a breath and unconsciously counted - something she was taught long ago when dealing with conflict, to count and be level-headed in the response.

Suddenly, drawn inward with her own breath in the enchanting and quiet forest, she remembered.

The hard branch Kartilaan used as a training sword struck her across the thigh, dropping young Sophie to her knees.

"Ow!" she yelped through clenched teeth, angrily.

"Now count, Sophie. Count until you are calm." Kartilaan, being seventeen, towered over her. Her raven black hair cascaded about her shoulders. Icy blue eyes stared at Sophie with no emotion. The eyes of a killer.he eyes of her sister.

"1, 2, 3, 4, 5," Sophie panted for air between breaths shortly, her anger holding her in its grip.

"Slower, you must breathe to fight. Every breath should give you more power."

"6, 7, 8, 9…10."

Sophie could feel the air in her lungs and the power it brought. Her blood slowed, feeling rich and full. She stood up and her sister smiled wryly. "Good. That's how we fight to win. Cold."

"Sophie." Zane's voice snapped her back to the stream she sat next to. She saw the red brown leather of her bracers over her strong forearms. Instinctively she drew a hand over her round bicep, noting how it felt as she crossed her arms. She felt a need to protect herself even though she knew there was no need.

"What?" Sophie was short in her response, sounding agitated.

"It's just, I wanted to tell you-"

"What? That you've been alive this whole time? That you're sorry you abandoned us? That you abandoned me!"

"No, it's-" Zane drew in a deep breath. "I want to tell you about what happened."

Sophie glared at him. "Fine, I'll listen." She sat hard on a fallen log, crossing her arms. Truthfully, she very much loved this familiar ghost of a man before her. His eyes and voice were the same ones she had kept in her memory for the last ten years. The boy she thought dead, that they all thought dead, had returned. Now here they were, in the same place again. Was she still that same little girl he knew? What of him, was he still who she remembered? Or was it like Elloveve's cookies, where they may have been better in memory than in reality?

So now, after escaping the town and camping last night in the dark forest, he wanted to talk. Inside she was screaming for answers, but as Kartilann had said, 'We win because we wait.'

Unbeknownst to the pair, or to the rest of the party, the thick trees in this forest were a rare Crimson Alder. The wood itself was enchanted and had been watched over by Dryads and their shepherds for ages. This forest was enchanted, but not hidden beyond the guardian streams where the elves shielded the world from the mystical land of Viridian. This forest was in the twilight area bordering the magical land itself, but still inherited some of its more special qualities.

Staying within close proximity of the Crimson Alder could enhance memories, making the peoples of the world almost relive those times, wrapped in their deepest emotions. Not good or bad, just the truth. It was also said the Librarians had unlocked the tree's properties even further at the Ivory Library.

Zane was staring off into the distance where the forest opened up into a glade. The birds' soft chirping and the cries of the occasional hawk were soft on the ears as the breeze was to the touch.

"I woke up on the back of a horse, bouncing with my hands tied. The smell of the horse and the dried sweat and blood caked to my face were enough to make me sick. And judging by the sight of that horse's leg, I already had been.

"I gathered that we had been riding way out to the east from the town, crossing into the mountains but not the desert is about all I could tell. Despite my nose's damage, I began smelling something else. Something muggy, like old dishwater. I could hear voices mumbling to each other. I don't remember much else.

"I was given to an old dwarf named Sillius. Sillius was rough and hateful. He'd smack you for breathing out of turn, let alone for stepping out of line. He showed us smaller ones how to go deeper in those mines than the 'tall folk.'

"We would slide these wooden trays in front of us and we scurried on our bellies in the dark. Gods Sophie, it was so dark. Blindly groping at the walls for ore to bring back to the smelter. Ore to make iron and iron to make steel. Steel to make weapons. Weapons for his army.

"Over time we grew accustomed to it a bit. Not like how the elves or dwarves can see in the dark, but we could almost sense shapes in the abyss. We could feel the dark; feel how close the walls were to us as we dragged our trays in that endless dark. I don't know how long I lived in that endless monotony, but I know it was a long time until one day an ogre took note of me.

'Hey, you there! Boy! Get up and fetch my mug.'

"I looked up to see a large ogre towering over me. My eyes were still adjusting to the light in the mine shaft junction where we brought back our collections. To be honest, I couldn't hear him very well. Being in those tunnels really makes you distant, like you aren't part of this world. I just kinda stared at him.

'I said boy, fetch!'

"I remember him hitting me across the cheek so hard stars danced across my squinting eyes. 'Zane' was all I could mumble.

'What did you say to me?'

"It felt so good to say my name that I almost forgot about the pain; I hadn't heard my own name in so long. I knew I could die, but I didn't care. This big lunk of an ogre would say my name, or I would die trying.

'My name is Zane.'

'You.' He grabbed me with one hand and threw me against the wall. I felt every jagged rock edge dig into my back while the wind flew out of my lungs.

"He cursed as he walked to me, drawing a cracked leather blackjack from his belt. I sputtered on the ground, unable to move. Then I saw him.

'Back down, Sledge.'

"The ogre stopped immediately and from behind him appeared a tall man in tattered black, tight-fitting clothing. A great club was strapped to his back, though looking at the muscled arms hidden beneath the dark leather bracers and cotton shreds, he didn't need it. His chest was protected by a dark set of charcoal chainmail with leather segments sporadically placed. It was his face-"

Zane paused for a moment, thinking. The smell of the trees was lost to him and the running brook at his feet no longer captivated him.

Suddenly, Zane snapped back and cupped his face in his hands, taking a deep breath of air. He shuddered slightly.

Sophie put her hand on his shoulder. "It's okay, it's okay." He looked at her and smiled.

"It was his eyes. They were blood red. He had no face. Well, none we ever knew. There was the same black gauze covering the helmet he wore, and the black horns were the only thing protruding out, curving down towards the front of the face like an angry bull.

"When he spoke, Sledge backed up, looking both disappointed and scared at the same time.

'Hmmm. we will keep an eye on this one.'

'Why wait, Maldros?' I saw Sillius hobble over, glaring at me. 'He's no good here. Maybe your pits would be a more suitable place for someone as irresponsible, lazy and generally worthless.'

"He jabbed me with the crooked stick he carried to drive the point of each word. Maldros sneered at me from behind that mask.

'Yes, why wait indeed.'"

"Hey!" Zorin's voice shook Zane back to reality.

He came up to them in a light jog. "Are you two ready to hit the road?" Sophie stood up and checked the fit of her swords briefly.

"Yeah, I think we are," Zane replied. "I'll have to tell you about the pits some other time."

"The pits?" Sophie looked at him in genuine surprise. "You mean you were actually a gladiator?"

"Yup."

"Ha! Did you run a lot?"

"Hey now, be nice." Zane smiled at the jest, throwing his arm around Sophie's shoulders.

"I had the help of some good friends, like-" Zorin paused. It had been a stressful few days and he couldn't remember the names of his friends who had helped him escape. Except for one name.

"Saza."

"Who? Who is Saza?" Zorin looked at him, perplexed. "Sounds like an elf name."

Zane braced a foot on a nearby boulder, adjusting the slender pewter buckle on his tall boots.

"Yeah, he was an elf. More so, he was a good friend." He looked at his two friends and smiled with a ray of hope. "He's tough too. I'm sure he's ok."

He shook the memory from his head. "Hey, let's get back to the camp. I don't know about you all, but there is something strange about these woods. Not sure what, though."

Zorin nodded. "Sure, pal. Meet you back at camp and we can get moving." Turning, Zorin walked back twenty or so paces to where Cordelia was packing their small collection of shared supplies in a small backpack.

"Zane," Sophie began softly once Zorin was out of earshot. "I can only imagine what you've been through. I hope you understand if I'm-"

She paused. Truth be told, she never stopped loving him, nor did she think she could. Little did she know, he felt the same for her.

"It's ok." He smiled. "I don't think we should jump back into where we were." He offered her a hug with a crooked smile she knew all too well. If she had any doubts this was really him, they were dispelled at that moment.

"Where we were? What, when we were ten?" Sophie sighed. "Let's just start here. We don't need to talk about then."

She smiled and pulled back, looking into his eyes. "Let's begin here and now. Will you stay with us?"

"Forever," Zane said with a smile. "I never want to leave any of you again."

Sophie laughed happily. "Then come, let's go."

"Friends?" Zane said sheepishly

Sophie laughed. "For now, Zane Shieldheart. For now."

Cordelia smiled at Benedict. "It's good to hear her laugh again."

"Sure is." Benedict smiled at their happiness. It was like a dream come true. They were all back together again.

The group traveled for four days in the forest and meadows, trying to stay off the roads themselves in case sympathizers from Pallus' army were near. On day three they rounded a hillside and could see a small encampment of dark armored soldiers tucked back in a glade. Nearby, a red dragon fed on some freshly slaughtered cattle. Zane noted that she was slightly smaller than Fury, and her beard of black horns wasn't nearly as full but older, much older.

A loud voice called out in the distance, "No stragglers, all clear!"

"Scouting party," Zane said to Zorin in a hushed tone. Zorin nodded in acknowledgment. They couldn't have been looking for just them, he thought, but maybe it was a good sign that others from the town escaped as well. He hoped he was right. Cordelia's face showed her curiosity as she stared at the crimson and amber scales of the dragon dining on the cattle. Zane smiled, remembering his cousin's fascination with dragons.

The group made their way past the scouting party carefully, smelling their campfires being lit and realizing the army was likely going to set camp here for the night.

A few hours later, once the campfire and voices had faded behind them, Zane broke the numbing silence.

"Hey Cordelia, did you see the beard on the dragon?" She nodded. " It's not as full as the one Pallus was riding. That means she's younger, not as powerful."

He thought about what he said and corrected, "But still way too dangerous, though. Not even the mighty Benedict could take her down." Benedict shot him a warning eye that made Zane laugh.

"Thanks, Zane. Real cute."

"There she is, gang. First Port."

They came out of the trees overlooking a rocky cliffside to the sprawling green valley below. The mid-afternoon sun, to their back and right, made the trees cast a cool shadow across the group. To their left they could see the port city on the edge of the expansive sea.

Zorin clapped Zane on his back, who was lost in thought, chewing a small blade of grass. Smiling in return, he pointed at the docks and they snickered at some private joke.

Benedict was in awe.

"It's so green. No wonder they call this land Viridian ."

They all stood silent. The birds softly called from the trees, and they could almost hear Elloveve's voice on the breeze and smell the elderflowers and honey that accompanied her graceful elven footsteps.

"She would have so loved to have seen this."

"I think she has," Benedict smiled, placing a hand on Cordelia's shoulder. "In fact, I think she's here with us now."

Sophie closed her eyes and smiled too.

THE FURS WERE SOFT ON Dabria's cheek as she opened her eyes. Her lover sat across from the bed in the dark oak and teak room that creaked. Nightblade's dark black hair was pulled back from her face as she sat in a chair looking out the small window. Dabria could hear muted voices outside and the occasional faint whistle. These blended into a sweet syrup of sound with the gently lapping waves against the hull of the ship.

Slowly Dabria stretched her arms out from the gray and white wolf pelt she favored that lay upon the soft cotton of the sheets above.

"Good Morning."

Her lover smiled as she spoke to her, taking a sip of the sweet mint tea she preferred to drink in the morning to settle her stomach. Nightblade turned to her, revealing her blue eyes, the same color of the sea they both loved.

Feet found the cold floor as she sat up, the shock helping bring her senses to the forefront. She shuffled and found her boots. Dabria's black muslin night shirt and pants were loose and comfortable. Looking at her black armor in the corner, there was no need for anything else.

The sun spilled into the room with a golden morning glow in the dawn's light. They were only three days into their journey from home and they had more days and mornings to look forward to. Just like this.

Dabria smiled at Nightblade as she ran a hand over her short cropped blonde hair and blinked her golden eyes.

"Good morning, my Sunbeam."

CHAPTER 5

TO FIND A PASSAGE

"Belz."

The man stroked his leathery face with one hand, brushing the edge of the thick salt and pepper mutton chops framing his cheekbones. Above them the icy blue eyes peered into Zorin's heart, searching for some reason to deny his request, he was sure of it. His other hand cupped the burgundy bowl of a long stemmed pipe. Zorin never saw the man light it, and he noted there was no thick smoke that seemed to swirl and stick greasily to the skin as he expected. This ship's captain absently chewed on the end of the prop and stared coldly back at Zorin.

"Why are you and your family going to the new country?" He squinted an eye. "To seek your fame?"

Winding up for the pitch, Zorin began. "Sir, we are leaving because-"

"Shut yer gob, boy." The old ship captain leaned in and in a strong, forced tone that reminded Zorin of a crashing tide on a rocky shore continued, "I can hear the winding of a tale like a fishing reel. Best to not lie to me." His breath was hot and Zorin's face went flush. He sat back, his voice softening slightly. "Your hands don't look like your fancy clothes." Zorin looked at the purple velvet tunic he was wearing. He had saved months and months of his own money to buy the soft garment last year.

The family said it was his money to save and spend as he saw fit. Of course, a few games of cards didn't hurt to expedite those savings. Or some dice.

He looked at his hands. The palms were calloused, though the nails were manicured. The plain silver ring on the right hand was dulled from years of work with his hands. The ring itself, Benedict had made from an old spoon.

"What else can you offer besides the gold?" Zorin stared at the pouch of their gold on the table as he played back the memory of the previous evening.

He remembered Cordelia walking in the front of their group, down an oily, oak hallway.

"Room twelve?"

Benedict called back, "I think it should be that last one." The door was a varnished black to keep the sea from rotting the wood itself. The smell was musty and the humidity gave it a thick, almost greasy feel. Cordelia gripped the cold forged iron and squeezed the thumb latch.

Entering the room, they saw the one bed and the faded carpet on the floor. Zorin pushed in and flopped on the bed. He kipped up almost immediately, laughing.

"Just kidding, Zane and I have work to do."

Zane looked puzzled. "We do?"

"Yup. We need to get to Belz and we only have 20 pieces between us all."

Zane nodded in understanding. "Ah. Gotcha."

"Wait," Benedict broke into the conversation. "No."

"For the umpteenth time, Benedict, it's not wrong when it's an 'agreed to' game."

"You could lose what little we have."

"Not now." Zorin looked at Zane.

"Oh no."

An all too familiar grin cracked the recently morose and distant Zane. Sophie smiled.

"No. No. No. "

Zane ignored his brother's moaning and turned to Zorin, knowing they were up to a familiar and much loved mischief they had both missed over the last decade.

"Four-legged kings?"

"No," Zorin smiled wickedly. "Empty sleeves."

Zane nodded, his grin spreading, and held his hand out to his best friend to shake heartily, both chuckling.

"Oh no, this is bad. No, no, no." Benedict was beside himself. He knew inside that those two would do any manner of illegal activities, including ending up in the local lockup empty-handed, their meager funds lost to their wicked enterprise. Cordelia's hand clasped her cousin's gently.

"You have to trust them."

"But they could lose everything. Then where will we be?"

Cordelia didn't know how to answer, but she looked at Sophie, who was listening to Zorin and Zane plot out how they were going to profit tonight. They were chuckling excitedly and Sophie's strong shoulders were relaxed as though she had set down a large knapsack of heavy goods. Her stoic and cold features softened and Cordelia saw her smiling. A smile long since missed. She smiled too and, turning back to Benedict, took his hand with both of hers.

"We will be right here, Benedict. Like we are supposed to be. Together."

THE TAVERN FLOOR WAS COVERED with dark-stained oak slabs, cut together seamlessly. Years of scrubbing with coarse stones gave it a smooth, matte quality much like the decks of the ships in the harbor.

"Blue cedar," Benedict remarked in admiration of the bar as he ran his hand along the surface. The bar itself was made of a single long plank of wood. It was a tree common to the Viridian forests and known for its natural resistance to rot. The plank was oiled and polished to a high sheen, illuminating the natural gray and blue hues of the ancient wood. The leatherbound arm rest was soft to Sophie's touch as she leaned on it.

Cordelia sat at the bar next to her, eating some green vegetables with a tart smelling sauce. Rosemary. She loved that smell, it took her back to their old kitchen in Port L'For.

"There you go, m'lady. A local mead from Akesh-bah-lol."

The barkeep sat down a plain pewter goblet with a honey yellow liquid swirling gently inside. He smiled gently at her, his elven eyes and high cheekbones graceful in the soft light from the iron braziers hanging from chains throughout the large room.

"You will find the currants sweeter than any other." He leaned in, drawing his golden eyes to soft slits. "As are many things in this fair city."

"Really?" She, too, softened her voice and he leaned in further. She whispered in his ear gently, "Just not you, right? I find you rather-" She wrinkled her nose and shook her hands as if freeing them from something wet and unpleasant.

His eyes flew open, his face growing flush. "Madam, I never would have insinuated that I would ever-"

Cordelia laughed. "It's quite alright. I thank you for the good laugh, and this wine is quite delicious."

Red-faced, the bartender bowed to her.

"Hey! Derry! Derry Goldleaf, you worthless excuse of a bartender, get over here!"

Thankfully, the jeering of the scruffy regular known as Mick saved his pride a little by calling him away from the awkward conversation. He began moving to the other end of the bar where he saw other patrons to tend to. As he slid a mug of the basic house draft of creamy ale, he looked across the room at the table of card players now drawing a bit of a crowd.

THE GAME WAS GOING WELL, Zorin thought to himself. The five other players at the round, dark wood table placed three cards face down in front of themselves. They each took turns drawing face-up cards and either adding them to their hidden hand or placing them in the center with coins to pay the pot.

Zorin could see Zane at a table of minotaurs over the shoulder of the player directly across from him. Boisterous and loud, they were regaling each other with stories in a common bonding ritual called "The Boast." The tactic was effective, but risky. Zane was giving Zorin signals of what cards he could see from that side of the table. The trick was not getting caught. It was the minotaurs' accelerated consumption of ale and Zane being half their size that had Zorin most concerned.

"Hey, are you going to fish or draw?" An impatient man's voice interrupted Zorin's thoughts.

"Oh! Well, today is a drawing day," Zorin coolly replied, staring at the player to his immediate left.

He could tell the card had four stars around a crown, that the dark haired Halfling three seats to the right had laid down the card he wanted. Her black and honey curled hair graced a dark brown scalp that was shaved around the sides and back, leaving the top in a dozen thick spiked and beaded tufts that bounced when she had raised the pot two more silver. Not that he needed it, but the man to his left most likely needed it more, given the slight inhale when she dropped it in the pot.

The man was furious. His wiry goatee seemed to twist like an auburn lightning bolt from his pointed chin. Now it trembled ever so slightly, his golden eyes flashing a warning to which Zorin smiled purposefully, discarding a lion reared back with two paws ready to attack. Taking a small silver coin shaped like a square, he gently tossed that as well into the center of the table, where the core of the wood was a light beige easily used as their pot for the game.

"The lion and one silver raised. Your turn, good sir."

The man drew a card from the deck he was calling a fishing hole. Mumbling, he immediately placed the same card in the pot. An axe leaned against the stump of a felled tree. Good, he's not playing axes like Zorin thought. He looked to Zane as the half-elf woman began her turn. Zane's hand was still a balled fist on the left thigh. Someone had the Stone. He had hoped that, by laying down the Lion, another of the major cards, it would lure them out to take it.

He took note that no one had fallen for the bait yet.

He was also noticing that Zane was beginning to sway a little.

"A pox on Pallus!" one of the minotaurs began.

"He has destroyed our fair cities and enslaved many to his dark army. I hope he chokes on his pride and drowns in his own blood."

Zane laughed. "He's nothing! I should know."

Zorin's heart sank into his shoes as he began to panic. What was he doing?

"Would you, now?" the minotaur retorted, his muzzle slightly sneering. "I fought for him five years ago until I lost this." He held up a stump of an arm ending in a brass, three-pronged fork.

"Cast me out to die, I reckon. I walked back here to First Port and have been here since."

"I was in Bloodwood." The minotaur squinted his eyes. He lowered the black horns on the sides of his head, crossed his massive arms, and leaned back.

"Bloodwood?" He snarled. "The mines must have been terrible with you there."

Zane laughed. "I'd be lying if I said I didn't do my part to make things a little harder for old doom and gloom there. Not just in the mines."

The Minotaur paused for a moment as he sat forward in his chair. Dipping into his memory, he could imagine Zorin in the gladiator pits. Something was familiar about the young man and he carried the arrogance of others he knew from the pits.

Smiling, he could hear the crowd in his memories calling out for blood in the underground fighting area of Darkovnia, where he had made a name for himself as well. He could hear the crowd chanting his name like the crashing surf of the northern rocky shores of his homeland.

"Jo-Lith, Jo-Lith, Jo-Lith"

Zane was telling the truth, and Jolith could respect the bold man's character.

Laughing, he clapped him on the back with a meaty steel colored hand.

"Salute, little man." The smaller horned female minotaur with the deep blue eyes tapped her mug on her ornate bronze breastplate. Her muscled body wasn't any less impressive than the others, Zorin had noted. The other two raised their mugs in salute to their newfound friend.

Zorin smiled.

"Oi! Fuzzy Face!" Zorin looked at the halfling known as Spindle, now standing on the chair and glowering toward him, her dark brown eyes burning like hot coals.

"Ante up! " She plopped back down with a grunt. "It's two to you while you were off daydreamin'".

She shook her hands and rolled her eyes. Zorin sighed, tossing two silver coins into the center pile.

The game lasted deep into the night. Benedict looked up from his mug and saw Zorin approaching. His gait was measured and slow, his eyes looking a bit sheepish. Holding up his hands, pleading slightly, he slid into the chair beside Benedict.

"So, there's good news and bad news."

"What's the bad news?"

Benedict's heart prepared itself for the worst. He could tell Zorin was trying to fabricate excuses for some hidden mistake. He hoped it wasn't one that they couldn't recover from, as Benedict prepared up the stern words for his friend's poor actions. Zane would be another conversation and he was preparing an even heavier speech for that. "After all, if there were no law, how could order exist with these two?" he told himself many times.

"I only made a profit of four gold after the bar tab, a certain halfling and I will never be friends, and your brother is currently vomiting in a bucket."

Benedict's eyes flew open. Now was his time to speak the pent-up rage of knowing this was a terrible idea to begin with. He would never admit it openly, but one could bet he might have felt even slightly good about his concerns being justified.

He glowered at Zorin as he let loose the chastising voice that only those closest to him ever saw.

"This was a colossal waste of time! We can never get to Belz on this! Way to go, genius!"

While Zorin was being dressed down by Benedict for his irresponsibility, Sophie worriedly looked at Zane bent over a bucket at the table. There were two smaller minotaurs laughing and clanking new dents in the soft metal of heavy pewter mugs. They were with a stoic female and a fourth at the table. The largest, she assumed, was the leader. He had three warrior braids ending in a large silver clasp and his scarred face showed the story of many battles. She noted with a smile he had his gray and black furred arm around Zane's shoulders, gently patting him with one massive hand. His other arm ended in a trident resting on the table.

"Zorin, who are they?" Sophie interrupted. Benedict froze as Zorin smiled his crooked grin.

He chuckled. "Well, that's the good news. Seems Zane made good friends with the first mate and some of the main crew of a ship called *The Sun God*. They sail to Belz tomorrow and said I just need to talk to the captain about passage and he may be able to work a deal."

Benedict laughed and shook his head. Cordelia smiled and looked at her cousin, the hero of the night, head first in a foul and sour smelling bucket.

THE WAVES GENTLY LAPPED THE musty and seaworn docks outside the warped glass window. The gentle call of seabirds echoed as they excitedly found the remains of the gutted fish being cast into the water by the old fishermen cleaning the morning's catch. The Captain pulled from his chocolate and cream-smelling pipe. It wasn't lit. He never lit the pipe when finalizing decisions.

"What'll it be, son?" the captain asked, already knowing the answer.

"Zane and I can help on deck and I'm skilled at the lines and ships boat duties. Benedict is a talented iron worker and Sophie can lend her sword if need be."

The captain nodded and thought before continuing. "And the raven-haired girl?"

"Cordelia is a-" he paused. The superstitious crew wouldn't take kindly to a wizard, he was sure. She'd be branded a witch and cast overboard as soon as they found out. "Healer. A talented and skilled practitioner of the healing magic of the world, of which I don't fully understand."

"That's what I wanted to hear. You all pull your weight to Belz and we'll be happy to have you as crew. Let's get started, we weigh in an hour."

The captain took a long draw from the pipe in thought as he turned to look out the small window to his right. It opened to the harbor where the dark mahogany hull of *The Sun God* was gently bobbing at rest.

CHAPTER 6

AN UNLIKELY CONVERSATION

The waves rocked the bow of *The Sun God* like a whale's deep heartbeat. Benedict smiled, looking out across the white crested waves as they cut a swath through the cerulean and azure ocean. The smell of kelp and sand was replaced with a familiar charcoal and iron as he bent the three inch o-ring into place on the anchor. Jolith, the pewter and onyx-haired minotaur, looked on with interest as he skillfully drove the hammer in steady blows, driving it to its proper form.

"There's a grace in what you do, Benedict. Thank you," he said, gripping one hand on his notched saber. The words seemed to push the seven foot giant into a state of peace. The scars on his face softened and the veins on his muzzle relaxed a bit.

"We are the ones who are thankful, Jolith." Benedict firmly pulled the glowing iron from the coals to place around the horn of the anvil. "My family is grateful for the passage to Belz."

Jolith nodded. He raised a hand to a female minotaur, who nodded back. She was on the other side of the wide deck next to the beige-clad Zane.

Zane had left his dark cloak below, and stood in the sun looking across the waves to the west. He sighed and cleared his throat before talking to his friend.

"Kiri. Do you think we all have a place here in this world?"

"Of course." She stood straight and her eyes smiled. "We all have our place. The water is life." She grinned, putting her hand on his shoulder. "But battle is also life, my friend. Is it not the same for you? To meet an enemy is one thing, but to clash steel together in combat..." She took in a deep breath and gripped the axe at her side. "That is when you know a man."

He looked at her. "Just a man? What about you?"

She laughed.

"What about me, my friend? Is it because I am female or a minotaur that you question?" She looked at the young man and could see he meant no disrespect. An awkward compliment maybe, or a slip of the tongue. Her eyes softened.

"Man, minotaur, orc, even the halfling. Do we not all revere the sea? The sea is a battle itself. The oldest of battles, am I right?"

Zane nodded. She smiled and drew closer. He could see the bay-colored fur around her muzzle brush gently in the salty warm air.

"Zane, the storm on the sea isn't good or bad. We just know that with it, we can travel, but against it will only bring tragedy."

He looked confused, and she smiled again.

"Not all is as it seems, Mister Shieldheart. Nor is its intention as clear as we wish it to be. Ride your waves, don't just fight them when they seem to oppose you." She threw her head back in a warrior's laugh. "This! Knowing this will at least keep you from drowning! That in itself is a victory you should claim. Survival is our greatest battle."

Zane smiled. Clapping her cannonball-like shoulder in a broad smile, he looked to the rigging above. Full sails whipped above him in the noonday sun, providing some shade.

Zorin looked to the rigging as well, standing to the rear and port end of the ship. His arms ached from restocking the six foot long harpoons by the ballista. Each was fletched with a triad of stiff leather fins, tarred with a dark pitch that, once cool and dry, could withstand water spray or impact. Last night the bindings must have broken loose in the squall, sending the steel tipped bolts sprawling. There wasn't that much cleanup; he noted this was the last of it.

He looked at the ship's armament of the ballista. Two eight foot crossbows were erected at the rear defense, with two more at the front on either side of the bow. All four corners were set. Zorin hoped it wouldn't come to it, but he had used these to repel boarders and even a huge sea serpent that threatened to capsize The Mako, the last ship he served on. That serpent had been the inspiration behind the ivory dragon he had carved for Cordelia. Until four weeks ago he had no idea what a real dragon actually looked like. Before that, he only had a memory of a painting mixed with the reptilian face of a large serpent. That was what he had assumed they looked like.

The skeletal visage of the black dragon with its blue-swept, thin horns. He paused and thought of Fury, the huge red dragon his father had partnered with.

"A partner? Ha!" He pondered the pairing. Was he jealous of the dragon? Jealous that Fury had access to the respect he dreamed of? Did he hope his father still retained a level of humanity beneath it all? He shook his head. The only partner his father had was death itself.

As he felt the taught fibers of the thick hempen cable of the ballista's bowstring, he noted the panels of yew with a core of ash making up the arms. An eight spoked hand crank could be used by one person in a pinch but would take a lot of strength. He looked out across the waves, thinking of Elloveve on the rooftop, firing arrow after arrow as he and Cordelia ran from the orcs rushing the courtyard. He saw Fury facing her, and her proud defiant face.

"Well, where are we going to go now?" He whispered the question he'd asked her when he was younger, and chuckled nervously.

The dull crash of heavy timber under the waves slammed the deck upward. "Woah!" Zorin shouted along with the crew trying to regain their footing.

The ship rocked heavily enough to jar loose a barrel rolling across the deck. Shouts from the crew became more panicked.

They all yelled as a second slam from something below the heaving waves landed again, but much harder. The cracking of timber under the strain below startled Zorin. He ran to the port side and saw a huge dark shape, much like an egg but of a size similar to the ship itself, pass under the hull. The deck groaned and heaved starboard. The captain appeared from the rear door to his quarters and ran up the stairs to Zorin. Sophie followed from the mainmast.

"What do you see, lad?" Fear raked Zorin as he realized, with much certainty, what he had seen.

"Whale?" Sophie, next to him, asked. .

"Good guess, but no. That was a dragon turtle."

The captain stamped and clapped his hands.

"Bah! Of all the rotten luck. Those things are greedy, and if they sense the gold on that little necklace of yours even they won't stop until it gets it for its rotten nest in the deep."

He looked at Jolith and pointed above. Jolith turned to Zane.

"Full sails, brother."

Zane nodded and ran across the slick deck to the mainmast. He was skilled at climbing, bounding up the iron rings to the first and largest sails. These were already dropping from the two shirtless, deep-toned sailors straddling the long arm. The wind was filling them, causing the mast to groan under the strain. Zane spun to keep going, his foot gripping the first iron rung and then the next, hands reaching for the rungs above to the next sail.

A third shock hit the ship full force, rocking everything starboard this time.

"Stand back!" Benedict shouted as he made a frantic grab for the small forge he had been working with earlier.

Benedict had long since extinguished the coals of the forge but his heart fell when the door flew open, spilling the remnants of warm black ash to the deck. No fire followed. Benedict thanked the Knightlord for his mercy.

He looked up and saw his brother 40 feet in the air from the swaying deck. He was untying the upper sails, freeing them. They flared below him as they took flight. Zane swung back to the mainmast with a cat's grace, descending quickly.

Cordelia ran up to Benedict. "It's a huge dragon turtle!"

She was both terrified and excited at the same time. Benedict's heart dropped as he remembered the red eyes of the sword's pommel, the pommel of the sword that killed Erebus.

Another slam into the hull lifted them off their feet momentarily as they sprawled to keep their footing. Benedict searched for Zane in the sails. He had barely reached the lowest sails when he suddenly lost his grip and plummeted twenty feet to the hard deck with a thump.

"Zane!" His brother's form was still on the deck as he ran to his side.

The huge maw of the dragon turtle came up over the top of the deck, and the smell of rotten fish and hot steam overwhelmed him. It drew in a deep breath but it roared in pain, a six foot pole sticking out of the nape of its thick, leathery neck at the base of the jagged shell. Benedict was horrified, frozen in place alone in the center of the deck, mere feet from the maw of this enormous monster. While standing in front and protecting his brother, he weighed his options.

He looked back at Cordelia. Her eyes were enormous as she mouthed, 'talk to him.'

Benedict was dumbfounded.

"What?" He swore she had just mouthed out for him to talk to it. He turned as the huge maw dropped down to his level on the deck. Its huge dark blue eyes peered into his soul. Its lips pulled back, revealing rows of jagged teeth when a voice rang out on the cold deck.

Benedict took a deep breath. "Wait! What do you want?"

The dragon turtle's dark green face turned toward him, pain in its deep eyes. "Help me!"

Time stopped.

Zorin froze behind the ballista. Cordelia's face was contorted with a confused smile. Sophie buried her face in her hands. Captain dropped the pipe from the corner of his mouth.

"What are you doing?" Benedict kicked Zane before he ruined one of the most amazing and precarious conversations of their lives.

"How can we help you?"

"The hurt." It motioned at the harpoon in its neck. "Please help."

It lowered itself onto the deck where Benedict cautiously approached it. He moved past the giant maw, now relaxed, and past the blue eye that looked at him, pleading. He gripped the two inch thick pole and pulled sharply and quickly, successfully freeing it from its neck with a groan.

"Thank you, my friend."

Zorin looked at Sophie sheepishly, shrugging, feeling a great bit of guilt.

"Why are you here?" Benedict questioned.

"Elves. Sea elves stole something from me and I thought you might be with them."

"We know of no sea elves."

The gigantic beast groaned slightly, as it thought in its mind. Once again, another dead end in the beast's search for their lost friend. They thought back over the past decade or more. The black conch shell was the last thing their friend had left, and was the only clue as to where they may have gone.

"Thank you, my friend. Please, if you hear of an onyx conch shell, come back to this spot and tell me."

Benedict nodded. The huge beast thought again of its lost friend as they finally slid off the deck into the water, leaving the ship to right itself on the sea.

THE DINNER TABLE WAS EERILY silent that night. No one could truly understand what had just taken place and it was easier to ignore the insanity. They stared blankly into the shallow wooden bowls cradling a few stewed potatoes and a chunk of fatty salted pork. Using a stale roll to mop up the starchy brine, they then chased it with bitter flat ale or water.

The stale air was moist and dank in the mess below deck. The myriad smells of thyme and lemon from the cooking were welcome amid the strong musk and salt their bodies smelled of after the day. The captain's pipe smoke added to the aroma.

"We have six days until we make it to Belz. Provided the wind stays favorable, you will be ready to start your new lives." The captain nodded at Zorin. "Thanks again, lad."

"Thank you, Captain Triscuit."

Zorin smiled and went back to his potatoes, noting they tasted sweeter for some reason. Three days, and they would land in the great and rich country of Belz. Cordelia knew the most about the clerics known as the librarians of the Ivory Library. She said there would be a price to use and research the knowledge they protected.

"It's said if you need to know something, they know that very thing. There's little that is not known by the librarians."

She had paused on the deck of the ship, clutching the ivory statue he had made her. He noticed the face was fading and a bit worn where her thumb caressed it worriedly.

"I will approach them and request entrance, as I'm the only one versed in the arcane ways." She turned to him. "We will get our answers."

He chewed slowly as he looked from the table to the corner of the room where Sophie sat with a limp Zane cradled in her arms. They both claimed to not be hungry and it was the first time since their first embrace over a month ago that they were really seen together.

"I'm dying, Sophie."

Sophie was mopping his cut and bruised brow with a cool herbal mint rag. "Zane-"

"Really! I feel like everything is growing cold and dark-"

She smiled and shook her head, knowing his excuses were just so he could spend more time in her care. She wasn't going to admit she was enjoying it as well.

"Zane."

Sophie pulled Zane closer to her chest and smiled slightly as she whispered.

"Just shut up."

CHAPTER 7

THE IVORY LIBRARY

Cordelia walked between the rows of tomes. Each binding varied from simple dyed canvas with silver corners to dark tobacco leather, a sunburst of oiled colors leading to bronze and pewter rounded caps and showing a lion and a bear on the front.

She lost herself in the blue cover, drifting on a memory from not too long ago when they entered the great port city of Bemil in the nation of Belz. The famous giant statue of an eighty foot knight greeted them, made from smooth granite. Faint silhouettes of seagulls circled about his head and torso, a sword in his hands pointing outward that bridged overhead from cliffside to cliffside, held out in a salute to those entering the city. He was to the left of the ship's bow as they came into the cove. She smiled, and corrected herself. Port. It was on the port side. She pictured Zorin's approving smile of her memory of that particular lesson.

Waves of water crashed against the hull of *The Sun God* as they sailed into the bay of Bemil. Cordelia remembered the deep blue green of the gentle surf lapping against the kelp and barnacle encrusted stone work at the base of the giant statue's feet. Even on the high deck of the ship she could barely see over the bridge of its feet. Each boot was as long as *The Sun God* itself.

"The knight watches over Bemil." Zorin read the large plaque at the statue's feet. "Benedict, your knight lord watches the platinum city. That has to be good right?"

"Absolutely." Benedict, ignoring the sarcasm, bowed his head in reverence to the holy statue. "And he watches over you too, my friend." Zorin laughed as he shook his head.

"Sure he does, ha!"

The memory dropped from Cordelia's mind as her fingers found a tome of interest on the shelf.

Cordelia was drawn in when she saw that the book was a recounting of the time during the Bloodwood and Veridian wars, thirty years ago. She had been given access to the rows of tomes soon after arriving in the Ivory Library, one hundred and twenty miles to the northwest of Bemil. They had come on foot, a refreshingly uneventful journey that had taken just over a week on the well traveled road.

She ran her hand down the deep tones of the book's ornate spine, remembering the tall bald man in the white robes. He had been standing in the front of the stoic, yet curious, group of librarians greeting her when they arrived at the Ivory Library.

The sun had been hot and high in the sky, and the tall towers of The Ivory Library reflected the sun's rays onto the parched earth leading up to them. She noted the legends were true, that one of the twin towers shone more brightly than the other in the sunlight. Supposedly, the other tower shone brightest when it was a new moon with the faintest of moonlight, though she had yet to confirm the story. Both towers were home to thousands of scholars, historians and mages all seeking knowledge. The Towers were built to magically help funnel power to these experiments.

"Welcome, Cordelia, shepherd of the flames." He stood slightly, smiling in the onyx and quartz hall beyond the dark oaken doors between the milky white towers outside. "Tell us, what do you seek?"

"Lord Pallus."

His eyes glinted as he nodded in understanding. "All in the past is written. Though the one known as Pallus wrote his tale over many years, not many have dared to help record it."

The librarians sought one thing. Knowledge. And the knowledge they collected was traded for other knowledge.

"I can speak of his attack on OallEnAkhan," Cordelia stated, nodding. They began to whisper. One woman with hair like fresh spun gold pulled back her hood, revealing one pale sightless eye. It was paired with a dark brown one next to it that flared defiantly.

"No one survived that. How is it- "

"I did."

They burst into discussion amongst themselves. The tall man stood silent, almost smiling and nodding in acknowledgement.

Zorin looked at her questioningly. If they needed information and that was the only price, why not let him discuss his whole life?

"Isn't that worth so much more?" He mumbled to himself, but Cordelia's eyes hardened with determination. Staring him in the eye, she shook her head slightly, demanding silence.

"Very well. You do know the ritual known as the telling is often fatal?"

Cordelia nodded and felt Zorin tense beside her. The rest of her friends would never let her get this far. Though she had omitted the risk when discussing it with them, they had to trust her. She would look for what they needed and hopefully get it back to them before she entered the test.

"Enter, Cordelia. You have been accepted as a librarian. Tomorrow, your true test begins. Use this time wisely. Research what you will need to face the reliving of your tale, for it to be recorded." The tall man bowed and waved her into the next room.

Cordelia began walking towards the double doors open before her, showing rows and rows of books winding the central tower and fading into the tall expanse until they were only a blur. Sunlight slipped in at regular intervals, refracting within large prisms that focused it into the central crystals, setting them afire with a white light and bathing the entire room.

"Wait! Cordelia, what do I do?" She turned to see the guards holding Zorin back. A thin, iridescent force field had been erected between them that blocked him from entering.

"Go back to the others. Tell them I will be testing tomorrow to join this order as a librarian. For now, I need to study." She smiled.

He looked at her with a concern he couldn't hide. He'd heard the word 'fatal' and that was enough to make him feel sick to his stomach. He looked at Cordelia's smile and sighed before returning a nod of support to his chosen little sister. Zorin turned on his heels and, nodding to the two guards in their ivory and gold plumage, left the room. Cordelia watched him go before she stepped into the vast library.

CORDELIA CLOSED THE BOOK. IT held only one passage of note. Three warriors - Pallus, Ash Delarosa, and Maldros the Dark - had been mercenaries for hire during this time.

"Great. It tells me he wasn't always the pompous justice we knew him as, but I don't know these other two. What of the dark cleric?" Cordelia muttered.

Slightly discouraged that this was the only verse about Pallus in the pile of recent tomes she'd read, Cordelia sighed and moved the unlit brass candlestick to the right of the table to make room for a large book with the six-pointed star familiar to her and the old country. If the more recent accounts didn't help, maybe the recounting of the world's dawn would. At the very least, it would liven up her boredom a bit.

The tome was dusty, but the leather creaked as it opened for her curious hands. Trembling, she took a deep breath and began…

> *When the world was new, the elements themselves comprised of four: Earth, Air, Fire, and Water.*
>
> *These four built the ground to stand on and the sky above. Over time, elements worked together and created mixed para-elements between them: Magma, Lightning, Mud, and Steam.*
>
> *They were happy, but they needed help with this great new world. From creation itself they found a clay that they were able to work with. They formed gods to help them control their new world and bring life to it. These were the Lion, the Bear, the Stone, the Thorn, and the Skull.*
>
> *Each of these new deities was to harness control of nature's personality. The Lion was proud, just and good. The Bear was good, yet followed no rules, finding what was needed for the good of all. The Stone was solid in its duty, regardless of good or evil intention. The Thorn aimed to find its own power, no matter who should get in the way. Finally, the Skull represented the chaotic free will of those dark entities required for balance.*
>
> *For many moons they worked to build their world together. The eight elements collected what was left*

of the clay of creation and made both the plants and animals. Soon they brought their children to help, adding their own special balance of gifts to the individual creations.

The Stone helped these masters build their forms, like the anvil at a forge. The Bear helped the fire heat and harden the clay, while the Thorn gave it desire. The Lion gave it courage while the Skull made sure it paid its toll with mortality.

Soon the Fey and many other creatures were born to help populate the land.

The Elements pondered the last bit of clay they held, and how best to build creatures to help keep the balance and protect the land they all built together. They were opposed again. Soon, younger para-elements began bickering with each other. Lightning struck out at the Mud in anger and the hot Steam tried to cool the Magma, all to no avail. The elements retreated to think.

The first-born, those deities who were born to the elements first and above all else, thought as well. The Bear and the Lion thought they could make beings, too. After all, they had watched the elements closely and were sure they could repeat those same holy actions with the intention to help. The Thorn and the Skull said they, too, would help make these creatures, as they were also part of the balance.

The Stone said it would not be any part of it. This changed everything. The great forge was crucial to what they knew of the process.

So the remaining first-borns had to improvise without the anvil as they had seen before. They fought over what elements to include and what form they would take. They wanted to honor their makers, so the form took the shape of wings to represent the Air, Fire dwelled within the belly itself, while Water and Earth combined together to make a fluid form which could fly. It looked fierce and frightening, as much as it was graceful, and thus came the first dragons.

Their forms were like great opalescent reptiles, shimmering metallic and rainbow hues glinting off their scales. A rainbow of colors, not owning one over another.

The master elements were furious. They saw in these creatures their mistakes of the past and reprimanded their children. They then looked at the clay, and there was only enough for one more creature. They turned to the faithful Stone and offered it to them. Stone looked over the gift and judged that they, too, would make a dragon... but not like their siblings. They would make a stone, not a serpent. They would use Water for a blanket, not the Air as a tool to fly. They had no need for wings. They handed the extra clay back, and made a dragon turtle.

The elements nodded in approval.

The elements went on to use the clay to make 'the people,' as they came to be called. The people adapted to their regions and took on forms to assist the lands they were sworn to protect and serve. The first-born, as before, placed their gifts into each one of them.

Those in the mountains seeking treasures in the earth became the dwarves.

Those in the swamps slowly became the orcs, immune to the harsh poisons.

Those in the plains became humans.

Those in the forest became the elves, dancing with the fey.

Those in the desert became the halflings, hiding in the smallest of shade.

Those in the oceans became the merfolk.

And those in the tundra became the lost ones.

The elements and the first-born looked, and were happy at what they created.

Cordelia closed the book in thought and slid it back into place near a small muslin and burlap-bound book. It was a soft tome, smaller than the others, tucked back into the bookshelf and possibly lost to time. Her heart leapt a moment thinking this could be a great find, something lost as it rested too far back, possibly forgotten.

It was a poem. There was a stanza on each page, with an illustration to accompany it.

A place of olde beyond our ken
    Whose feats inspire the minds of men
    Set to rest on four-fold favor
    'Til did rise the tumored savior

Gripped in jealous wanton ire
    Tore the veil with Parci's sire
    But not of ends shall we yet speak
    For of beginning's truth ye seek

Before t'was thought of heart and soul
    There was a place called Eridul
    Where o'er the dark the one did sweep
    And with a song birthed high and deep

Four quartered then so none could hold
    The key to pass beyond the fold
    There Parci droops in sanguine flight
    Whilst Azilix the mountains smite

Then flowed the Ningalix along
    Whilst Bubbling to Lananna's song
    Of heart and hearth of craft and heat
    Of winged and bound and flowing feet

A truce of eons they did make
    'Til Azilix maligned its fate
    And stalking low in cavern deep
    A plot dispatched to rule the three

I cannot bear this scathing heat
    How pleased if thou wouldst hide from me
    Where shall I go to give relief
    Indulge our friends to salve my grief

And so impetuosity
 Gave birth to seasonality
 Then did the three come last to know
 When joined as one their powers grow

It rested then the Azilix
 A second phase but with a twist
 Upon this task it toiled away
 Whilst dusk turned night and night to day

Whilst swooping cross the barren sky
 The Ningalix soon sidled by
 This constant swirling vexes me
 Perhaps wouldst pause and hear my plea

I cannot stop phlegmatic friend
 For I must circle end to end
 The deal is struck and binds me so
 I cannot wander to and fro

Once seeing poor Lananna's plight
 The Ningalix sued Parci's might
 And after many cycles spent
 The Parci did at last relent

With groaning feat and push and pull
 The three combined their powers full
 Till Ninga's fingers stretched and strained
 And waters swarmed across the land

Then did appear the earthly lord
 The Azilix pounced with a roar
 Since what was mine has now been lost
 You shall repay to fill the loss

The three agreed but with a shudder
    And asked the price it would require
    The Azilix grew keen of eye
    And bid them wait for its reply

Then cycles passed and once again
    The three returned to make amends
    Have you yet set the bounty price
    Bid tell us how we can make it right

This place I fear remains so bare
    'Tis hands I need to make repair
    Come join with me in noble feat
    What I've begun you must complete

Then led them to its darkened lair
    Where deep within it had prepared
    Ten legion statues standing strong
    Just give them life to right this wrong

The three looked on in welling grief
    An army's host stood at their feet
    So yearned did they to have it cease
    They joined as one to keep the peace

A sudden horrid groaning sound
    Tore from the three across the ground
    And struck each stony golem shape
    Breathing life conceived from hate

A grand stone army then arose
    Answering to their lord alone
    With one command he ordered them
    Enslave the three in Azilem

And so their curiosity
    Gave life to pain and misery
    Contented then the Azilix
    To rule the three with stony fist

For eons three did wilt in chains
    Their ardor tuned to bitter strains
    As chafed they were from captive state
    Their minds still whirred to change their fate

As they required but one small piece
    From Azilex to make complete
    A living fulcrum to retake
    What they had lost in their mistake

Designs they sought to turn the tide
    From Azilex's eye they first must hide
    For o'er the loam swept to and fro
    Its gaze of coals its mind of stone

First the Parci made its request
    A boon on which its head could rest
    A lump of clay I wish as gift
    And in return the winds I'll shift

Not long 'til Nana came to beg
    A single stone it wished to take
    And in exchange a spark of light
    To light the caverns through the night

Then coming last the Ningalix
    A vein of silver it did wish

And fill it would the barren depths
With waters deep to feed the rest

These offers did the Azilex
    Consider all the asks and gifts
    Agreed at last the monstrous Lord
    Bestowed the three their meager hoard

And so the land began to right
    As mountains grew to towering heights
    An ocean filled the molten deep
    Great clouds bore rain to cool the heat

And wondrous things did populate
    Verdant forests and crystal lakes
    Then did the Parci open wide
    Whilst Nana filled the vibrant sky

Yet one last deed the three prepared
    With stone and clay and silver rare
    A piece from each they did bestow
    To bring to life the Avinol

And from them stretched a ring of light
    It burrowed deep and shimmered bright
    A twisting maelstrom soon arose
    That cracked the Azil's home of stone

Then came the Lord of high and deep
    What hast thou done together three
    We've bound you to your stony lair
    And taken back the surface fair

> *Then screamed the Azilix once more*
>> *You've trapped yourselves you pseudo lords*
>> *To my domain all things are bound*
>> *To my command they all bow down*
>
> *Laughing then the three took flight*
>> *As Azilix was pulled from sight*
>> *The great stone hands he once had hewn*
>> *Now buried him in iron tomb*
>
> *And from the Avinol soon spread*
>> *A stream of life from fountains head*
>> *And then did birth the ancient ones*
>> *From where all life has first begun*

Cordelia shook her head in confusion and gently placed the book back on the shelf. Was this some sort of folklore? She placed it back on the worn, dark wood shelf and took a minute to notice the lack of dust on the glossy, oiled surface.

Taking a deep breath, she pulled out another tome that caught her eye on the shelf below. This one was a brown leather with gold leaf on the edges. It creaked when she opened it and fell to the first page.

> *The Great Sunder as told by Aechelus VII, Chief Historian of the Ivory Library*
>
> *The personalities of the deities had grown much over time and became the entities we, the civilized West, have come to know as such. The Knight used the might*

of righteous war to drive peace while the Prince applied the selfish war for his own aims. The Maiden in her flighty youthful imperfections was still good at heart, while the Hag was the first, therefore the foremost power of the elements themselves. The Judge used the gavel and the scales to ensure fair justice regardless of right or wrong while the Ferryman waits for us all on his river of death.

We were their children, as were the dragons.

While all six of the holy pantheon stood, a question arose. Some say it was the Ferryman, whispering something to the Maiden that she turned away, repulsed, while he snickered at her reaction into his dark musty sleeve.

Whatever it was, it has been lost to time. What is more important is the outcome.

The gods shouted at each other and began splitting away from each other, the Knight and Maiden on one side and the Prince and Ferryman on the other of their great hall. The Judge watched on, looking for balance. The Hag, worried about her children, stepped back as well.

The gods called to their children, the dragons, to take their side and assist in the judgment. To their surprise the dragons split perfectly even, to each of their parents.

The children of The Knight were judged half to be strong bastions of valor and good. The other half were found guilty of enslaving the people of the desert (and possibly some halflings, we suppose). As the gavel struck, the dragons split into Gold and Blue. Blue as a mockery to the color's indication of honor.

The Children of the Maiden were judged as well. The evil ones had enslaved a dark race of elves, corrupting them until both races fell in love with the art of poisoning. She drew tears as she banished both of them underground. Their scales became green to remind them of the forest they now left. She gave the good dragons a hue of brightest silver like the moon.

The Ferryman's children had corrupted the swamps with acid and poison, much to his delight, but there was the other half that had tried not to corrupt the land and instead tended it until it grew and overgrew, protecting itself. The Ferryman made them bright copper, knowing that when it tarnished in death it would show a sickly green. His loyal dragons became jet black.

Finally the Prince stepped forward, positive that his dragons were all on his side. It would be absurd, he thought, to have any sort of betrayal. When the gavel struck, he found they had already been waging a war in the northlands and some dragons had been experimenting on the lost people. The people had split into smaller dragons, snow white in color but smaller than all the others. Others had grown in size immensely, becoming ogres and giants. Proud of their ingenuity, the Prince laughed joyously until he saw that exactly half were in fact not guilty, choosing to stay in their homes in the sand. Furious, he made the corruptors Red to show his favor. The others turned into brass, as he wanted them to be weaker than the steel of war.

Closing the book, Cordelia sat back and smiled, staring at the candlelight cast from the table. There was the answer. They needed the good dragons to join them in the fight against the hordes of Pallus. Her smile faded as she remembered that no one had seen one in hundreds of years. She stood up, determination spreading across her young face, and strolled to the window facing out of the huge library. She looked out across the night where the stars and moon shone down on the dry valley below.

Taking a deep breath, Cordelia looked to the right where she could see the spanning bridge between the two towers, four or five floors below her. Turning her gaze back to the valley, she could see for miles across the rolling hills and dry plains. She closed her eyes and imagined flying across the valley, gripping the neck of a dragon in glittering metal scales of silver or gold.

"We will find you. We will. I know it."

CHAPTER 8

THE LONG NIGHT

Cordelia stood in the center of a stone disc. A six-pointed star of blue and red energy pulsed as it rotated slowly, hovering about her ankles. She could smell the tall hedge of the labyrinth before her, the entrance directly behind the three librarians leading this ceremony.

She knew only a little about this ceremony from what she'd found in the library. She knew the labyrinth itself was made of magical trees from across the sea that could interact with a person's thoughts, springing memories to life as if the owner was physically reliving them. She noticed that the acorns were brought over from the Forest of Memories in Western Viridian, which made it so much clearer why they had all shared memories in that forest on their way to First Port.

This trial would be stronger and more focused, she told herself. "Don't get overconfident."

The tall man from yesterday, known as Rue, nodded and the crowd grew silent.

"Cordelia, today your story will become part of our library. First, we must free the memory from your mind."

The woman with the blonde hair and blind eye stepped forward.

"We only record the truth. Any story that passes our lips is tainted with some untruth. Our lips betray us, and before we know it we have lies. Lies are no good to the library."

The third librarian stepped forward and pulled back their hood to reveal blue-black hair and the chiseled angular features of the elves.

"Your memories are shielded in layers of emotion, encapsulating it. It protects the rest of your sanity from being infected by the most horrible of memories. Sometimes these filters can alter the truth. These trials are designed to peel back the layers and record the memory as it plays itself."

She took in a deep breath, mentally steeling herself. She had told Benedict of the good dragons, that they had to find them. He had agreed with her, but no one had seen them for centuries. Now, for that nugget of wisdom, she faced her price- reliving her darkest night.

"You may enter the labyrinth, Cordelia, but be warned that what you face is very much real. To not treat it as such would be foolish." They stepped back and waved her toward the opening in the high hedges.

As soon as she stepped over the threshold the silence was deafening. The canopy of growth barely allowed slivers of light that danced across the back of her arm. The lemony scent of the leaves in the cool moist air was welcome.

Cordelia turned and the hedge closed beyond her. The tall boughs were dense and thick, not even allowing light from the other side. Cordelia was alone.

"ANOTHER LEFT."

Cordelia sighed. She had been walking for what felt like an hour but had yet to stumble upon anything other than the occasional twig in the meticulously clean dirt floor. The dust rose to her nose but smelled clean and fresh, as though she were walking in lavender with no flowers to be seen.

She looked up and saw a man standing down the road watching her approach, a red cape over his broad and armored shoulders. His familiar raven hair was short-cropped, crowning the handsome face of her cousin.

"Benedict?"

He smiled. "They sent me to assist you, Cordelia. Apparently it's to test us both."

She hesitated. This wasn't the way she had heard about. One memory to pay. She reached out and felt his arm. It was real. He was real. He laughed.

"I'm wondering about this puzzle. What do you make of it?"

"Ok, let me look at it."

Benedict nodded and pointed to the wall, where there appeared to be a stone doorway. The door was shut tight but emblazoned on it were the words: *If I drink I die, but if I eat I'm fine.*

"I can't think of anything that fits that. Maybe a type of cactus?"

"Fire." Cordelia stated gently.

"What?" He was surprised by her sudden knowledge of the answer.

She smiled. "It's fire. Water puts it out, but it needs fuel to burn."

Her hands produced a small flame which she blew gently to the wall. It set the words ablaze as the door swung open.

Together, the two walked down a short hall to another door. This one was midnight blue with deep burgundy colors.

You cannot see me, hear me, or touch me. I lie behind the stars and twist what is real. I am what you really fear. Close your eyes, child, and I come near.

They paused. Cordelia closed her eyes. This answer wasn't easy, though it seemed like it should be.

Benedict's eyes grew wide.

"The dark." Benedict was looking at her. "That's it, right?"

She smiled, somewhat uncomfortably, as she nodded.

Drawing breath, she snuffed out the candles to either side of the doorway one by one, plunging them into darkness. The door swung open, revealing a dim light from an unknown source. Like starlight.

Behind the door was a long hallway. The wet stones seemed to glow internally, but when examined closely they were reflecting. Reflecting each other, but also reflecting nothing. Cordelia was perplexed as she ran a hand along them. The moist air in the hallway stuck to her skin, a musty smell of stagnant water and old moss filled the air from the wet stones.

As if sensing her need for understanding, blue-green flames ignited the iron-caged torches along the wall, alternating right to left every twelve paces. In the distance she heard chirping. Much like a bird but more guttural, and deeper. Benedict tensed as his eyes narrowed. The sounds grew louder and seemed to be around the right turn at the end of the corridor.

He looked at her, concerned. "Do you hear that?"

"Yes. What do you suppose it is?"

He slowly clenched his hand around the hilt of his great sword, drawing it from the sheath.

"I'll scout ahead."

Benedict sped up his pace to a slight jog, peering around the corner before turning back to her and smiling.

"Come here! This way!" he laughed. "It will be easy, there aren't that many!"

Benedict bellowed a battle cry as he threw the gleaming silver sword over one shoulder and charged around the corner. The chirping became shrieks mixed with ringing steel.

Cordelia's heart dropped. She ran around the corner and stopped in shock. Ten reptilian bodies lay on the ground clad in dark leather armor and gripping small javelins, none of them more than four feet tall. Their reddish orange scales blended with the blood on the floor, mouths agape in death. Benedict cleaved through another who stood defiant against him. She saw that it was protecting something.

Behind the place where the kobold had stood moments prior, there was an unarmored female guarding two terrified children. Benedict raised his sword high with a roar.

"No!"

He spun on her.

"We are free of them, don't you see? The evil in their wretched little bodies is gone. I have purified them!"

Her terror turned to anger. Benedict's face twisted and his eyes darkened. He laughed and walked to her.

"This is as much my test as it is yours, remember? If you stand in my way of completing this test, I will be forced to defeat you as well."

Cordelia's eyes flared as his face contorted further, the grin twisting impossibly to his ears and red eyes glowing from narrow slits.

"Little cousin-"

This was not her cousin. This couldn't be the kind-hearted Benedict. She looked down at her arm and was surprised to see the sword tattoo on her wrist, the same tattoo her mother had.

Instinctively, she touched it and a sword of pure orange flame erupted in her hand.

Benedict roared and lunged at her. She sidestepped the large sword and brought the flame across his back in one stroke.

With a cry of protest, he exploded into a shower of green sparks, disappearing into the floor.

Cordelia stood in silence as the sword disappeared back into her hand. A woman's voice rang out.

"Cordelia."

She looked up, wondering where the familiar voice came from. The female kobold smiled as she hugged her children.

"Thank you."

The scene around her melted away and left only a third sign before her. There was nothing else but an endless void surrounding it.

I can bring tears to your eyes, resurrect the dead, make you smile, and reverse time. I form in an instant but I last a lifetime.

This one was both easier and harder as she realized the answer.

"Memory."

The sign faded, and in the darkness she felt the ground once again beneath her feet.

Cordelia stood in a red brick kitchen with a long, oiled cedar table in the center. The room was filled with merriment and laughter. Everything seemed slower than normal, peaceful, like gently swaying in the tide. Sophie had her arms around Zane; they were next to a smiling, kind-faced Benedict laughing at one of Zorin's stories.

"Cordelia!"

She saw Elloveve at the stove, stirring a large pot. The elf paused to shout something at Zorin before shaking her head with a smile. She looked at Cordelia, her eyes twinkling with the life she always remembered.

Cordelia started to walk towards her lost friend when she felt a hand on her shoulder. Turning, she saw her mother's smile as she gently moved past her to kiss Elloveve's cheek gently in greeting.

"Mama?" Tears welled in her eyes.

She felt a squeeze from a large powerful arm and looked into the icy blue eyes of Erebus Shieldheart.

"Father?"

He smiled and gave her a warm hug. She lost herself in his broad chest and felt his shirt become damp with her tears.

"I love you, papa. I wanted so much to tell you that."

He nodded.

"One more time."

She saw his own tears as he mouthed silently, 'I love you too.'

Elloveve called Zane to help set the table. He grumbled and looked at Sophie pleadingly before she laughed, pushing him to his station. Erebus shook his head with a smile.

Her mother's lips kissed her cheek. Lorahana Shieldheart silently motioned at her heart with a smile.

'We are so proud of you,' she mouthed silently.

Cordelia's heart broke into a thousand pieces. This was all she ever wanted. For everyone to be together. All of them.

"I wished for this every day, mama. Every day."

Lorahana nodded and Erebus looked at her with saddened eyes. Cordelia wiped her eyes and drew in a deep breath, peace settling over her. She knew they couldn't speak because they were spirits of memory. Her memory. She knew what had to happen next.

"Papa, is it time?"

He looked at her with the warmth of the forge's fire in his eyes again, and smiled. He stood up straight and nodded. Her mother joined him, her hand in his. Together they walked outside, Cordelia following close behind.

"Good luck, Cordelia!" She turned to wave at Elloveve, who smiled back, stirring that large pot and nodding. "We all love you!"

They stepped out into rain falling from the dampened moonlight above. Standing by the familiar old tree outside of the smith shop, the exterior of the house in Oallan-Ak-Khan appeared as it always was in her dreams. A great bonfire crackled and sputtered. Three orcs were in mid-sprint, frozen in time. One swung a huge great ax at an invisible target in a wide arc.

The dark armored foot of Lord Pallus was kicking something on the ground, also frozen in time. She looked down the road and saw six cloaked bodies hiding just to the other side of the fence with a small horse.

"Oh, Buttercup." She sighed under her breath, tears welling at the bittersweet memory of the horse that led them to freedom. Erebus's hand fell on her shoulder.

Turning, she hugged her father one more time. Choking back the tears to show her strength, she knew that she needed to be strong for them too. She held her mother's hands before they both silently sobbed in each other's arms. Cordelia then began to walk to the cloaked children, becoming increasingly aware of her legs growing damp from the tall wet grass. Looking down, she remembered something. Something that would piece this nightmare back together in her mind perfectly. It had to be perfect, she owed that to the library.

"Mother!"

Cordelia ran to her. Her mother looked surprised as Cordelia held up the sword tattoo.

"You will need this."

Her mother smiled and nodded, extending her hand. The tattoo faded from Cordelia, reappearing on Lorahana's wrist once again.

They parted ways. She saw her father kneel before Pallus while her mother walked to the field where the orc's great axe gleamed. Cordelia approached and knelt behind the smallest of the children, her black hair dampened from the rain, and gently wrapped her arms around her.

"Don't worry. I'm here too. We both are, now."

As she spoke, trying to hold back tears, she could hear her voice blend with her younger self. The younger raven haired girl seemed stronger than she felt right now and Cordelia allowed the memory of her younger self to help hold her up.

"We will leave together."

Her mother looked at her before touching the tattoo, the sword flaring like a mighty torch in her hand.

Time resumed, as the worst night of her life played itself out all over again.

SOPHIE NERVOUSLY LOOKED AT THE opening to the labyrinth. She instinctively fidgeted with the tattered threads of the faded bracelet on her wrist. Their friendship bracelet.

"Cordelia has been gone for a few hours. Hey, Rue, is she ok?"

"Yes. Your sister is more free now than she has been in a long time."

"There she is!" Zorin pointed at the opening as Cordelia strode out, proud and strong.

Benedict stood up with a slight tremble and walked to her. Cordelia threw her arms around her beloved cousin, dispelling the last thought of the dark version she had defeated.

"Congratulations, Cordelia. Your story is recorded for others to learn from and gain strength by." Rue stated solemnly.

Belinial, the one-eyed librarian, stepped forward. "Your debt is paid, you are a librarian here. You may study whenever you like."

Cordelia nodded.

"Mr. Zorin, this letter came to us for you." The elven librarian held out a folded letter sealed in wax with a large letter E.

Zorin looked confusedly at his comrades, who all were curious.

Zane shrugged. "It's not gonna bite you, open it up!"

The rest of his friends exploded in variations of, "Yeah!" and, "Do it!"

"I'm being invited to a tournament just south of here in Ellington. It's for the bravest of heroes." His friends smiled and nodded, looking closer at the letter.

"That's just a week or so away!" Benedict said. "I'll go with you. Cordelia can use the time to study and the rest of the group can rest up." He put a hand on his friend's shoulder. "It has been a long journey."

Zorin smiled and looked around at his friends, thinking of the future.

EPILOGUE

Far away, a mailed hand held a similar letter by a river. He stroked the gray beard at his chin. His purse was lighter than he wished. and the prize could help him on his way. The white and steel-colored mane of his armored warhorse felt soft under his palm. He thought of someone, and their gentle grace. He reflected on their warm memory as he mounted.

A different strong hand put away the letter before jumping on the back of a small pony in the grasslands. The bald head, bulbous nose, and less than charismatic attitude kept many away from the dwarf. It made him laugh. He had no family, no friends of note. But this contest should bring some livery he hoped, clutching the ax in his hands.

In a forest, an owl clung to a thin, elven shoulder through his robes. He knew this tourney would be another step in his journey for enlightenment. He smiled as fire danced across his knuckles in perfect time. Standing, he began to walk out of the trees to the valley below cradling the sprawling rich and robust town of Ellington. The owl leaped from his shoulder and took flight to scout the path best suited to the wizard.

Thinking of the future.

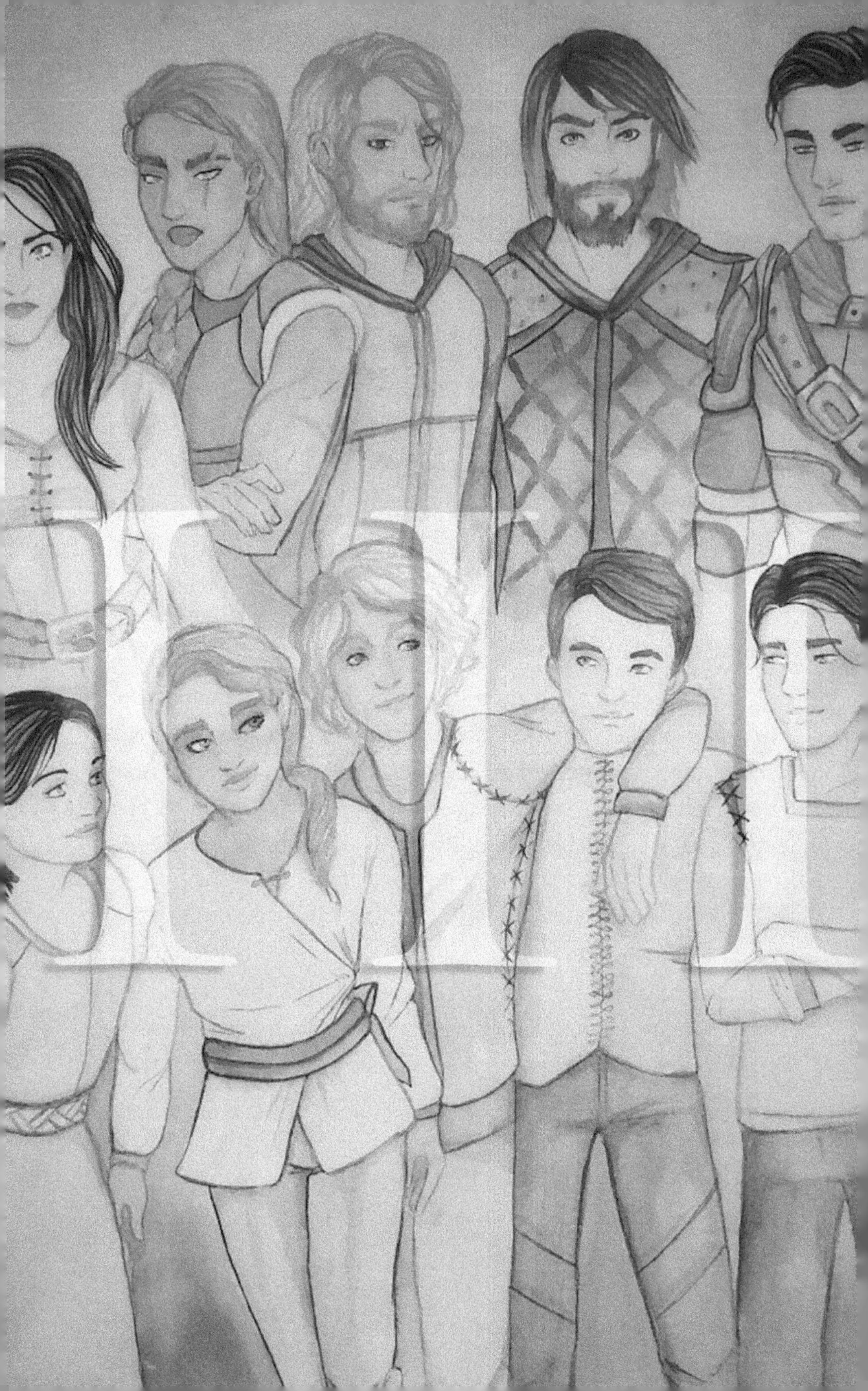

CHAPTER 1

THE GAMES

"Boy, is that loud!"

The deep brown-haired girl sat on the barstool, peering to her left out of the nearby window at the city outside. She could see down the wide cobblestone streets to the market square a good mile away. A huge crowd was gathering, watching some acrobats perform.

"Aye, Lassie. That crowd loves a good show and the good lord of this land is always happy to provide it!" The bartender grinned. The gap in his teeth where one of the ivory beads was missing was becoming more prominent as he spoke.

"Always?" she questioned. "Are there these challenges often?"

The bartender guffawed and shook his head.

"Nay! I see what yer askin'." He winked with a kind face. "Not like Trull, Bloodwood or Wolfling gladiator pits. Our challenges aren't bloodsports. We are civilized, ya see? They truly test skill and allow the cream to float to the top."

"Unlike yer flat ale, eh, Lamprey?" The stout man at the table laughed with his two friends.

The green and brown of Lamprey's hazel eyes seemed to flare as he turned his smile to his regular patrons.

"Ha! And if you ever want one to taste as good as that last one, you best shut up and drink it, Joey!"

The room erupted in jovial laughter. Jessica smiled, knowing the threats were all in jest. She was new to this town and was a bit apprehensive about the invitation in her pocket that had brought her here.

She was a priestess of The Maiden, a healer and defender of the faith. She had taken vows to stand up for good, no matter what any other power or law may dictate. Her order was known for kindness and, equally important, free will.

While she pondered her purpose here, she almost didn't notice the door open to admit a tall figure who walked with otherworldly grace. Many patrons stopped talking as the figure's gentle footsteps tapped across the polished wooden floor right next to her.

"Oh, my," she breathed out in recognition.

"A mead would do me some good this day, Lamprey." His silky smooth voice poured out, but she already knew him without needing to hear his voice.

"Mr. Silvertongue?"

He turned to her, his eyes pools of the deepest oceans.

"I'm a huge fan."

He inclined his head toward her. "I do hope you are here for the games, are you not?"

"I am."

He downed the mead in a single gulp and stood.

"I hope to see you at the stage when I begin playing. Though-" He tapped the paper in her hand and smiled. "Today, I'm playing for you. Good luck. "

Her eyes followed him as he left, but all other eyes were trained on her.

"You are competing today, miss?" The bartender asked with glee in his voice. "Hear that, boys? We've found a champion to root for!"

The tavern cheered as they all raised their mugs to Jessica.

"Aye!"

IT WAS WELL INTO THE afternoon when Jessica walked closer to the raised circular stage used for an arena. The smell of the apple and mincemeat pies was sweet, drifting in the warm breeze from the vendors. The cinnamon especially, she noted. She was getting hungry, but there was one last combat battle she was to attend.

Cinnamon reminded her of home. The aromatic and dry scent danced lightly over the slight breeze. She closed her eyes and saw a smooth pine door swing open, revealing a sunlit grassy plain and rolling hills. There was a clay oven baking outside the door with a sweet smell of raisins, but more notable was the cinnamon and clove scent in the cookie dough.

Opening her eyes, she took in another deep breath as she thought of the remainder of the day's events.

Jessica had already witnessed and lent her healing skills to a few of the battles. She was called upon in between rounds to tend to their relatively superficial wounds, to which she would smile. It was a reasonable way to show off her healing skills. She was proud when she saw Lamprey applaud, along with her new friends from the tavern, from their elevated platform directly above and behind her.

They shut down early to come and give her support. Lamprey had said, "Ain't nobody comin' today anyways but the occasional sourpuss who can't stand a good time, I reckon."

He was a tough man but had a certain kindness about him. The jagged scars on his forearms told of tougher times than just running a tavern from the barside. She could tell they were from someone else's blade, and many different blades at that.

Jessica prepared to see the next combatants come out. The arena was raised with an area for her and the other healers to stand, one of whom had left early after growing ill all of a sudden. She sighed. Her competitor was a strong healer but seemed to panic easily under stress. Jessica believed that was the truth behind her sudden absence as she looked at the empty cement station in the pit.

The Pit, as it was respectfully called, ran alongside the arena and sat about five feet lower. Jessica could barely see the wide granite floor beyond the hardened steel chain that stood as a barrier. On the opposite side of The Pit, the stadium seating began with a long railing in brass and iron running along the perimeter. Brass lions stood holding the rail in their mouths every twenty paces or so.

Suddenly, the crowd erupted in cheers and she craned her neck to see over the lip of the stage. Soon, a bald head appeared followed by the stout boulder-like body of a dwarf. His pudgy nose had been broken several times in the past and when he held his axe high she could see gaps in his teeth almost as wide as those missing. The matted braids from his beard shook on both sides like writhing snakes.

The announcer broke in, "A ruthless dwarven warrior like no other, his smell alone could kill an orc! Roar with Skotmir! Berserker son of the Garnet Mountains!"

She looked back at Lamprey, who was laughing and leaned over the rail to shout at her.

"You will have your work cut out, whoever comes out to fight that one, Jessica!"

The crowd quieted down as she heard the soft clanking of thick heavy plate mail. The man was tall by most standards, even from her position on the ground looking up. His armor was worn and tarnished to a dull tin color that was almost black in spots. The armor hung close like a second skin on his entire body and a red cloak flowed over his shoulders and draped to the knee, covering the dirty cream muslin of the belted tunic.

The man was completely armored, except for his black and gray-haired head. Unlike other armored combatants, he chose not to wear a helmet. Though a short beard hung from his chin gently, his cheeks and upper lip were free of any of the salt and pepper whiskers. A strong jaw tensed as he looked out to the crowd with deep blue eyes that held a secret, she was sure.

Jessica looked back at Lamprey. He was staring intensely, trying to place what stood before him.

"He wouldn't tell us more than his name, folks. Give a warm welcome to Keldor!"

Jessica joined the crowd in welcoming him with a cheer. She looked behind and saw her friends cheering.

All except Lamprey. Her cheer slowly faded along with her wide smile as she fell into his intense stare. Her heart went out to her new friend as his face now trembled with a smile of recognition from the other side of the high iron railing. He was now standing straight, with his hand in a balled fist across his heart in a soldier's salute.

THE BATTLE HAD BEEN CALLED a draw, both winning favor with the judges. Jessica noted that they looked back to the Duke, who was standing and applauding for once.

She admitted to herself that she had no idea what they were trying to achieve in the arena. Both fighters were very skilled in their very different fighting styles. She could tell Skotmir, the dwarf, was a crazed fighter of some sort, letting himself fall into the blanket of a relentless rage like a boat in a storm. Keldor was the opposite. A skilled swordsman, the large sword he carried was able to deflect against the dwarf's double bladed great axe. She smiled as she cheered, as well. It's not that she didn't enjoy it, she just wasn't familiar with the sport.

"I suppose in a real battle this could have ended much, much worse."

She prepared the medicinal herbs at her feet that, unlike the usual cinnamon aroma, were much more spicy and bitter smelling. The overpowering odor of sour tree bark made her nose wrinkle. It was strong in an ammonia smell, but she knew that's what made it work the best.

Following the battle, she met both Skotmir and Keldor to tend to their wounds in the same pit. As a healer, her test as a champion was tending to the wounds of the combatants.

"Ouch!" the dwarf winced, as she brought the warm soapy water to the grazed cut on his elbow.

"Oh, I'm sorry, I didn't mean to hurt you-"

"Hurt?" The dwarf laughed and shook his dirty bald head, the braids of his beard whipping to the side. "Nay!" he winked at her. "It's clean now! My beautiful mud is gone!"

She smiled at the awkward joke. Not the cleanest or politest of company, he was at least kind.

"You should be thanking the kind lady, friend." Keldor smiled, resting his mailed hands and leaning on the great sword turned down to the ground in front of him.

He looked at her, his smile widening. "Thank you."

"Uh, yeah! Thanks." Skotmir jumped up and walked to Keldor. "That was fun. I would have won, you know."

He laughed with a deep resonance, smiling. "For sure, brave Skotmir. Absolutely, you would have."

Skotmir turned to Jessica. "Hey, the rogue challenge is next. Come, let's see what they are gonna do! I've never been that sneaky," he joked. His broad smile revealed chipped, gapped teeth behind his coarse beard.

"Sounds good," Jessica said, stifling a chuckle at her new friend. As they turned to watch, she glanced behind her to see her friends cheering, but she noted to herself that Lamprey was now gone.

"THIS IS AMAZING!" SKOTMIR SHOVED the pie into his mouth, mashing it partially on his face.

Crumbs and globs of warm sweet apple filling and crust fell, sticking to the hairs across his broad chest. Jessica's eyes were focused on eating the steak and kidney pie wrapped in parchment without a mess. She hadn't eaten since the morning's small breakfast of a few eggs at the Inn, and she was feeling quite famished.

"It really is," she responded, as she hungrily took a bite while walking through the wide aisle between the stands. Keldor strode next to her with a leg of turkey in one hand and a crumpled cloth in the other, periodically mopping the grease from his cheeks.

"There. We should be able to see from that spot." Keldor pointed to a place next to an elf in a long dark robe, a single tawny-colored pauldron attached to his right shoulder.

Jessica walked in first next to the elf, followed by Skotmir and Keldor.

A loud shriek cut through the air, startling Jessica.

"Woah!" She clasped her mouth in surprise at the sound coming from what appeared to be the feathered shoulder of the tall elf dressed in sky blue robes. The pauldron spun its feathered face towards her revealing itself as an owl. The elf smiled at her.

"Hello." He smiled from one corner of his mouth at her.

"Um, hello," was the only reply she could muster in her shocked state.

"Hey there!" Skotmir chimed in, almost dancing with excitement as he laughed. "Your owl looks real tasty."

The tall elf rolled his green eyes under jet black hair. The owl leaped from his shoulder to sail upward and above the stage as he sneered out, "Go." After a moment, the elf turned his eyes away from the sky to look at her inquisitively, in a similar way that a bird of prey might look upon a mouse.

"I am Jessica." She smiled.

The elf composed himself and regarded her. "Yes, I saw you earlier. You did well with your healing arts. I am Vix, Master of the Arcane." He bowed.

Skotmir grunted. "Why do you have an owl?"

Vix looked at him. "You should have one, too." He leaned down. "With it, you can see what it sees."

As he stood back up Jessica asked, "What does your owl see now?"

Vix looked at her with a smile. "The same thing as you and I. Only," he looked at Skotmir, "Higher." Skotmir glared at the joke as Vix laughed.

A hush fell across the crowd.

"Ladies and gentlemen, a swashbuckler from the old world will now attempt to remove all the bells without ringing a single one."

"The rogues must be very agile to perform these tests," Vix said under his breath to Jessica, noticing her smile. She acknowledged him with a nod as she watched Silvertongue himself walk out with a young man who appeared to be no more than twenty. He had a short, dark beard and a burgundy tunic. Once a fine piece of clothing, it now showed some harder wear of the road.

Silvertongue placed a hand on the man's shoulder.

"Zorin, if you would please."

The young man nodded. The crowd went deathly silent.

Silently, he stepped across the tile floor. After a few steps, he paused as two guards each poured a bucket of gravel all over the tiles. Then, still silent, he cautiously proceeded. Approaching the tall dummy, he methodically plucked a bell from it, muting the tongue with his thumb and slipping it into his tunic. He repeated this action for all ten bells, then held up his hands.

The crowd erupted in cheers.

Silvertongue walked out onto the stage. "We only test the rogue, never compete. Rogues either are experts or they are not. Though if you ask one, they would all claim to be experts. Provided you didn't wear a badge." The crowd laughed.

Horns blasted from the Duke's platform above the stage. Silvertongue looked to the Duke, who was now standing, clad in red and gold velvet, with his arms outstretched.

"Citizens of Ellington and beloved visitors to our festival, time is short and a decision must now be made. I have seen enough. I have seen our champions.

"I've seen the strength one powerful fighter has, in the skills only a seasoned veteran could have. I have also seen the raw power of unbridled rage. The warriors known as Keldor and Skotmir, step forward, both of you."

Keldor and Skotmir smiled at each other as they stepped forward to the edge of the balcony.

"While they fought, there was someone there to help who showed the love and care that only a true follower of the maiden could give. Step forward, Jessica."

Her head bowed, she stepped forward next to a grinning, gap-toothed Skotmir. "Knew it would be you!"

"And, finally, a weaver of the arcane."

"Well, isn't this awkward?" Vix breathed out from behind his stoic and proud face.

"Step forward, Master Vix."

Jessica knew the three of them were likely to win, but she hadn't seen the Wizards' skill contest earlier in the day. She chuckled, "Well, we are all right here, aren't we?"

"Yes. Aren't we." Vix sighed.

"Finally, we have our rogue. Thank you, Zorin."

The crowd cheered and the trumpets blasted.

"I must meet with our champions. Please, Elias Silvertongue, begin the celebration!"

The Duke walked away as the crowd began to dance. Jessica and the others were gently ushered by two smiling guards to the Duke's keep on the other side of the grassy square.

THE CHAMBER WAS LINED WITH dark, musky-smelling wood. Traces of a sweet pipe smoke still lingered on the walls. A small fire was in the stone hearth, surrounded by a sculpture of a knight bowing to a maiden on one side, with a similar maiden handing a rose to the knight on the other.

Jessica smiled. The depiction of her faith was favorable. The followers of The Knight were known to be locked in good and just law, whereas her beloved Maiden bowed to no one, only powers of the good and righteous.

"Thank you for joining me. You are all strangers here, but not to me." The Duke smiled, cupping his hands gently around the goblet he cradled as he walked to the window. The light cascaded across his gentle face. A close-cut beard of dark black hugged his cheeks, framing his strong jaw and dark, kind eyes.

"This world is in peril. A dark force is rising under one known as Lord Pallus." Jessica noticed that Zorin looked downward, almost guilty. The Duke continued.

"In the nearby nation of Darkovnia, one of the many barons is guarding a treasure of great power somewhere beneath his mansion. One that could give us the edge we need to defend Belz against the dark rising force. We need you brave four to retrieve it."

They all nodded, but Jessica looked puzzled. "Excuse me, your grace. There are five of us here before you." He smiled and nodded. Gracefully, he walked to her, placing a gentle hand on her shoulder. The glint of rubies danced across his knuckles in the beams of the dying sun from outside.

"We are aware," a familiar resonance rang out, beyond the open oak door. In walked Elias Silvertongue.

"Jessica, we wish to offer you a place here, aiding this city and its people by teaching them in the ways of the Maiden."

She was shocked. "But the existing temple, what about those who-"

"Our temple honoring the gods has lain dormant since our civil war 50 years ago. It is time to return to the people their faith. Would you walk this path with me?" He smiled and knelt before her. She nodded and offered her hand.

Skotmir grinned wide, unashamed. Keldor's eyes glinted with sincere happiness as he smiled. Vix nodded in stoic agreement. Zorin smiled and shrugged.

"Sounds like a pretty good idea."

"Absolutely, my lady. " Keldor bowed.

"Good luck with your church."

"It is decided, then. Lady Jessica shall stay here to assist in our rebuilding of the faith. The rest of you will journey to Darkovnia." He paused. "But first, gather the rest of your friends, Zorin."

"How did you know about them?"

"There's not much I don't know within the walls of Ellington. You arrived with a certain squire in training named Benedict. I assume there are more of you than just a righteous paladin and someone of your talents." Zorin and Elias chuckled.

The Duke clapped his hands with a big smile. "Good luck, my heroes, and may The Knight and Maiden watch you now."

PURPLE AND BLUE LIGHT GLISTENED on damp walls of cold stone. The woman's polished bootheels clicked in the familiar corridor as she walked with steps that held purpose.

The musty smell was fading into the welcome smell of the running underground stream beyond the end of the hall. The sound of rushing water began to grow in her ears, but not before the sound of a jagged and cruel halberd striking the ground. A dark armored form stepped into the dim light from the edge of the hall. A guard. Her guard.

"Mistress Valya!" His tone was filled with malice behind a thin veil of respect.

"Are they here?"

He nodded. The dark onyx and sapphire skin of the dark elf wrinkled slightly around emerald eyes in the dim light that cast about the room.

"They are being set up in the chamber as you planned."

"Separate sides? Are their stones being embedded into the walls?" She stared at him through her red eyes. Her prize, awarded from the sun lord, had to be perfect. Too much was riding on it.

"Come. Show me."

They walked the edge of the cliffside on an ancient rope bridge. The water cascaded below in several waterfalls, churning a frothy rapid that served as a natural barrier and secure location for their outpost. The pair of dark elves lived in the reaches beyond the sun, but they were not alone.

Turning the corner, three of their people were hanging a steel gate in front of a large chamber. Inside were another dozen, dragging large faceted gemstones to hang in recesses within the walls.

"Perfect. Their life forces will power the enchantments I've placed on the room."

She looked at the guard next to her for a moment as he nodded in blind agreement. He had no idea what these were. To him, they were just simple gemstones. He noted that two of the five oversized crystals were the size of most of the workers, but the stone was opaque. Valya told everyone she had brought them back from a surface raid.

One of those leading the installment looked at her and smiled, nodding knowingly. One of her closest guards. A secret keeper. His cruel red eyes gleamed in the light as he motioned behind her.

She followed his eyes to a giant forest-green set of scales that disappeared into the shadows. A snake-like tail, like the largest of tree trunks, slipped into the inky darkness just out of her keen eyesight.

She cackled delightedly as she went to inspect their work. Her platinum hair danced across midnight shoulders that held a jagged staff, glowing with power.

CHAPTER 2

THE BARON

The road before them was well traveled, the stones worn smooth. The many rains spread the tan and red soil flat between the stones, allowing the sun to bake it into clay. The trees and grasses on the sides of the road allowed some shade from the late summer sun.

Cordelia walked, her eyes looking into the trees at the light bouncing from the leaves. It had been several days since Zorin and these newest members of the party joined the rest of them. Given the urgency of the mission, she was thankful there were more people there to assist in their cause.

"Hey Cordelia, what are you thinking about?"

"Something I read at the library."

This wasn't entirely untrue. She did have a copy of the book with her that she had been reading. The one-eyed librarian had handed it to her when she left, claiming it reflected her theory of what the great treasure could be.

That night, they set up camp in a small clearing in the trees about 50 yards away from the road. Keldor and Cordelia cooked some venison and potatoes for everyone as they all shared stories. The savory smell of the potatoes and lightly spiced meat on the fire, mixed with the smoke, made them all smile in anticipation.

After the dinner they assigned watches for the evening. Cordelia opted to take the last watch, giving her time to review the book more thoroughly.

Illuminated in the campfire light the leather tome creaked as it opened to her anxious hands, the arcane transcription springing to life.

> *The War of Champions as told by Vindalas the Golden, Commander of the Veridian Dragoons recorded by his squire Folas Belam*
>
> *The following is as written by his bedside testimony during the First Moon in Spring of the year 937.*
>
> *In days that only us elves can remember and man had forgotten were times of great despair and death. Dragons, giants, dwarves, elves and men engaged in battle, slaughtering many across the landscape, both good and evil alike. The western continent became a focal point for this warring, in particular an ancient Mesa known only as 'The First Stone.'*
>
> *Standing hundreds of feet high, it was a sight to see with its perfectly flat top and large, smooth horn, which jutted from one side and pointed to the east. It stood in the middle of the continent upon one of the many hills of the central forest. A forest, I am sad to say, that met its end during this time. But wait. I get ahead of myself.*
>
> *This 'First Stone' was black like the night itself, but flaked with peacock-colored flecks in multiple hues. It was impossible to break, and emitted a strange*

power all about it. An ancient power. My lord at the time looked at it with a reverence I had never seen before. He saw something both great and terrible in this monolith.

So did the rest of the world. Some wished to use it for good or evil, claiming it could do great things. Some refused to let anyone control it, for fear of the good or evil it could do. It became known as the god's forge, supposedly a way for mortals to ascend into godhood. Regardless, war would be waged to determine its end. And end, it did.

No one knows what truly caused it, and those that saw it are gone now. Some say there came a great flash from the heavens as a smoking, flaming fist of the gods struck. Some say it looked like a great ancient giant's hammer, while others say it was created by man as a weapon known only as 'the destroyer of worlds.' Still others say that someone tried to ascend, and lost their challenge to the gods themselves.

We lost many in that war, but more in that moment.

Regardless, the result was the same. In that flash, the 'First Stone' detonated and expanded, pushing man, giant, elf, dwarf, rivers and mountains outward, along with those beautiful trees. It rippled from the center to form the Great Glen Valley we know today.

The remains of the 'First Stone' settled in five places. We made a truce with man, and a promise. We would never let anyone gain control of the 'First Stone" again. Its pieces would be guarded by erecting five citadels on top of its remains. Each was named for the color of its foundational stone.

The Celestine Tower in the center was the tallest, built to oversee the entire Glen at once. Towering thousands of feet in the sky, it was one of the few things taller than the ancient giants. The Ivory Library, where the world's chronicles and science were collected and stored. The Jade Temple, where one's spiritual journey could find an epicenter, also guarded the way to and from the Shattered Lands to the north. Garnet Keep guarded the bloody lands of the south, and The Obsidian Fortress watched over the wild and unknown northwest.

This ended the war and began our current calendar, as we know it today.

Soon following this, the countries of the west began forming outside the Glen. The rich aristocracy of Darkovnia formed with the baronies and became the primary trade route linking the east and the west through the port city of Belz and Ellington, respectively. The trolls, orcs and bandits populated the south in Trull. The reserved martial artists for peace dwelled far to the west. One of the lost northern peoples, known only as wolflings, settled outside the gates of the Obsidian Tower and named the land after them, remaining reclusive behind that great dark bastion.

Closing the book, she still felt lost. It did explain that Belz and Ellington were once a part of Darkovnia, but is it the giant stone that she should be thinking of finding? Or, should they be looking at the five sacred towers?

"This is so frustrating!" she exclaimed, as she got up to take a quick pace around the campfire while her friends were fast asleep.

All but one. Vix heard her words behind his closed eyes and his silence. Something inside him was burning, like the long-thought dead coals of a forgotten flame.

THEY HAD TRAVELED INTO THE early afternoon. Despite an attempted raid by a small party of bandits, the journey was relatively uneventful. They had paused to make preparations to complete the last three miles posing as nobles to enter the Baron's dinner party this evening.

Benedict had remarked, following the battle, "You truly are a master of the greatsword, Keldor. I hope to learn much from you." Keldor smiled briefly, rebuckling a loose line for the vambraces on his left wrist.

"There is not much more to learn, from what I saw. You are a skilled and promising warrior, Benedict."

Benedict smiled and nodded. Despite the praise, he internally vowed to ask again in time.

"Oh, this is ridiculous!" Zorin stepped out from behind the bush he was using for modesty to change behind. The outfit was made of alternating colors of bright pink and mint green in hard contrast.

Zane and Sophie were laughing. "I think you kind of rock that look."

He stood up and modeled for Sophie. "How do I look? Stunning as ever?"

Sophie laughed and squeezed his hand. "Simply dashing! We shall be the toast of the night."

"Yeah, if by toast you mean we will be burned at the stake like the fashion disasters we are, sure."

"Calm down. You look terrible, but no worse than normal," Vix chimed in, with a curl of his lip. "Besides, we should all appear comfortable or else it will become obvious we do not belong, am I correct?"

The group sighed. Vix was curt and to the point, but was right about at least one thing. They had to blend in at the ball tonight or else the entire mission could fail.

Zorin grunted and stormed off to collect and stow his pile of gear while Sophie and Zane giggled, returning to gather theirs as well.

ZANE AND SOPHIE LEANED WITH one shoulder against the smooth granite wall of the ballroom. From here, they could see their friends and watch safely away from the crowd, while not drawing too much attention to their spying. They spoke softly over each other's shoulders.

"Seems Benedict can't loosen up, wherever he goes. He's standing like a statue at the edge of the dance floor. If he denies the cocktail waitress one more time, they may ask him to leave on general principle."

Sophie chuckled. "Well, we chose the wrong time to visit Darkovnia. No one serves milk, apparently. Poor guy." Her gaze scanned to the right. "Keldor seems to have made a friend."

Keldor was speaking to a woman with jet black hair, silver streaking at her temples. She wore her curly tresses pulled back under the hood of her blue and black attire. Her face was a deep, rich umber with clear matching eyes that smiled warmly as she spoke to the powerful and wise old warrior. Keldor smiled and bowed, taking her hand and leading her out to the dance floor, where they began a slow and gentle cadence.

"Keldor is quite the gentleman. I wonder where he learned how to dance like that."

"Like how?"

She studied their movements. They stood side by side, facing opposite directions. Their hands were the only thing that touched, held back to back while their fingers gently arched toward their faces. Keldor held his other hand behind his back as he smiled over his right shoulder to his partner. She returned his smile as they stepped forward and backward, swaying together like a child's swing in the wind.

Sophie knew this dance to be one practiced only by those of noble birth.

"They are performing a dance of the Glen."

"The Glen?" Zane paused. "I guess there is more to Benedict Senior than meets the eye."

Sophie chuckled while Zane smiled, proud of his joke. He took a sip from the tart wine in his pewter cup.

"Well, at least Skotmir did the smart thing and decided not to dance."

They had passed Skotmir off as one of their servants, at his request. He was back at the guest room, sleeping soundly after the great feast they had partaken in. The taste of the turkey and pies probably still lingered in his dreams, like the drool from his wide mouth.

Sophie's hand went to rest on his shoulder, snapping him back to the task at hand.

"Cordelia is enjoying herself. She's sampling the fruit at the table and talking with a few scholars, it appears."

"Seems we are the ones standing out," Zane said briskly. "We should move."

He looked over his shoulder, slightly panicked.

"Not yet," Sophie said calmly. She gently turned his bearded chin back toward her blue eyes with her fingertips. "Not yet."

Zane sighed with a smile and nodded.

Yes, not yet.

KELDOR LOOKED DOWN AND SAW their feet on the moonlit path of the garden. The crickets gently chirped and, though the dance was over, people were still up talking and drinking into the night. It was nice to talk to someone. Someone like Shae.

"Tell me, Keldor. Tell me your story. I feel I do not know you as well as you know me tonight."

He stopped and looked into her dark eyes. They reflected and amplified the dim lights of the night. She had told him she was a Baroness and a widow; and that she had three children, the eldest being a colonel in the local guard and the youngest, a priest. Her lands lay to the east and she had come here to maintain the uneasy truce of herself and the others.

"Can you hear them?" Sophie whispered to Zane, as they perched in the darkness on the nearby rooftop.

"Yeah, you?" He put his arm around her. She smiled and leaned into his soft embrace.

"Yeah."

Keldor sighed and smiled.

"Dear Shae. Thank you for this evening. It has been wonderful, truly."

He sighed again. Why did he feel so disarmed with her? He felt so calm, so at peace. He smiled and resumed their walk. Smiling in return, she again took his elbow.

"I was once pledged to a great lord many miles away. I served him and four others, pledging my life to them, their lands and my faith. I cared deeply for them all, they were everything. Especially one–" He grew serious. "I hope at our age you did not take me to lead you on in a romantic fashion."

She chuckled with an honest smile. "Nay, gentle Keldor. What I gained this night was a friend. That means so much more to me than another gentleman." She squeezed his muscular arm gently. "Besides, it sounds like we both have our hearts pledged to another, regardless of what's considered polite or not." They chuckled together. "What was she like?"

He smiled and patted her arm gently before continuing.

"She was the gentlest of breezes, yet the strongest heart I ever met. Her smile could melt the ice on a northern pond and her eyes could see through the hearts of anyone. She knew truth and valor as her siblings and she–" He stopped, thinking. "She believed in me." He smiled.

She smiled back at him. "So tell me, should I call you Sir Keldor?" She could feel the slight tremble in his arm at the mention.

"What makes you think–"

"Keldor, you can't fool this old woman. You are a Knight of the Glen." She stopped and looked into his eyes. "And a handsome one, at that."

He blushed and looked away, embarrassed by his crumbling façade.

"Your secret is safe with me, brave Sir Knight." She straightened up. "Well, may I trouble you to walk me back to the gallery? I suppose I should say hello to the old crooked-nose himself."

They chuckled together. "Yes, of course m'lady."

They walked back in silence, passing by the smaller braziers and torches lining the garden path. As they approached the entrance, they could smell the sweet elderflowers at the doorway. Keldor smiled in memory before walking inside.

They did not notice the two spectators above them on the roof as they passed by, who were silent now, sharing a soft kiss under that same moon.

VIX WALKED THE HALLWAY BENEATH the main floor. He had no need for the party and instead cloaked himself in arcane shadows to get a head start on the exploration. He had only been successful in finding a few guestrooms, the servant quarters, and the kitchen; most of the night had been spent dodging the frantic servers from the kitchen or cellar, and the stoic patrolling guards.

He felt the air grow colder as he proceeded, until he came to a seemingly dead end.

"No moss, or cobwebs," he remarked. It was ancient, and completely barren. The musty smell of the hall, like that of an underground spring, had faded and was replaced with a dry dusty scent.

"Shee-fa-tef-shak," he hissed, as the edges of a glowing door frame appeared in the wall. He pushed gently and the wall responded, sliding to the left to allow entry. He stepped into the pitch black room. A moment passed that felt eternal before, one by one, blue flames erupted from torches descending down an endless staircase.

Vix smiled. "Well, hello. Time for us to go."

CHAPTER 3

THE DEEP

"It's just down this way."

Vix called to them softly as the party made their way down the musty stone corridor, looking back briefly to make sure they were all together.

There was power in numbers, after all. He saw Sophie in her chain and plate armor now, the jovial court attire stowed back in her guest room. She had seemed a bit apprehensive when Vix fetched her to talk of the discovery in the deep. The apprehension only grew when they fetched the others, one by one. All but three joined them late that evening, around the witching hour. Zorin and Zane had been too tired to rouse, snoring in concert with each other. Keldor, little known to them, had gone out to the courtyard alone to think of another time under the stars while slowly puffing on a long stem pipe.

"I don't like traveling this far from the others," Cordelia said plainly to Benedict.

"I agree, but they may be safer where they are," Benedict said over his shoulder, as he ran a gloved hand over the rough gray stones of this lower hall. "Besides, we shall come back to retrieve them once we ensure Vix has found it."

"Found what?" Cordelia asked, exasperated.

"His sense of humor?" Skotmir added, chuckling to himself.

"Oh, shut up! Short and smelly. Bah! So doubting," Vix snarled. "Of course I found it."

"I just wanted to find some more of that turkey, honestly," Skotmir retorted.

"I hope you did, Vix. And I agree we will need to come back for the others as soon as we can."

"They'll be fine. Something tells me they will be fine," Benedict reassured the others. They had come to trust more in his intuition and faith over the past few months. There was a peace that followed Benedict when he prophesied that could calm the spirit.

At the end of the hall the smell disappeared and the dry dust of time lingered in the air. Vix approached the door and, drawing a wide diamond with his hand, spoke, *"Shee-fa-tef-shlak."*

Answering the arcane words, the door shifted to the side as it had done before. Vix looked back with a proud grin.

"Come, my unbelievers. Let us press on to confirm just how right I shall prove to be."

THEY DESCENDED THE STAIRS FOR what seemed an eternity. The twenty minute hourglass Cordelia carried still dropped its dark red sand and only showed three quarters empty. She nodded to them that they still had time, and they continued into the dark depths of the endless cavern on those stone steps. The steps hugged a rough cavern wall and were wide enough for two, though everyone marched on in single file, partly due to the sheer drop at the other side of each step plunging into darkness. The blue green fire of the torches never revealed the end of those endless stairs. A wet and musty breeze gently flowed around them as they descended.

They could only imagine the size of this cavern, as the torches disappeared far behind them in the distance.

Sophie had moved to the front of the group, in case of any danger, and now led them down into the depths. She was driven by curiosity as much as the mission itself.

"Look at that," he whispered to Benedict, close behind.

"By the knight's shield, Sophie. Is that a town?"

Sprawling far below them, the faint glow of many fires was beginning to illuminate the fog. "It must be. It's not unheard of to have those people of the underground build settlements of immense size. Though I never thought I would see one."

Skotmir ran his hands along the rough cut wall.

"This isn't the work of dwarves. Too rough, too... hasty." He spat on the ground in slight disgust. "The stone deserves better than this. So-"

"Crude?" Benedict assisted without thinking. Skotmir looked at him, his eyes glistening slightly. Benedict's heart sank a little, to match his shorter friend's. He was visibly upset.

"Crude would be somewhat natural, I think. This seems like it's mocking it. Or, the stone is laughing at us."

"What? Laughing at us?" Benedict looked around at the stonework.

"No tool marks, you see? But yet it exists. There is nothing indicating a natural cause for this. No river or air. It's ancient, but why is it here? I don't like it. It's like the stone made it. With just the stone."

He looked at Benedict, his eyes back to their familiar strength.

"That's what bothers me, buddy. Why? It makes no sense. Like a creature of stone made it. "

Benedict looked out into the darkness and judged the circumference of the room. Assuming the curve hadn't changed without him noticing, it would be wide enough for the entire Pig and Turtle to sit end to end. Including the guest wing would make this impossible to imagine. *The Sun God* could sail down its murky depths without any challenge.

A chill ran up his spine as he imagined the size of an ancient massive creature of stone, scales and claws, and what it must have looked like.

Continuing on, they completed the stairs to find that the ground transitioned into a polished cobblestone street. Buildings flanked either side of the street, with many people walking along to various merchants or stepping inside the small shops of the marketplace.

The people themselves varied, from elves to dwarves, some with gray ash-like skin and red eyes and others in the more familiar tones they themselves bore. Halflings worked some shops and occasionally humans dressed in dark robes would bring baskets of glowing fungus to various shopkeepers, who smiled back, taking a share with a nod.

They soon came to a long building with a few barrels stacked outside on its long deck, additional storage for the tavern inside.

"Hello, there." The voice startled them slightly as one of the humans in a long dark robe approached them. He was followed by a female elf with long, dark red hair. His eyes were like pale sapphires and, as he spoke, they glinted from underneath his hood.

"You are the heroes of Ellington, are you not?" They hesitated before Sophie spoke. "We are here seeking a-"

"Seeking a great artifact." He smiled. "Yes, yes I know, and we are here to help you." He nodded at the elf to his right.

"This is Jade. She will be a light in the darkness for you. She has come to know this world very well and can guide you."

Benedict bowed as the others nodded gently. "Welcome, Jade. Thank you." She nodded and walked to the rear of the group to stand by Cordelia. Cordelia and Jade smiled courteously in greeting.

The man opened his hands and three flames the size of torches sprung above his palms, glowing and illuminating his face in three colors. Red, green, and blue.

"There are three paths presented to you. On the first path, an old man needs help with marauding bandits who are plaguing his home, thus providing a slow and small impact on the world around you. On the second, a merchant guards a path to great riches, provided you can allow yourselves servitude to him. The third path can heal the heart of your world, though it may come with great risk and sacrifice."

He smiled, allowing the glow of the lights to illuminate his face gently. Benedict could sense a powerful holiness about this man, as if pure light had manifested in a single person. He was perplexed and fascinated, but oddly calm.

Sophie turned to her friends. They all burst into discussion, talking over each other in a cacophony of sound that was meaningless to anyone witnessing it that wasn't familiar with the close friends.

"What should we do?"

"Should we help the old man? He's someone that needs help?"

Vix burst in suddenly, drawing silence as he snarled at the group. "I won't be anyone's servant, no matter the prize."

They all turned toward the tall, dark haired elf. After what seemed like an eternity stuck in a stalemate, Benedict just shook his head, mumbling to himself as he turned away.

"Unbelievable."

Sophie sighed and stepped forward, flexing her powerful biceps under her crossed arms, trying not to look nervous. To her, there was the obvious choice. One she believed her friends would support. She looked back at the man's crystal clear eyes.

"The blue flame has the great risk, correct?"

He smiled. "Are you sure, Sophie? I foresee a path few can understand, let alone tread, but one that you will have to walk yourself. Though you will all be together," he nodded at the group, "You will feel absolutely alone."

Sophie closed her eyes and took in a deep breath. She thought of herself alone in Olan-ak-khan, waiting for her sister who never came back home. Waiting for Zane for so many years.

"I am no stranger to being alone. I..." She stood straight. "I know it better than anything else."

The man closed his eyes, nodded, and smiled gently. Sophie saw the red and green lights dim for a moment, the man's eyes darkening and the sockets showing through the skin. The outline of ivory teeth became more visible. Though his visage was more ghastly, it didn't seem malicious but all knowing. She shook her head, and it was gone. He looked at the rest of the party.

"Are your minds made up, too? Will you accompany Sophie on this journey?"

They smiled and nodded in agreement.

"Then step into the room behind me, adventurers. I hope you find that which you seek, and can heal your world."

They looked at each other before stepping through the door and into the abyss before them.

ZANE SAT IN A MEADOW of white flowers as a bright midday sun shone on his face and shoulders. The sweet grass he gently chewed in the corner of his mouth was welcome, mixing with the perfume of the flowers and nearby lavender. He turned and saw Sophie in a white dress. A white bridal dress, he noted. She held a small bird in her hand, gently stroking the brown and red feathers of the robin. She brought it up to her cheek for a gentle caress before setting it free to fly. It spread its wings and softly ascended into the warm light.

Sophie walked over to him, the dress billowing behind her, dancing in the gentle wind. She knelt down to him, leaning in to kiss his cheek gently before sitting next to him.

"Zane-"

But the familiar deep baritone voice was not what was expected.

Zorin was gently shaking Zane to wake him up.

"Zane!"

Zane startled up in a soft bed of billowing down. His was just one of many in the manor Baron Venere offered his various guests.

"Huh?"

Zorin's face showed a level of concern Zane hadn't seen in years. Not since they couldn't find the old scroll case that he 'borrowed' from his father.

"They're gone. Everyone went down in the cellar. Vix left a note saying they were going to explore and be back but they aren't."

Zane shot out of bed. "We've got to go. Is it? I mean are we? Is it just us missing?"

Zorin counted in his head quickly and nodded.

"Yeah, I think so"

Zane nodded seriously. If anyone could find their missing friends, it was them.

Zane and Zorin peeked around the corner of the kitchen where they could hear some of the preparation for the next day beginning, though the sun itself was barely peeking up. The beige and white outfits those in the kitchen wore were covered in flour as they kneaded out the dough into loaves to bake.

There was a sweet smell of cinnamon and cranberries floating from the room. Zane was washed in memory. Zorin smiled and nodded, almost reading his mind. They knew they had no time to steal one of the breakfast pastries, and it appeared these were made for those working in the kitchen and that didn't seem like a very nice thing to do, stealing someone's breakfast.

They waited for the bakers to turn and load the large wood fired oven, then made their dash down the hallway. They smiled as they reached a long musty corridor, almost as though they could read each other's thoughts.

"Those rolls sure smelled good!" Zorin whispered, behind his dark bearded grin.

Almost a perfect match, the blonde whiskers on Zane's chin danced as he laughed. "Like the ones back home from the Howling Mountain Inn!"

"We would have snagged them for sure, ten years ago. I bet they taste great."

The two old friends chuckled as they made their way down the long stone brick hallway.

"WHY DID WE COME HERE again?" Cordelia was furious.

They were sitting down on the side of a dimly lit pathway cut in the floor of a long cavern. The light of the luminescent mushrooms and lichen cast a blue green glow about the walls where they were. In front of them, the path ended thirty feet in the darkness of the cave opposite themselves. Behind them, Benedict leaned against the cavern wall that once was the doorway they used to enter the room.

Despite all they tried, that way was now blocked.

"I don't understand. It was a tavern, you saw it!" Sophie turned to Cordelia.

Cordelia's eyes glared daggers at her oldest friend. "Yeah, I saw it, but not as much as I saw you just trust old blue eyes back there." Cordelia shook her arms in frustration.

Skotmir was chewing on a leathery piece of jerky, thinking in the silence before adding his unsolicited opinion.

"He was a pretty cool fella. I probably would have–"

"Shut up, Skotmir!" The pair spun on the wide-eyed, surprised dwarf. Jade stepped forward, her red hair flowing down her back.

"All of you, quiet!" Her voice rang out like a bell. This was the first time Jade had spoken to them since joining the party and the sudden change in her demeanor was surprising, even to herself.

There was no time for that now, however. She could tell the slight change in the air, the smell of oiled leather and cold iron. Something was coming from the darkness. Something not friendly.

"What is it?" Benedict asked, as he cautiously stepped from the wall. Vix spread his fingers from balled fists in anticipation.

Jade drew the bow from her back and, drawing the arrow back to her cheek, she spoke a single command.

The arrow glowed like a torch without heat, radiating an amber light in the darkness. She fired into the dark hall, the arrow illuminating the cavern walls before disappearing. They could hear it land with a thud, followed by a deep groan.

"Ambush!" Sophie yelled. Cordelia and Vix began weaving their hands as Benedict and Skotmir charged into the darkness with Sophie.

The opening erupted as six pitch black forms sprung out as though made of the darkness itself.

"Callay," one hissed, as a web sprung around their feet, anchoring them to the rough floor. Cordelia let a bolt of fire fly before she lost balance, falling backwards into the sticky web.

"Aktay." Vix flung his arms in an arc and a wave of superheated fire drifted at two of the assailants. They shrieked in pain, one of them dropping to a knee to clutch a smoldering cheek. The other caught Vix across the face with one gauntleted hand, dropping him into the web as well.

His vision blurred as he saw Sophie, Skotmir, and Benedict all fall into the web. He could feel himself being rolled up in the threads and found himself unable to move. His vision was darkening now- some tranquilizing effect of the webs, he imagined. They rolled him face up, a hazy green blue illuminating the ceiling. Stepping into view, he saw one of the onyx colored assassins take off their hood. Silver hair bounced across their shoulders, red eyes reflecting in the light.

"A surface elf," she chuckled menacingly. "What a rare treat to meet you, my cousin."

Another shape stepped into view, this one a huge monstrosity. Vix recoiled internally in horror, his eyes paralyzed and frozen open.

"Shall I take them back, Mistress?"

"Yes. We shall get them ready for the slave market, I think. There should be a nice price for this lot."

She turned and walked away as the large muscular arms of the other shadow reached down to pick him up. His fears were realized as the monstrous man's arms were covered in red-eyed spiders.

CHAPTER 4

CHAINS OF DARKNESS

D rip. Drip…
Benedict groaned, rolling from his right side to the left, no longer facing the rough and jagged edge of the wall. The wall was smooth like glass and, in parts, dangerously so.

Skotmir was disturbed at how foreign it felt to him, remarking, "It's almost unholy. It is not like any stone I've seen."

The stone was opaque and, when light would grace the twenty foot chamber of the cell, it shined blue and gray streaks. From some ancient flame, no doubt. Benedict noted it was like a smelter's slag, the runoff from smelting raw iron ore.

Benedict wondered what could have melted it to form this room, though. He assumed an ancient fire or a dragon's breath, but the young knight was careful to assume he did not know everything.

He opened his right eye. Even that motion sent waves of pain to his overworked back and legs.

For days they had been loading carts with various crates of supplies. The dark soldiers were always watching their work and driving them to perform at a pace slightly faster than possible with a load slightly heavier.

Dark elves, he told himself. Silver or lavender-haired, their eyes were green, red or even amethyst, he noticed. Protected by ornate and cruel armor, their skin was all shades of darkness in a moonlit sky. The most notable trait was their drive to test their prisoners' limits in their seemingly meaningless tasks.

Benedict tried to resist and found it easier to just submit to their wishes and load the carts. Sophie and himself being the strongest and tallest, they were the ones driven the hardest. Skotmir was kicked around cruelly by their pointed black boots. He didn't seem to care though, he wouldn't show them if he did. He never changed his pace.

Benedict saw Vix sitting and staring at the floor with his hands clasped in his lap, his head hung low. Though they were all quiet the past few days, no one was more reclusive than Vix. The deep elves had Vix and Cordelia gathering various local flora for their supplies. Cordelia's hands looked blackened the first day and began to blister the next from some reaction to a local plant. She had ripped fabric from the base of her dirty white dress and made some hand wraps for herself. She never let the pain show on her face.

"We need to get out. There must be a way."

A smile tried to crack his chapped lips. His cousin was tough, for sure.

"Hey Cordelia, are you up?"

"Yeah. Wish I wasn't, but yeah."

He sat up on the glassy floor. She sat on the long rock bench along their side of the wall. Sophie sat next to her, with unfocused eyes staring at the ground. Jade was ever-quiet, just sitting there in thought.

Skotmir was spread eagle, lying on his back and snoring loudly.

Benedict shook his head, half smiling, before whispering under his breath, "Nothing bothers that guy."

"I feel so stupid!" Sophie's voice resonated off the smooth glass-like walls as she broke the silence.

"This wouldn't have happened if I hadn't… it's all my fault." She stormed across the room, shaking her arms in frustration and anger.

Cordelia felt the bracelet on her wrist that Sophie had made her so long ago. Not wanting to further enrage her best friend she pleaded gently, "Wait, Sophie, I didn't mean-"

"No, you did!" She looked at her best friend, her face masked in guilt over her misdirection. Toying with the frayed ends of their friendship bracelet on her wrist, she smiled shyly, "And you were right. I shouldn't have trusted that man."

Sophie turned to stare at her own despised reflection in the dark glass, almost seeing someone different beyond the opaque sheen. A face the size of a child with curly hair appeared to be asleep within the wall. She shook her head, and the vision was gone.

"We all had a choice." Vix raised his head. "Didn't we, squire."

"I-" Benedict hesitated at the veiled insult. "I'm not a squire. Not yet anyways."

Vix chuckled. "Great. Not much else for us to do now. We're all doomed."

"Don't say that, you-"

"Oh I do know, little mage." Vix's eyes grew cold as he continued.

"These are the forgotten ones, those of my people that were banished long ago. Doomed to lurk beneath the earth further than our cellars, or our graves."

He looked back to the doorway. "They were the poisoners of The Skull. The god our young knight-to-be knows as the Ferryman."

He sneered as much to himself as to his companions, leaning back towards them. "I tell you, we now walk with death close behind."

Sophie walked back to the group, her steps ringing out with purpose as she approached. The sulking elf shook his head, visibly shaken.

"Stop. I see you quake as you talk of such things, as if you know them. But I am not stupid, Vix. I will not be fooled by your façade."

She stood in the center of the floor glaring at him, her eyes ablaze and her blond hair falling in several dirty matted locks across her shoulders. Vix was shaken. If one was astute enough or had the tools they could see the granite-like ego split as if a great sledge had struck it. She had the upper hand and she knew it. She leaned in.

"You are scared."

He stood, enraged. *"Fatah-bah,"* he shrieked, with hands outstretched as he leaped at her. The magic failed, as all magic had in the room over their time in imprisonment. Sophie could only guess Vix was trying to scare her. She used the attack's momentum to put him firmly but helplessly on the ground with a grunt.

"Please. Stop. We need all of us to get out of this."

She stood up and glanced back at a wide eyed Benedict and Cordelia. The sound of Vix's struggle was interrupted by applause as it rang out from someone on the floor.

A very awake Skotmir was standing now, laughing and applauding. "That's right, Sophie! Together!" He strode over to Vix, who lay defeated and broken on the ground.

"C'mon Vix, gather yourself."

With a slight grunt, the powerful dwarven berserker helped the much lighter Vix sit up on the ground. "Regardless of who they are in this godforsaken place, we need to focus on getting out and we gotta be together in it."

"Psst." A shock came across everyone's face as they looked at each other, frozen like statues rooted in place.

"Who?"

"Hey!" It came from the doorway. Silhouetted against the light from outside the cell bars was a familiar face. One they hadn't seen in days.

"Zorin?" Benedict ran to the bars. "How did you-"

"I was told by an old man in the town to come find you here. Zane and I made our way in and separated after..."

Sophie stepped forward, her eyes pleading as much as her words. She had come to expect the worst, after all. "Zane? Is he-"

"He's fine," Zorin said calmly. Sophie's hand clasped his tightly in greeting as well as in reaffirmation of her love's wellbeing. She took a deep breath and, after a parting gentle squeeze of Zorin's hand, stepped back.

While everyone was quietly greeting and rejoicing with their long lost friend, they didn't notice Vix staring at the dark walls in the back of the chamber.

The walls were shifting their opaque curtains like a slowly clearing fog, revealing the sleeping eyes of five unknown faces within the walls. He looked back at the group. They still had their back to him.

Vix.

A soft wraith-like voice called out. A voice he recognized. A voice that made his skin crawl.

"Not you."

The room froze. Vix walked freely in the cold cell but everyone else stood as if frozen in time.

He saw the street before him, cobblestone. A single torchlight illuminated the body on the ground. Her body.

The red ruby around her neck glowing slightly.

He turned and saw the wall of the cell again. The childlike freckled face of a halfling with frizzy auburn hair slept inside the dark glass. A red light began to glow faintly at her neck. A light with no source.

What did I tell you?

"I-"

Say it.

"You can't just leave."

The halfling's eyes opened suddenly, revealing empty voids of black nothingness, their mouth trapped in a twisted, silent scream from beyond the dark glass prison in the wall.

His fist came down on the glass, an attempt to free the hidden prisoners in the wall. A shrieking wail answered, ripping through his mind with the remembered sound of a hundred ravens taking flight. He saw the cobblestone streets of that distant memory, where the shadowed shape of that voice stood. A young woman's shape with bloody talons.

Vix opened his eyes, looking across the dark cell. Zorin and Benedict were discussing the lock.

"Ok, just stand back. I'll see if I can get it open."

"What are you doing?" Vix shrieked out. "We can't just leave!"

The group was stunned by the sudden outburst from the now-standing and panicked elf staring at the wall.

Benedict ran to silence Vix before he alerted the entire underground world with his outburst.

"So help me, I will do what I must to make sure you stay quiet!"

To his dismay, voices could be heard from beyond the walls and they were growing louder. The clamoring of blackened chain and dark steel plates made their way towards them now.

"Shh, everyone down." Zorin's voice was terse, quiet and quick to the point. One they all knew was true but hoped in their hearts wasn't.

"They are coming!"

Everyone scrambled to a normal position in their cell while Zorin panicked, looking around. Behind him was the walkway up the cliff face to the cell's location. Off the walkway was a sheer drop. Wide eyed, he gulped the air.

"Oh boy."

SOPHIE NOTED THAT MINUTES SEEMED like hours as they heard the approach of the Deep Elven Guard. She sighed audibly when she saw who accompanied them.

The woman stood slightly shorter than the rest of them, but it mattered not given the power that radiated off her and her station. Her red eyes were almond shaped and peered into the cell as she leered at them.

"And what seems to be the matter? What bothers my dear pets this evening?" They all sat silently, staring at the floor. Vix shook his head, freeing himself from the panic.

"Mistress Valya." The guard spoke from behind a dark cowl that cast the top half of his face in shadow. He pointed to the edge behind her with the pointed foot of his twisted halberd.

She turned slowly, like a snake coiling to strike, the blue black velvet of her cloak cascading from her shoulders to ride at her calf. She stroked his cheek.

"Move, Janick, you fool!!" She shoved the man, who stumbled out of the way.

"Thank you, my lady," he mumbled, bowing while stepping back quickly, allowing her past to look down over the rocky edge into the dark abyss below.

Suspended there was Zorin, dangling from the cliff face, his teeth clenched in silence and his fingers locked like iron to the edge. His arms screaming from fatigue, he clung to the edge with all he could muster. He saw her dark red lips peel back in a sneer across the ashen gray face, revealing a set of perfect ivory teeth.

"Hello. And who might you be?" She gently stroked his knuckles with a pointed boot. "Oh no." She shifted her weight slowly, crushing his hand, holding it in place and disabling him at the same time.

Zorin cried out in pain as he struggled to keep his hold on the ledge. Sparing a second to look down, he saw only an immense void below and could hear crashing water against jagged stone.

"I... I..." He sneered as his heart filled with rage. Not thinking he retorted, "I am the prince of the world, you dumb ox!"

Her eyes flared from the insult as she swung her foot to kick out his grip.

Vix mumbled and gently waved the fingers of one hand. The anti spell magic in the room stopped all spells but the very smallest of manipulations in the world. He hoped this would be one of them.

Valya's foot suddenly felt heavier than normal, throwing her weight off center. With a shriek, she flung herself over the side.

Vix smiled at his success. He saw that the guards seemed too afraid to react, or knew something he didn't, when he noticed they didn't move. Soon his heart sank.

"How clumsy of me." Valya appeared over the stone edge with her arms outstretched, levitating. Effortlessly, she floated up and out, returning to the edge and peering down at Zorin.

"Seize the outsider. And put him in with the others." The guards nodded. Two of them pulled Zorin up and held him with his arms behind his back. She smiled like a cat with its prey as she ran a single black fingernail across his cheek.

"I look forward to our discussion in the morning. See you soon."

She turned and strode back up the trail to the building illuminated in the darkness with the fire of blue torches.

IT SEEMED LIKE HOURS, BUT Zorin had no idea how much time had really passed. The last few days, he had simply slept when he was tired. Zane would be looking for him soon, he supposed. They had agreed to meet about four miles away at the edge of a huge underground lake before they had to sleep. Zorin was beginning to feel tired, a sign time was running short.

He walked silently to the gate and peered down both directions. All seemed quiet. He walked back to Vix.

"Time to go. Are you ready?" Vix nodded. They all looked at him. "How? They took all our gear."

Cordelia looked distraught. "I have no spellbook."

Skotmir shrugged. "Or my Axe"

"I believe it would be foolish to retrieve them. First we should escape. We have survived with less," Benedict said, putting his hand on Sophie's shoulder. Zorin nodded and, reaching into his boot, produced a single lockpick. Sophie smiled.

"Let's get to it, then." Zorin slid the pick into the tumbler and felt the cold iron reluctantly move into place. The gate slid slowly on its rail.

"Shh," Zorin hissed back to everyone, a reminder as he slipped onto the pathway.

Sophie sighed, thinking of her sword, but then looked at Cordelia. She was helpless without her spellbook except for the handful of less powerful spells she had memorized. Vix, on the other hand, seemed oddly confident.

They made their way down the path to the small guard house. Zorin motioned for them to stop and lower themselves to the floor a moment. He quietly approached and noticed two figures in the darkness playing a familiar game.

"Axes. Axes again, huh Dode?" He recognized the voice of the one she called Janick.

"Heh, yes. Yes, another Axe." This voice was familiar, but Zorin couldn't place it.

"Tell me Janick, how do you feel about our dear mistress?"

"Why? She's strong-"

"Yes, very strong."

"And.. cruel."

"Heh, indeed. Very cruel, isn't she?" He saw the other figure lean in.

"The way she treats us all, especially the way she treats you?"

"I... I suppose."

"There, I lay down the Skull. And let's pause a moment."

Janick sighed. "We won't always have to listen to her gloat, will we?"

"No, I have a feeling we won't." The figure pointed at the table in front of him.

"Look here, there's something I wish to show you." Janick looked at the table.

Zorin froze. The other guard looked directly at him with two icy blue eyes. The ash colored face nodded at him. "Go." He knew these eyes but couldn't place them.

Zorin ducked down and waved for everyone to follow him. They crept in the darkness out of the prison they had known as an unwelcome home these past few days.

"Dear Janick, do you see now?"

"I understand. Truly I do." Janick knew now that this revolution would start in blood. "But must it be-"

"Must it be you? Yes. As I told someone very dear to me, all things must end sometime."

KELDOR WOKE UP IN HIS room and put on his things to walk to the breakfast hall. He could smell the sweet pastries glazed in honey and berries and, the familiar favorite, cinnamon rolls. He smiled, rubbing the beard on his sleep-worn chin.

He exited, shutting the door gently behind himself. Walking down the hall, he heard a small voice.

"Heya!" He turned to see a halfling no taller than a young child waving at him. She carried a small lute strapped to her back that looked more like a mandolin, he thought to himself. She was dressed in the dark greens and browns of the forest. Deep burgundy hair came to her shoulders. Around her neck was a small corked glass vial.

"Are you going to breakfast? Me too! Um, can I join you?"

He smiled.

"Absolutely, but I'm getting ahead of myself." He knelt down on one knee and bowed to her. "I am Keldor. And who might you be, my new friend?"

She smiled, standing straight, and took his hand to shake it happily.

"Lorvana Birdsong, traveling minstrel." She nodded quickly, adding, "Well, let's get moving! Those goodies aren't gonna just eat themselves."

They chuckled together as they walked down the hall, following the welcome smells and voices in the banquet hall just beyond the marble walkway that overlooked the garden he had walked in last night. They spoke of the fine sunny morning weather. Keldor smiled gently at the pleasant conversation.

A conversation that no one seemed to notice was missing several honored guests.

CHAPTER 5

CITY OF THE GREAT FORGE

"It's good, I'm sure. Just... ew."

Zorin turned the mushroom over in his hand. It was the size of an apple, now toasted a chestnut brown from the small campfire they had made. It smelled like aged cheese and probably was just as sharp and creamy, Zorin told himself with a smile. Cordelia had pointed these out as non-poisonous ones, but was relying on knowledge from the memory of a book she had read.

"It will suffice," Vix chimed in, as he peeled a chunk of the flesh of his mushroom and carefully placed it in his mouth. He chewed with his eyes closed, trying to place the flavor. His eyes opened and he saw the group staring at him intensely.

"What?" Vix stopped chewing momentarily and looked at the intense stares from the group.

"Do you feel strange?" Benedict asked

"No, should I?"

"Sick?" Sophie added

Skotmir became excited, his grin getting wider as he imagined something. "Like you are going to shrink to the size of a mouse?" Benedict gave him a questioning look, prompting him to justify his comment. "Uh, I heard that happened to some girl a long time ago and-"

"Shut up, Skotmir. And all of you, for that matter. I am fine," Vix snorted, going back to his meal. "Despite what you may have heard, elves are not all weak. We have a very strong constitution, in fact."

Jade cocked an eyebrow at the needless brag and laughed, rolling her eyes. She couldn't remember much, but knew that statement wasn't always true. Elves, humans, and dwarves all could suffer equally from toxins that they weren't accustomed to. Only the orcs had any advantage in that regard, especially those in the deadly swamps.

As they ate, the gentle lapping of the underground lake on the shore was rhythmic and soft. The campfire was made of small twigs and a broken board they had found. Wood was a scarce commodity here in the dark underbelly of the world. The meal was pleasant, but there was the nagging realization of the last few days. They were lost, and Zane was nowhere to be found.

When Zorin had returned to the waterfront of the lake, they had found evidence of a fight that someone was dragged away from. Jade could track six smaller bodies the size of Skotmir and noted they were similar in weight. The tracks were made by the steel heels of their heavy boots in the loose dirt.

She turned to Zorin. "There was oil from a lantern that spilled here on the ground, probably half a day prior."

Zorin looked at the silty ground as he spoke. "Zane had a lantern."

Their hearts gripped in worry.

Jade noted that chains bound the taller person at the ankles before he was dragged into a four wheel cart and finally away, down the coastline of the lake.

"Zane! Oh no." He looked up. "Jade, you are positive they came this way around the lakeside?"

"Yes."

The lake was immense, with no sign of change in the coast's direction for the last day's worth of travel.

"See, the tracks still travel that way." As she directed their eyes, they could see there was one set of tracks with a set of large wheel ruts. She then pointed at another set twenty feet away. The feet were turned opposite, but similar.

"The wagon ruts are more shallow. Not as weighted down and going the other way. That's where they most likely came from. They picked something up. Probably close to 200 pounds, based on the ruts."

Zorin smiled at her surprising accuracy and confidence. She was an impressive tracker. "Great. Thanks, just-"

"Zorin, we will find your friend. I promise." She sat down. Jade didn't understand how she knew they would find him but she did. Moreso, she was questioning why she cared so much.

The next day yielded a welcome change of scenery when they came across an old pier. The cart's tracks ended here, where the wooden cart itself sat as well. The pier had three small, wooden row boats moored along the left side. Skotmir noted these were dwarven in make, well crafted but plain.

"I'm used to seeing the shipwrights mark or some strong dwarven design. These are so perfect, but empty." Skotmir was very disturbed by this. "Dwarves are proud, and function as well as beauty are important. It's so soulless."

Benedict put a hand on his shoulder. "Skotmir, do you see that light in the distance?" He pointed across the lake, where a faint orange glow was on the horizon.

Skotmir smiled. "Aye. Jade, is that a city?"

Turning, he noticed Jade energetically nodding in affirmation as she inspected the dark wood of the boats for any leaks before their next journey.

The glow of the city became brighter as they made their journey over the next few hours. Soon they could see four giant pillars of stone ablaze with fires that ebbed and flowed from within. They towered hundreds of feet towards a ceiling that was lost thousands of feet in the darkness above. Sprawled at their base were comparatively tiny houses, fifty of them. Sitting end to end, they would be the width of just one of these great pillars.

They heard a large crowd bustling around in the distance, the occasional muffled shout carrying across the water to their ear, gently cloaked in darkness. They were rowing towards a large harbor filled with ships of various sizes, with one thing in common.

"No sails. Well, I suppose that makes sense, actually." Zorin saw the largest ships had easily forty to fifty oars per side. Far to the left of the city was a dock not in use, cast in the shadow of one of the large ships.

"There. Let's dock there and we won't be too obvious coming in," Zorin suggested.

"Maybe we can blend into the crowd!" Skotmir offered excitedly, ready to explore the underground city.

"Hmm, speak for yourself." Vix was wrapped in his long robe, staring at the approaching harbor, trying to anticipate what they would encounter in this glowing city of fire.

CORDELIA GRUNTED AS A THICK bodied sailor pushed past. They had soon noticed all the different shapes and sizes of inhabitants here in this lively port city.

"I've easily seen ten or so of these cities on the surface, but never imagined one underground." Skotmir looked curious.

All the dwarves were ashen gray with cold, dark eyes. White, wiry beards shot from their chins like the coarse mane of a horse. "I have heard of these cousins of mine. That explains it."

"Explains what?" Benedict questioned curiously.

"There's stories about those of us that live in the dark beneath the mountains and hills. They lose the love of the sun and the love of pretty things. All things have a purpose, and to make it pretty is just a waste of time."

They passed by a fishmonger shouting at the crowd and holding a large pale squid on the end of a long hook. The smell was coppery and strong, but bidders were throwing hands up as fast as the auctioneer could rattle off his gradually increasing price.

"We need to find a place to lay low," Benedict said, looking around. "What about that place there?"

Zorin smiled slightly. "The Pale Ale. Let's try it."

They walked up the creaky wooden steps of the inn to the iron bound door and slowly opened it.

Inside, there was what appeared to be a small tavern. Three round tables stood empty and eight bar stools were lined up at a clean and oiled deep mahogany bar. The welcome smell of a meaty stew and potatoes wafted to their noses.

"Hello." A grunting voice came from the bar as a bald, gray haired dwarf stood up with a white beard hanging straight down. The hair almost made a perfect triangle at the end against his black, muslin apron.

"Come on, step up. What will it be?"

Sophie was wide eyed as they all looked at each other in realization. They had no coin or weapons. They had been hiding and avoiding every creature of the darkness with only a flint, steel, and a dagger found at the raided campsite.

The dwarf cocked an eye at their confusion. "You are the surface dwellers Dode was talking about." They looked at each other. Zorin froze. He had heard that name before.

"Yeah, it's gotta be you. Librarian, two elves, ugly dwarf and the rest of ya. He told me to take care of ya. What'll it be?"

They all looked at each other, hesitating, save a very excited Skotmir.

"Well, what's cooking back there, smiley?" Skotmir laughed as he sat heavily in a bar stool sized appropriately for his height.

THE MEAL WAS SATIATING BUT a little bland to anyone but this group. The meat was sweet and the potatoes savory, every bite brightened the palette and the dash of salt excited the tongue. The stew was served with a coarse soda bread they softened by dipping it into the thin broth. The pasty mess was hastily shoved in Benedict's bearded mouth with a smile. Zorin smiled at his friend, his mouth full as well. The warm broth matted the hair at the corners of their mouths as they both nodded in approval.

They all were happily eating the stew while Kegog, the barkeep, shook his head.

"By the stone, it wasn't that good. Those fools must have been touched in the head," he grumbled to himself.

Soon they finished, sitting back in their seats with smiles on their faces. Even the cool and collected Vix looked happy.

"That was amazing," Jade said, smiling at Sophie.

"It sure was!" Sophie's eyes beamed at her new friend.

"How 'bout some drinks? Hey Kegog, can we order some drinks?" Zorin added excitedly.

"I'll be there in a moment, hold yourself down," Kegog retorted while hidden under the bar, as Benedict mopped his dark bearded cheeks.

"Ha! Hard to eat with a beard, huh?" Zorin laughed. "You gonna keep it?"

"No. The next thing I'm dreaming of is a bath and a shave."

"I'm dreaming of a bed!"

Kegog approached the table, wringing his hands in a wet muslin towel. "That'll come soon enough. Now, what'll it be?"

"Ale for me!" Zorin said

"And for me!" Skotmir added.

"I'll take- " Benedict paused, trying to picture a cow in this underground landscape. He shuddered. "Just water will be fine."

"I will take a mead," Vix said cautiously.

"As will I." Cordelia chuckled at the Irony of agreeing with Vix for once.

"I would like a red wine, please," Sophie said, then instinctively looked at Jade, who sat there thinking. "Jade? What would you like to drink?"

"I... would like a red wine as well. That sounds good." Sophie smiled at the memory of sharing a glass of wine with another elven friend, what seemed ages ago in port L'For.

Benedict followed the bartender back to the bar.

"Excuse me, Kegog, we are looking for a friend of ours."

"Dode told me. The boy called Zane who went looking for ye."

He gripped three tankards under a large keg as the bitter liquid poured slowly, building a white frothy cap on top.

"If he was taken back to this town he wouldn't be in a tavern, for sure. He'd be at the slave market if he's not sold by now."

"Slave market?" Benedict was stunned. Only the cruel and evil had slaves; there were servants and workers of all types back in Port L'For, but never slaves. Kegog continued.

"The market opens in twelve hours, an hour after that is the auction. If I were you I'd be there for the whole thing. Dode said to take care of your every cost, but I don't know where you'll get the money. You can charge the cost back here for him to settle if you-"

He paused in thought for a moment before he shook his head to clear it. "Where was I? Oh, oh yeah, you were supposed to get this." He set the tin tankards down and reached under the bar, lifting a heavy sack of coins for Benedict.

"From Dode." He turned back to his work and mumbled, "Just remember all things must be paid back to him. He always makes sure of it."

"THIS IS YOUR ROOM. KEEP it quiet, and don't disturb any of my other guests."

Cordelia found it interesting that she hadn't seen any other guests, but nodded in agreement with Kegog's statement.

"Rest well."

Silently, they all moved into the room and their eyes opened wide. The room had a bed for each one of them. There was an unfamiliar smell, not unlike chamomile and lavender tea with cream and honey. The temperature was warm but not too hot, almost cozy amongst the tobacco brown walls and slate gray furnishings. Polished brass shone in accents throughout the room.

A doorway led to a separate hall entitled 'bathhouse.' Benedict sighed happily as he walked toward it, unfastening his armor for the first time since entering this world beneath worlds. It groaned as much as he did as the pieces dropped to the floor outside the doorway. He noted it seemed the only entrance was through the rooms. meaning only patrons had access. He was no stranger to defending himself or others with nothing but his fists, he was willing to take the risk. There was soft steam wafting from the hallway when he opened the door to the bathhouse. He saw a small lump of soap, a bowl, and a small razor on a tray by the doorway next to a pile of large towels. The gentle steam made the wooden varnished table wet with warm dew, even from this distance.

"Be back in a bit. I'm-"

Skotmir's loud snoring told him, before he turned around to confirm, that everyone was already fast asleep.

"A PROMISE, THEN," THE VOICE whispered in Zane's mind.

He sat in the dark alone, feeling the cold stone beneath him. It felt like an eternity since he had seen the light outside the cell. The musty smell of stagnant water no longer burned his nose and he almost feared any light that would come in at this point. The chains around his wrists bit into his skin as he rubbed a cheek.

"Two souls for the price of one." Two icey blue eyes seemed to glow in the darkness before him.

Zane thought for a moment. His dry mouth opened as he drew breath in the musty air.

"Yes, two for one."

CHAPTER 6

THE PRISONER IN RUBY

The market bustled with the sounds of people selling wares from their various carts, which were opened to one side to reveal their contents. They all had similar designs- carts, booths, and platforms made of a dark gray wood that seemed to mimic stone. They passed a small street barrier made of a similar material as they entered the square. Benedict pointed one out to Skotmir.

"What is this wood? It's stronger than any I've seen, yet not brittle."

"Stone birch," Skotmir replied. Benedict looked at him questioningly, as the name was unknown to him.

"Never heard of it, eh? It grows under the hills. See, it has what you would think of as roots growing into the earth, but it's actually upside down. Its bottom looks like a huge boulder on the surface. You would never know it was actually a tree."

Benedict thought briefly of his craft as a blacksmith, and what a great wood it would be to grace a sword's pommel, or maybe a hammer. He smiled for a moment before remembering their grim purpose today. The large podium at one end of the market was where individuals would be put on sale for purchase. He shuddered slightly thinking of his brother Zane, again in chains.

He looked at Zorin, who appeared a bit pale. "Zorin, how are you?"

"I honestly feel like garbage, but I'm sure it will pass. I think it's the air of this city."

Cordelia nodded. "Yes, this air is foul, though the market seems to be helping a bit. Come, let's look at the fruit vendors' wares. You could use something fresh." She turned to the others. "We will catch up in a moment."

They nodded and continued toward the podium while Cordelia and Zorin approached a cart where a halfling stood proud on a large crate, talking to a short-haired deep elf.

The smells of exotic fruits and spices lifted through the air, a welcome change from the hazy smoke of the giant furnaces. Zorin took a shaky breath, filling his nose with the identifiable cinnamon, oranges and cloves. There were other savory scents similar to rosemary and basil, and sharp, cooling hints of mint. He smiled. This was much better.

"Hey there, can I help you?" The halfling turned to the two of them with a smile on his round and ruddy face, a gesture they hadn't seen in a long time.

"How much for the mint?"

"Gimme a gold and you can have it, my friend." He winked at Zorin. Zorin looked pleadingly at Cordelia, who smiled and nodded.

"Okay, it's a deal." He placed the gold piece in the small, childlike hand of the merchant. The halfling grinned before rubbing the coin against a gold tooth in his mouth, then grabbed a fistful of mint and placed it in a burlap pouch.

Zorin squeezed the pouch gently as he brought it to his bearded face with a deep draw of breath. The soft cool vapors eased into his nose, cooling the burning from the foul sulphuric and smoky air.

Sophie walked stoically through the crowd, her eyes trained on the worn, dark gray podium. The crowd was gathering around the foot of it. She saw many gray dwarves and dark elves talking amongst themselves and pointing at the stage.

"Please be here. Please. Please don't leave us again."

Her heart rate was fast. She hoped upon all hope to see his face again after all these weeks. Her hands were balled into fists. She realized it and quickly wiped her palms together and across the armor on her thighs.

Vix and Skotmir looked on as well, but Benedict looked anxious. The crowd grew louder as the auctioneer walked out, a white wiry beard laid across the round belly of his armor. His heavy iron-shanked boots fell heavily on the planks, calling attention from everyone.

Zorin walked up to Sophie, leaning in without drawing too much attention.

"Listen, I'm going over to the other side where they can see me better. If he's there, we don't give up until he's free. Sound good?"

She nodded and he turned to walk back into the crowd.

"Hey, Zorin?" Sophie stopped him for a moment. "Thanks." He smiled and winked at her, disappearing into the sea of gathering people who, she imagined in disgust, were there to purchase the other people soon to be displayed, like a simple iron kettle or chipped vase.

The ashen gray dwarf announcer walked out on the stage, the heavy fall of his boots thundering from the wooden planks. He tugged at his beard before pulling out a scroll and barking at the crowd.

"Starting off, we have a prisoner who has served his sentence and is looking to atone for his wrong-doings with servitude. Servitude brings humility. Humility brings purpose. Purpose is life."

"Purpose is life…"

The crowd murmured at these last words. Sophie saw the gray dwarves in the crowd nod and beat their chests in agreement. The prisoner was another gray dwarf, standing proud in a muslin tunic belted with a rope cord at the waist. His red eyes glowed with a fire.

"Let's start the bidding at five gold pieces."

The crowd erupted with hands. "There's five, do we have 10?"

Thus the auction began. Sophie bowed her head.

"Zane, please be here. Please."

The auction proceeded with several dwarves, an orc, and even a deep elf craftsman going to the various bidders. A hush fell across the crowd as they heard the shuffle of chains across the steps behind the stage.

"Oh!"

Sophie's heart burst as she saw the bearded face of Zane appear. His golden hair hung in matted locks about his shoulders. He was clad in the same dirty muslin tunic as the others. His face was dirty and his eyes were still adjusting to the light of the marketplace. Sophie felt something squeeze her hand. Looking down, she saw Benedict's face crack a hopeful smile.

"Zorin has this. I know it." He shook his head. "It's a gamble after all, and no one knows that better than him."

The auctioneer rubbed his hands together at the sight of a fresh face. Never-smiling but still pleased.

"Now here's a rare treat. A surface dweller. Let's start the bidding at 20 gold pieces."

The crowd hesitated and Zorin's hand shot up.

"There's 20, is there 25?"

The crowd was silent. There was no need for the novelty of a surface dweller. He didn't look like he could do the work of the others, and this brought no purpose for the purchase.

"I have 25." The voice rang out from a cloaked dwarven figure standing on a stack of crates. The wiry white beard flowed from the blue black hood, obscuring his face. Zorin looked back at his competition.

"30!" he shot back before the auctioneer could respond.

This was all they had left in their purse from the inn. The man looked at him, his icy blue eyes locked on Zorin.

"40."

Zorin's heart sank. Then he thought for a moment. He could sell his new dagger, and Benedict could sell his sword. They did say it was magical. This could work.

"That's all we have. It has to work." His hand shot up.

"50," he said. He saw the look on Sophie's face. She nodded nervously.

"50, going once." Zorin looked back at his competition, still standing on the stack of crates, and saw the dwarf smiling before he disappeared in a small surge of the crowd. His familiar eyes were etched in Zorin's memory. Again he was lost in thought about why he knew them.

SKOTMIR WRUNG HIS HANDS TOGETHER while they waited in the cold stone lobby of the auction house. The granite benches were perfect in every way, he noted, running his hand along its side. Not one pit or rough spot. He sighed. But devoid of any maker's mark or decoration.

"This place is awful," he muttered. "Sooner we can get out of here the better."

Vix nodded. "Indeed."

The door behind them opened, and Zane walked out smiling with a grinning Zorin.

"Zane!"

Sophie threw her arms around him.

"Sophie."

He smiled over her strong shoulder as he breathed in the honey and lavender smell of her freshly washed hair.

"I couldn't bear to lose you again."

He pulled back and smiled.

"Never again, Sophie. I swear on the sky and moon itself, I will never leave you again."

He was shaking as he pulled her back to his embrace.

"Never."

"Thank you."

Vix turned from the two lovers to confront Zorin. "So, what deal did you make? Our new equipment still lies with us. I thought for sure you would have sold my robes off my back if you had the chance."

"They aren't worth that much Vix, come on."

"These are lined with Chikaran Silk, you fool! See the maker's mark?"

"No."

"It's right here-"

"I mean, I don't care."

"What do we have to do now, Zorin?" Benedict's voice broke up the exchange and was followed by a moment of silence.

Everyone turned to Zorin, who smiled an awkward grin, trying his best to mask his guilt.

"I have offered our help to the marshal, to aid them in clearing out the sewers."

Skotmir stood up angrily.

"What! I am no plumber or thief. Find someone else to get dirty with-"

"Stand down, Son of the Garnet Mountains."

The woman's voice was strong, and carried from behind Zorin as she stepped into view. She was a female dwarf, clad in dark iron armor that consisted of hard angles around her short muscular frame. Snow white hair was pulled back in a single ponytail from her ashen gray face, and her eyes looked at them with deep blood red irises.

"I am known as Ferra. Ferra Ironstone, marshal of the King's Guard."

Over one shoulder was a warhammer, blackened gray like her armor; the large rectangular head was simple and rounded from years of use. It was attached to a thick wooden handle studded with brass to enhance the grip in battle. She set it down on the ground in front of her, leaning on it with her hands crossed.

"I offered to pay for your friend's freedom after Zorin and I spoke about your ability to help us with a rather worrisome issue."

Benedict stepped forward. "What troubles this city?"

"There is a foul magic creeping into our hearts. Many of us have left the forges and become complacent." She looked at the ground, contemplating.

"Even our king is sick. He refuses to see anyone, and keeps to himself all day. He has not sent out his tasks in months, and many of our people looked forward to his mighty commands. It gave us- "

"Purpose," Cordelia interrupted gently. The red eyes flared.

"Yes." she hissed, setting Cordelia back a pace now, understanding not to question or interrupt the powerful commander.

"Our purpose, outsider." She sighed. "As I was saying, we are all slowly falling victim to this apathy."

"What do you need us to do?" Benedict bowed slightly in respect of the marshal's station.

She sneered and shook her head at the unneeded formalities. "We believe the source is somewhere deep in the sewers below the city. Clean it out." She stared at Benedict, who nodded.

"Thank you for freeing our friend. We shall do this immediately. " She nodded and, casting a final glance at Skotmir, spun on her heel and walked back into the auction house.

"WELL, THE SMELL ISN'T SO bad now, at least." Zorin spoke quietly, his voice reverberating off the stonebrick walls that arched overhead just out of reach.

Hours had passed as they made their way by torchlight, led by Zorin at the front who periodically paused to inspect the smooth stone wall. They had found an entrance to another set of tunnels from the main sewer shortly after entering the system. The entrance was trapped magically and had been triggered recently by the dead guard lying on the floor.

Benedict leaned down, clutching at his chest where once his silver pendant had been. Lost, when they were captured by the dark elves. His hand felt empty, but he filled his heart with faith.

"Knight Lord, please welcome this weary soul to the anvils of your realm."

"Bah! We have no time for the dead." Vix brushed his hands on his robes briskly, freeing them of the chalky dust that clung to them. He drew in a deep breath and looked around as he stood just past the insulted Benedict.

"We must do this deed and get on our way."

Jade looked at them with purpose. "I agree, we must continue. Zorin, let's go."

They ducked into the dark hallway that Zorin pointed out, and moved into the darkness beyond.

They traveled for hours until faint voices grew down the hall, and the faint glow of distant fire light reflecting off the far wall at the end of the passage became more apparent.

"Hold up." Zorin forced a whisper at the top of his breath to reach everyone. Benedict motioned to stop Cordelia and Jade, both nodding at the rear of the group.

There was a charcoal taste in the air, as though something were being burned down the hall in a well ventilated room. It seemed there were multiple voices in the distance- all gravelly, male voices.

"I'll scout ahead," Zorin offered. Before anyone could respond, Vix spoke from the safety of the back of the group.

"A grand idea. Don't take too long."

Skotmir shook his head at Vix before tapping Zorin's elbow with a smile.

"Be safe, my friend."

Zorin nodded and, handing his torch back to Skotmir, faded into the shadows.

"What the-" Zorin's voice was barely under his breath as he peered around the corner. He had to blink several times to adjust to the light of the room. The room was immense, not unlike the inside of a tall chapel. Tall pillars towered into the air, supporting a ceiling hundreds of feet high like the tallest buildings in Port L'For, but now buried underground. The pillars were at six points around the room, pressing into the floor with their fifteen-foot bases revealing a six-pointed star. Connecting them in the center was a platform raised just beyond his height, surrounded by steps leading up to the backs of four chanting gray dwarves dressed in dark robes.

Zorin looked back at his friends and motioned for them to come up quietly to his position. He then ducked into the room, sticking to the left wall to work his way around the perimeter for a better view. The stone was smooth and, unlike above, there were carvings in it depicting various scenes.

He ran his hand along the side of a cow being led by a young maiden to a nearby stream. He then saw a woman kneeling in a graveyard. He could feel her loss of a sister in his heart as his hands passed over. In another one he saw a man in strange clothes, a sleek jacket with a long collar folded to the shoulder and what he guessed to be a thin scarf tied around his neck. The knot was triangular and directly in the center of the man's throat. He was unfamiliar with this style. He was behind a desk, threatening a smaller man dressed similarly with a small sculpture in his hand. As his hand ran over it, he could hear a voice echo in his mind.

"Jynx!"

He shook the imaginary voice from his head. Whatever the enchantment, there was no time for sightseeing, even if it was being done by his hands.

A shrill and bloodthirsty voice rang out in the center of the room.

"We beseech you! You, the true queen of the void, please answer our call and grant us your blessing. Dark Queen, hold this unbeliever in your stony gaze. May he taste the poison air from your breath. The elements at your command, my beautiful Queen!"

Zorin snuck closer, bracing behind a pillar. He spied a chest at the top of the stairs that he could stay within the shadows of. He made his way, crawling up the stairs. Peering around the side of the chest, he could see the five-headed dragon on their robes and froze. He thought of a night, very long ago.

"Come, child, and let me show you the power of my queen," the dark cleric said, standing by his hated father's side.

The dwarf threw his arms back and howled. "We shall free you, our Queen! You will rule the air again! You will take your rightful place alongside the dark prince, together ruling this world and above."

The dwarf cackled maniacally, his red eyes wide and arms outstretched towards the fire, hiding a crooked staff of ash. The altar at the center had a dark black tapestry covering it, but something glowed red faintly from beneath the dusty shroud.

A creaking groan came from across the room, sounding like a giant piece of steel and stone sliding against each other. Across from Zorin, a huge humanoid form leaned against a pillar. Standing twelve feet tall and holding a large mace in one hand, the two heads of the giant turned to each other and snarled out of boredom. Zorin's heart was racing. He looked back and could see Benedict at the entrance, slowly sneaking in with Jade and Skotmir.

He waved a hand, careful to keep it out of sight, silently telling them to stop when the sound of a trap's jaws, metal crashing into metal, alerted the room.

Benedict yelled out when the trap sprung, sending a large metal claw into his calf.

"Intruders! Kill them!"

"Greta will kill for the Dark Queen!"

Cordelia paused for a moment as Vix stepped forward.

"Ty-sah!"

Three spiked balls of energy shot from his hands, knocking one of the dwarves into the air to land lifeless on his back. His experience with the arcane was apparent; she smiled, glad he was on her side. Cordelia pulled a familiar bolt of fire into her palms before releasing it into another cultist. Zorin watched in horror as Greta the Giantess slammed the spiked mace into a pillar, barely missing Benedict as he dodged. Benedict spun up and drove his sword into the ground, releasing a blast of magical energy that slammed into Greta's exposed flank.

Her heads bellowed in unison, reeling back to show filed and broken teeth.

Zane and Sophie charged into the fray. Zane had his two daggers drawn while Sophie's new longsword was over one shoulder, both of her hands preparing to strike as they met the group of cultists. Sophie dropped the blade into the first dwarven cultist at the shoulder while Zane leapt from the side of the pillar, driving one blade into his neck and finishing the job.

Skotmir roared. His battle axe gleamed as he drove it into another cultist, sending him to his back in a heap. Zorin ran up to the last cultist, who was preparing a spell in a dark language.

"Ak-stah-fo-nes-tah!"

A bolt of lightning shot out and struck Skotmir hard in the chest, driving him to slide on the smooth marble floor of the platform.

Skotmir yelled and shook his head wildly to clear the biting sparks in his mind. The smell of singed hair snapped him out of it as it burned his nostrils. He saw Zorin drive his rapier into the cultist's back, dropping him dead almost immediately.

"You can't stop me, little man!" Skotmir saw Greta swing wildly at Benedict.

"Skotmir, send me up!" He turned behind him to see Sophie dashing at him. Without thinking he crouched down, offering his hands at the floor. Sophie stepped into them and with one huge effort he sent her into the air, her sword raised, aiming to strike the back of the large giantess.

Greta roared as the blade cut deep into her back, passing easily beyond the moldy, loose leather armor. She fell to the ground, dropping her mace to the floor. Benedict struck one of her heads with his great sword, rending it silent. Sophie roared as she picked up the huge mace with both arms, bringing it down on the other head in one final stroke.

All was quiet, save their racing and labored breaths.

They continued to pant in that silent room, surveying the scene. Sophie smiled and nodded at Benedict, who smiled back, both of them pleased at how well and fast they worked together.

"Hey everyone, you aren't going to believe this."

He was standing next to the altar and had thrown the dusty shroud from it, revealing the bars of a cage made of solid ruby. They pulsed with a deep red light, revealing a tall silver-haired elf sitting inside.

CHAPTER 7

THE SONG IN THE DREAM

The monkey chirped from his shoulder, both in happiness for their freedom and in worried anticipation of the liberators. Not completely trusting, it shrieked at Cordelia when she tried to come near.

"Abu doesn't like you. I'm sorry."

The cold voice of the tall elf who was once trapped in the ruby cage was quiet and hushed. He said his name was Eralin, and he looked like one of the Viridian Elves. Though, Vix noted, something was different. He was tall, standing almost seven feet, and his white hair made him look more like the dark elves except for his plum-colored eyes and blue-gray skin.

"You are taller than most, and your hair and eyes are not common to our people. Are you from this place?"

Eralin turned to Vix and cooly regarded his question.

"If you mean this underground prison, no one is truly from here. Though I've found that in my time imprisoned here, many who come to visit eventually-"

He turned to Zorin.

"Thank you again. I have no idea how many years have passed since I've been trapped in that cage, praying for release or vengeance."

"Where are you from?" Benedict asked. Eralin paused. "I was a sailor. My ship was The Nautilus. Our beloved Captain fell to a band of pirates. I myself was imprisoned, tortured." He paused in silence, looking away to the distant hallway's darkness. "They bound me and I ended up here. I know not much else."

Nearby, Zorin opened the chest he had been hiding behind. He easily picked the ancient lock and the large ornate brass clasp creaked from its post, freeing the lid. It was heavy and dense, but free of age and rot despite the layer of dust.

Inside, he saw an ornate rapier. Green and purple gems graced the sterling silver guard and scabbard, glinting in the light. As if stepping into a familiar dream, he smiled as he lifted it out of its resting place.

"That's a gorgeous weapon, Zorin."

"Thank you." A lady's voice seemed to dance and resonate in Zorin's mind.

Zorin stared at Benedict for a moment, wondering where the voice came from.

"I,uh-"

"Well, don't be stupid. Tell him 'thank you,' silly!" the voice gently jested.

He looked down at the sword. The voice was coming from the sword. He quickly looked at Benedict

"Yes! It is. It is, isn't it?" His voice started earnestly but trailed as he found himself neck deep in thought and questions. Questions he was afraid wouldn't have answers.

"Yeah, it suits you."

"See? We were meant to be together. Your friend even thinks so."

"Did you hear that?" Zorin asked Benedict, forcing himself to stay calm.

"Hear what?"

Zorin raised an eyebrow, testing the waters. "A voice?"

"Nope, just us."

"He can't hear me, silly!"

"I, uh-"

"Are you sure you're ok?" Benedict approached him. "Maybe the air is getting to you. I could-"

"I'm fine!"

Benedict paused, his eyes raised in mock surprise at his friend's outburst. Zane smiled, finding humor in the situation.

Zorin smoothed out his tunic and cleared his throat, forcing himself to calm his demeanor.

"Thank you. I'm fine, just a bit weary. Thanks." He stumbled off to sit on the steps with his new blade.

Benedict shook his head with a chuckle. "Ok, old friend. It's ok."

HOURS LATER, THEY WERE BACK in their room at the Inn. Skotmir sat at his bedside thinking, looking out the window at the large, underground city. The flames rumbled periodically from the towering furnaces, sending plumes of fire and smoke rolling into the air.

He thought of the marshal's face when they told her they had completed the journey and what they had found. She looked very disturbed by the news, though her voice carried the same stone-borne strength he had come to expect of her.

"Get some rest. We will meet here in the morning to discuss our King." She had turned away, he noted, and brushed her cheek. "I fear this has had no effect on his condition."

She was worried and cared about her king, that was certain, but Skotmir was still bothered by the overall sense of apathy that laid low with everyone that lived here.

"Boy," he mumbled to himself. "Stay here much longer and I'll become a boring old stone like the rest of these dwarves. Silent and empty."

He yawned, noticing the rest of his friends were asleep.

"Benedict can really saw some logs over there." He chuckled at the paladin's gentle snoring. With a smile, he flopped back onto the bed and closed his eyes.

SKOTMIR FOUND HIMSELF IN ANOTHER underground city as his dreams washed over him. A city similar to the one where his mortal body lay on its soft downy bed, but this one was decorated in fine stonework gilded in gold. Silver and brass sconces lined the room, throwing multi-colored light to cast dancing silhouettes on the massive cavern walls. This was familiar. This is where he once called home.

Great fires erupted as the clanging of steel anvils rang below the balcony he stood at. Looking down, he saw the forgemasters wielding hammers on giant gemstone crystals. The shards were carried to grinding stations where they were given facets and finally settings in the blades or hammers of the weapons they made.

Skotmir saw his father in front of the great forgehammer of their people. To his right was Thotmir, his brother. They were identical save for Thotmir's dark blue armor and dirty blonde beard, which he wore in a single braid. Skotmir never liked the feel of their traditional armor. Too restrictive.

He was a Boar's Head fighter. A berserker who did better without being trapped in armor and who was known for the ferocity of the wild boar in battle. They were outcasts. He shouldn't be in this room.

"Thotmir?" Skotmir said, with a quake of uncertainty.

"My brother, why are you here?" Thotmir's eyes studied him uncomfortably. "You left us. Why do you return?"

Before Skotmir could reply, Thotmir raised a hand to silence him.

"It matters not." He looked away and back at their father on the huge podium. "We need you not."

Their father stood with his back turned to them. His long white beard was braided in the center, pulled neatly from the golden crown on his head. He set the jeweled hammer down on the anvil and turned. Skotmir had never seen this hammer. He knew in his heart it was only a legend, but that knowledge didn't cease his amazement at its beauty.

Gemstones lined the shaft above a sharkskin leather-wrapped handle. The head of the hammer was wide and commanding, with six cuts of marbled rose and teal jasper outlining the settings for large garnet stones. Behind the head was a long pick of brass.

"Ah, Skotmir. Do you know why you are here?"

"Father, no I-"

"Hush, boy!" His father's patience was growing thin. Skotmir noticed his feet were anchored to the rock itself as if he, himself, and his family were carved from the same block of stone.

"You are here because you need to collect and bring back the last of the six winds, an artifact that has been forgotten in time. You have found one of these. Press on, before it is too late. This is not a place for mortals."

The room went dark, replaced by the glow of the hammer on the table. The gemstones gleamed like a pair of bright blue sapphires now, above a glistening smile of white diamonds.

LORAHANA SAT IN THE CHAIR mending a seam on a white tunic, just as Cordelia remembered.

"Zane is so hard on his clothes." She chuckled to herself, rocking back and forth.

"Mama, tell me about the dragons."

Lorahana looked at her with a slightly tired expression. She paused, then smiled, succumbing to the pleading voice of her child.

"Oh, all right. What do you want to know?"

"Their magic." Her voice changed; she felt control over this dream now, over this memory.

"Remember, dragon magic is powerful magic. A magic that can pass through time and over great distances. Magic weapons in many ways are forged from dragon magic, whether actually touched by the dragon's spirit or just mimicked. At its core, dragon magic can work wonders and even may, upon its destruction or freeing, grant wishes."

She stopped rocking and thought for a moment.

"It's probably for the best that dragons haven't been seen for so many years, my sweet Cordelia."

BENEDICT COULD SMELL THE HOT coals before he felt their warm, familiar heat. His hand was resting on a rough oak table where a four inch red eyed Dragon Turtle carved of pure silver sat.

A great arm brought down the hammer to the red hot iron, sending sparks scattering away.

The deep voice resonated, "What are you looking for, Benedict?"

"An artifact of power. But that's all we know. "

Erebus laughed as he thrusted the iron back into the fire. The deep burgundy rose to a warm cherry again.

"I suppose the real question is, what do you really need?" Benedict thought for a moment. Erebus taught him that a solution wouldn't be found by looking directly for it. Instead, he was to find the path or tool and work toward it.

"A light. A light for this terrible darkness."

Erebus nodded as he pulled out a raw, jagged iron rod from the table.

"You have always gone through life yearning for something bigger, but you've never found what you had within first. Only then can you find what you are without." He walked towards the work bench. A familiar workbench, Benedict could smell the oil that was rubbed into the oak over the years.

"Take this iron. By itself, it seems strong." He thrust it into a crook of the wooden plank at the end of the bench. "And can do the job in most cases, I suppose." He shrugged.

In one swift movement he struck down on it with the hammer, shattering the iron.

"But under a different force, it's actually brittle."

Erebus then pointed a single blackened finger at the hammer. "But if you work it in the smoke and fire, it becomes steel."

Benedict watched as he walked toward him, realizing for the first time how young and small he was compared to Erebus.

"Smoke and fire are simple things. But they need to get inside the iron. You are this iron, but now you've found the fire of the Knight Lord, have you not?"

Benedict nodded, a little embarrassed at himself. Erebus patted his shoulder, smiling.

"Then, Benedict, maybe you have already found what you came for."

IN THE MORNING, THE GROUP all shared their stories with each other. Each of them in turn were entertained, if nothing more, by each other's company. All save for Vix.

"You all never cease to amaze me with your silly stories." He stood up, clutching a towel from the pile and leaving for the bathhouse. "I'll return shortly, then we best get moving to marshal Ironstone. She doesn't seem to be one who likes to wait."

The group sat there in silence for a moment.

"I dreamt of my family too." Zorin sighed, knowing he couldn't keep it from them any longer.

"Though it wasn't as pleasant. I saw a boy, about ten years old, sneaking into a room he should not be in. It was a room of oddities surrounding a desk. Brains in jars, small hideous creatures in jars with labels and unpronounceable names. It was me, but as if I were out of my body. On the central oak table was a basketball-shaped object covered with an embroidered cloth. The object seemed to slightly pulse in size as I approached, mesmerized.

'Pooooor motherless Child, come here Child,' it hissed at me, like steam from ice in boiling oil and just as dangerous. *'I can help you. I will love you. Come to my arms, let me whisper sweetness in your ears and cover you in kisses you never had.'*

"As I raised the edge of the fabric, I saw a faint green light fading in and out, in and out like the waves on the sea. I had never seen the sea back then. Bands of script appeared in a bright gold, contrasted against the green fog within. I wanted to reach in so badly, tears streaming down my face, as that voice became sweeter, more motherly, familiar.

'Please son, won't you let me hold you?'

"Footsteps in the hall broke my trance. I gasped and looked around sharply for an escape. None could be found readily- the only way in or out was the hall where the footsteps were coming from. This was my father's office. I was never allowed in my father's office. I saw a small table next to the cushioned bench used for reading or guests he never had. I dove under, hoping it was enough.

'With this I can control dragons for you, as you do, my love. The boy? He is weak, nothing like his mother.'

"The boy began to sneak out of the room but bumped the table leg, causing a small candle to rattle in its mooring. The giant man turned around, noticing the boy under the table. With a mighty arm he flipped the table up and out of the way, exposing him to the wrath of the much larger man.

"His voice was eerily cool, but it rang like thunder. 'What have I told you about being in my study?'

"He kicked me into the bookcase with a single strike, a small cloud of dust from the neglected tomes rising from the impact."

"From outside I heard a call, 'Hey there! Can Zorin come out and play?' The knocking at the door caused my father to pause."

'Go away, Zane!' he boomed toward the front door, then turned slowly with a maniacal grin toward the boy. 'Zorin can't play today.'

"I knew if I even whimpered I would just get more of the same, if not worse. I gritted my teeth and vowed I would never carry my father's name as a huge fist crashed across my brow. Then, it all faded to black."

Zane was staring at his friend.

"I remember that day." He wrapped his arms around his friend's shoulders. "I'm sorry."

Zorin brushed his eyes before looking at his best friend. "I'm not. He will be the sorry one."

Zane's blue eyes were gentle and calm as usual. "Did you dream of anything?"

Zane laughed. "Naw, I was out. What about you, Jade?"

Jade thought for a moment while restringing her bow.

"Yes, I had a dream," she said, looking outside. "But I assure you, it was of no importance. It was of another time. Another life."

Cordelia raised an eyebrow but quickly smiled. "Let's get moving. The marshal's waiting for us." As they all gathered their things, Jade remembered more of her dream.

A dream of dear friends, from a long time ago.

They were all poised on the ridge astride six warhorses overlooking a huge barbarian army in the green valley below. Their shouts and jeers were muffled at this distance by the gentle breeze. She remembered it was spring.

Jade saw the village in flames behind the raiders, her keen nose filling with the iron and smoke of the slaughter below. She noticed the raven haired mage at her right turn away as they saw a few knights' bodies being paraded around. The raiders celebrated the slaughter they all came to atone for.

"It is just us, then?" a knight asked plainly, turning her head to the black haired leader.

Her dirty blonde hair hung gently to the shoulder, cut in a short style to ensure mobility in the heavy plate on her torso. It was a style all but Jade and the mage were wearing. That knight carried a polearm with a swooping blade at one end. It was a glaive, Jade remembered, but couldn't remember the knight's name.

Or any of their names, for that matter.

All she remembered was that this was her tribe, her family. Next to the mage, a tall honey haired man drew his longsword, a sword that looked like the emblem of crown and sword they all wore on their tunics. Finally, on her left, the short dark hickory-colored hair of another man blew gently as he prayed. Her heart leapt slightly when his blue eyes fell on her and smiled from beyond a golden set of armor.

CHAPTER 8

THE DEEP KING

Vix heard the gentle crunch of the autumn leaves beneath his feet, drifting across the smooth white marble of the stairs to the large, pillared gazebo. The trees bent of their own accord toward the center, almost in their own reverence to the man sitting on the throne. He rose, his yellow robes cascading to the floor, gently revealing delicate golden embroidery that shrouded him in gentle sunlight. There was no roof to this structure, only the cool autumn sky far above those tall tree tops.

"You are an abomination to our people," he stated through clenched teeth. "You practice the magical arts, but at your heart you are only footsteps from the dark path. For all intents and purposes, I should have you exiled." Catching his anger as his words escalated he smiled, remembering his manners. Politely pouring two goblets of sweet white wine he smiled again with a slight bow, passing one to vix.

"But." Regaining his composure, he continued. "Vix, there is a war coming and I believe, despite all your faults, you can still be a great asset to your people. I charge you to seek out a way to control their dragons. Do this and report back to me. Only then will I allow you to undergo your telling at the Ivory Library. I have heard of a competition taking place in a small barony to the north of here in a few days. It's possible that this will put you and your cunning on the right path."

Growing serious, he continued, "Those librarians are their own people, but I have kept my place among their council. They will not allow you through their gates unless I allow it."

Vix's eyes narrowed and in a shaky tone he replied, "Yes, Lord Hyro."

The elegantly clad Lord Hyro, lord of the Silver Maple Woods, turned away to look out into his red and gold forest.

"Do not fail me or be discovered, for I cannot help you." He stood and motioned for the guards to lead him away.

"Vix."

"Yes?" Vix looked around. The dream from last night was still haunting him. He wouldn't admit it to the young mage Cordelia, who was staring at him, that he was in fact daydreaming.

She began to explain, "We were-"

"Your friends were just saying that you may be familiar with this symbol."

The King's marshal held up a scrap of parchment, burned at one end with a dark red S-shaped symbol.

He scanned the room, embarrassed that he'd drifted off. They stood in a granite chamber with a large map of the city on a dark wooden table. Torches lit the walls and the smell of a sweet oil was burning in the large ironwork brazier hanging by thick chains above their heads. Light shone through the iron framework in panes of thick glass that held the clear oil itself. He looked back at the symbol.

"It seems as if it is just a stylized S-shape, but what concerns me are the five parallel lines cut downward ending in arrowheads."

He pointed them out on the paper. "That's a glyph of summoning." They all looked at each other uneasily.

Cordelia looked at him. "Vix, have you seen this before?"

Vix returned her gaze, but heard ravens on a moonlit street. The voice of the blue skinned scholar he was traveling with called him to the building's side.

"Look, Vix. This can't be good."

He saw the same symbol. "A glyph of summoning."

"But summoning what?"

Screams ripped through his mind as he shook his head, bringing himself to the present.

"The sooner we get out of here, the better! I can't think straight." He turned to Ferra Ironstone. "Where did you get this?" he asked.

"It was found in the King's throne room. The paper style seems to predate my time as marshal."

Cordelia stepped forward with a hand outstretched. "May I?"

The marshal handed her the parchment. Cordelia passed a hand gently over it; the edges of the parchment glowed with a blue light.

"This is blood. But from about a quarter century ago."

"Has it been that long?"

"What is that, marshal?"

"Many years ago, the King took a bride. She is different from most of us- a wizard. Keeps to herself, but I bet she knows what this means." She spun on her heel, snapping her fingers. "That's it. Go to the keep, find out from her what she knows." They all nodded.

"The guards are told to attack anyone crossing the bridge. They will move for you if you carry this emblem." She handed Zane a small square of dark gray fabric. About as wide as an arm's length, a pair of silver hammers was embroidered on it with hair-thin steel thread. Turning to leave, she paused at the door, looking over her armored shoulder.

"Please, bring us back our King."

SHAR WRUNG HER HANDS TOGETHER as she paced in the cold stone quarters of her room. The dust of the room was settled and still and the smell of the smelters outside was welcome. The smell of power. She smiled. She thought of the carts of blades and crude armor, sized for larger humans and orcs being pulled to the portal. A plan progressing without any challenges was always a good plan, she thought. Reaching down, she pulled up a short stool made of a dark purple wood cloaked in a single wolf pelt. Sitting down, she pivoted an ash gray leg to swing facing the mirror above a small desk made of the same plum colored wood.

Shar stared into the red eyes of her reflection. She thought back over half a century of being trapped in this prison of her own making. She brought them here to this twilight world that blended the lines between the living and the dead. Her gray hand gently dabbed the corner of a soft cloth into a crimson paste. She drew the skin around her red eyes taut as she smeared a sharp curve of the makeup below each eye.

The crimson reminded her of something. Rather, someone. She saw a girl, a single braid of flame sprouting behind a head of ebony and ash. The girl smiled, but only briefly, as she went back to scrubbing what appeared to be a huge bowl. The girl was ten feet tall, but half the size of the rest of the giants in her tribe. These giants of the mountain flame were terrifying, but Shar knew them all too well.

They were her partners in this plan. They would run the weapons to the trade barons and fuel the great warmachines while she was safe. She smiled. The girl was of no concern, she told herself.

A creation of magic that was just that, a creation. An experiment. Shar had used magic to create a half-giant. Physically, Popi, as she came to refer to her, was half the size of the other giants but, unlike them, she had no parents, only the weave of magic that created her. Because of this they despised her, thinking of her as less than them and, in some cases, an abomination.

Shar had abandoned her, then. Left her creation to find her own way and survive or not, as was the will of the chaotic weave she served. There was no time for such pets, after all, and there was so much to do.

Shaking her head, she cleared it of the girl's memory and reached for a waxy violet lip gloss which she applied with another small cloth. She saw the reflection of the stone around her neck. A red stone that had been split. She remembered that its sister had a spirit trapped inside, a vengeful spirit of a bird-headed woman. Talons like razors gripped the vertebrae of a deadly and wicked spear.

She smiled at this memory. She remembered the feel of air under her wings. Shar remembered the taste of blood, but she also remembered him. His blue eyes that shone like lit sapphires in a glacial pool.

Slamming her hand on the table she screamed in anger at his memory. She took a moment to collect herself before standing. Blue green fire gently pulsed between her fingers, like waves on the sea.

Smoothing the pleats on the front of her dress, she sighed before she chuckled at her outburst. She shouldn't be upset. As she turned toward the door, Shar told herself this wasn't a prison.

This place was a sanctuary.

THE SMOKE BILLOWED UP FROM the molten iron, pouring far enough below that the heat wouldn't cook them as they crossed the bridge. The bridge was wide enough for eight carts, and it would take them a few minutes to cross.

Skotmir knew without looking that the iron was being funneled into the huge furnaces in the city behind them. Similar methods were used in the Garnet Mountains he called home, but nothing this grandiose. Their mines were geared more toward the rich gemstone deposits riddled with gold and the occasional platinum veins. His people relied on trade for most of their raw iron.

"Seems we have a welcoming committee." Benedict gestured cautiously towards the five rows of Dwarf Infantry standing at attention on the other side of the bridge.

An intimidating sight, the helms only allowed their white beards and red eyes to show across all fifty soldiers. Short fighting spears with broad bladed heads were held in one hand and tall square shields were secured to the other.

"Here goes nothing," Zane mumbled, taking out the cloth and, almost wincing behind it, displayed it with two hands in front of him.

The officer in the front rank stepped hard to the right, standing ninety degrees from their path.

"Make way for the marshal's envoy!"

Zane looked back at Cordelia with a chuckle, and now also with a cocky swagger in his step.

As they crossed the stony courtyard, the soldiers parted to allow the group to enter. Jade looked behind her and saw the ranks close behind them as they walked. They were in perfect form, like the flow of a slow moving rockslide.

Upon reaching the massive twin doors, two guards worked a hand wheel on either side which swung them open to allow the group entry into the receiving hall of the keep.

The hall was lit with large iron braziers, similar to the ones in the marshal's office, hanging from the sides of the tall and towering pillars holding up the domed stone ceiling. The main floor was wide, easily spanning the same space as it was tall. The burgundy and gold floor runner led up to a raised platform upon which were two stone thrones, side by side. Next to them was a podium draped in a red velvet cloth, something round hidden beneath it.

Eralin saw the guards scattered throughout the hall exchange a look of concern. Their nervous shuffling in thick plate armor reverberated dully in the hall. One of them pointed at Zane, more importantly at the small banner he carried. The smell of charcoal in the braziers reminded Skotmir of his home far away. A similar hall he noted, just not as dark. The pillars of his home were encrusted with red gemstones and gilded with gold embellishments.

The figures on the throne became more visible. The dark midnight blue hues of the king's robes cloaked his frail body. His cheeks were sunken and the white whiskers of his chin were sparse and wiry. The other figure sat in a black and red cloak, her hand on a bronze staff. Cresting at the foot of the stairs were the four king's guards, identifiable by a helmet adorned with three deep iron ridges. Sweeping back, they came together as a single wall, their spears together in unison.

"Who approaches his royal majesty?" the woman stood up and hissed.

Sophie looked at the guards. "You know you don't want to be here for this." Zane held up the banner. They lowered their spears and looked at each other, then turned to the king and bowed before marching away in unison.

"Cowards! Come back!" She looked at the imposters.

"You! You worms have no idea who you are playing with!" An unfamiliar pit churned in Benedict's stomach as he noticed the king was trembling in his throne, staring wide eyed at the woman.

Her hair was spun platinum, gracing her beautiful ash gray face. Her red eyes began to glow and they noticed her canines begin to lengthen as she held her hands outstretched.

"Please, Shar. Let us reason with them. Please don't do this-"

"Stay down, your highness. This is my fight now. They cannot have you!" Black leathery wings sprouted from her back.

"Wield me."

The voice came to Zorin's mind directly, but he knew it was the gleaming sword at his side. He took a deep breath and drew the blade from the scabbard.

"Yes. She is deeply evil and not of this world, my love, but I can protect you. Keep me close."

Zorin dropped into a defensive stance. The group followed suit, drawing their weapons or readying their spells.

The woman shrieked and lightning forked from her hands at Sophie, Benedict, Zorin and Skotmir. The smell of ozone ran into Zorin's nose as he stood bracing for the impact of a blast that never came. He looked and saw Skotmir drop to a knee as Benedict and Sophie were blown backward, sliding on the stone floor and cursing their false step.

Vix and Cordelia both fired off six blue fiery bolts that slammed into Shar's body, followed by a volley of well placed arrows from Jade and Eralin's bowstrings.

"You dare to oppose me, mortals!? *Fess-tah-goh!*"

Clapping her hands together, a thunderwave rocked out and knocked everyone to the ground, their ears ringing. Zorin saw Zane braced against the podium's wall below Shar, out of sight in the shadows. He nodded at Zorin, his two daggers drawn. Zorin knelt there for a moment.

"Get up. Go to her, my love."

Zorin began to stand, only to be greeted by a blast of blue fire. Shar shrieked as the torrent hit Zorin, only for it to be split around his body by the sword in his hands.

"What?! It can't be!" The king was at the shrouded podium clutching the velvet drape. "We must call Beryl!"

"Yes! Do it!"

Throwing off the cover revealed a black stone the size of a large melon. It seemed to rotate with a greenish blue glow from deep within.

Zorin froze. The king placed both hands on the stone, throwing his head back as the blast of energy filled his being.

"Beryl! Come to our aid!"

Eralin felt his heart clutch, freezing him in place. He couldn't take his eyes off the glowing stone.

A deep, thunderous reverberation of giant wings deafened the hall. A roar rolled through the chamber as they all froze in place. A huge serpentine form burst through the doors behind them, its deep green scales a vivid contrast to the mustard yellow underbelly and webbing of its wings.

"No. The green dragons are gone," Cordelia protested in disbelief.

"Yes, driven from the forests they once ruled by their silver brothers and sisters."

Shar leaned over the railing at Cordelia. "But they are with us, the sunless, now." The great dragon crawled towards the podium.

"You called me to your side, King of the Iron City?"

The King trembled as he raised a single finger at the adventurers. "Beryl, kill them. Kill them all!"

"Yes, gladly!" She slammed a claw into the stone, leaving a five foot indentation where Benedict had just been. Beryl hissed, swinging her tail in a sweep towards the party.

"Down!" Vix yelled, throwing both himself and Cordelia down, feeling the air move as the massive tail sailed barely overhead.

Arrows flew from Jade as she deftly dodged another slam of a claw. Sophie struck out at the dragon's underbelly, driving the sword deep into her flesh. Roaring, the dragon swung to a side, wrenching the blade free and sending both it and its owner sliding on the floor.

"You cannot leave! You will die here together!" Shar raised her hands, summoning a gale force wind that slammed into the party. They held onto the ground with all the strength they could muster. Behind the Dragon a rift opened, revealing a night sky that swirled as it was framed in fire.

"My love. Look at the King."

Zorin saw a shape emerge from the shadows behind the king, holding two gleaming daggers. Screaming with effort, Zane struck the king down in a single blow, pushing him to the side.

"You deceiver!" the king screamed, lying on the floor like an overturned turtle on its shell.

He was struggling to right himself in the mass of cloaks and capes he wore for his station. Ancient and faded, they probably were once very bold. Faded axes and hammers of long lost clans were embroidered in thin metallic thread that now lay flat and tarnished.

Zane drove his orcish blades into the stone. Sparks flew from the impact, sending Zane reeling back.

The stone was completely unharmed. Zorin was shocked.

"My love, send me to your friend." The sword spoke to Zorin from his hiding spot several paces away.

"You cannot stop us!!" Shar shrieked as she stopped the gale. "Beryl, now!"

Beryl drew in a deep breath; they had no more time to think.

"Now! Let me free you of this shadow world!"

Zorin winced slightly before casting the blade in a gleaming arc to his best friend.

"Zane! Use this!"

Zane grasped the hilt of the sword out of the air and brought it down on the stone.

The king screamed, "No!"

"Live well... My love..."

An explosion of green light erupted in the room. Sophie felt herself tumbling end over end in the growing darkness as everything went black.

CHAPTER 9

THE PROMISE

Zane coughed as he brought himself to his hands and knees in the room. At least he thought it was a room. As he looked he realized he was outside, but felt like he was inside. Inside something. Looking around, he saw his friends lying side by side in a covered cart. They all seemed to be sleeping.

There was a campfire. Sitting on a log at the campfire was an armorclad friend he hadn't seen in months.

"Keldor. Oh Keldor!"

He tried to go to him, and realized his legs wouldn't obey.

"Ugh, what the-" Zane was anchored to something. "Oh, come on. I need to go, I have to-"

"Hello, Zane."

The familiar voice sent a chill through him. It was the same voice from the prison. He looked up and saw a man in a black robe, the folds held together by a dark gray hempen rope. His face was pale and gaunt but his eyes were familiar. They blazed like two lit sapphires. Zane, realizing, spoke quickly and fervently.

"I haven't forgotten."

"I know. I know you haven't." The man stood there staring at him coldly. "Two for one, that was our deal."

He walked to the sleeping friends. Brother Benedict and his best friend Zorin. Sweet cousin Cordelia and their new comrades Vix and Skotmir. His heart warmed a little when his eyes fell on Sophie.

"I can't choose two of them just for my selfish life. Please don't make me."

The man looked back at him with blazing eyes.

"Zane, it is not their lives we trade."

He opened his left hand and in it were two coins.

"These two come from my domain. One was meant to be there, as it was her time. The other was imprisoned there by those who wish to change the order of things."

He walked to the clearing of trees and gently placed the coins on the ground. With a glimmer of the dawn's light there appeared the bodies of Eralin and Jade, lying in the tall soft grass.

Zane drew in a deep breath. "For me, right? That was the deal. I can do that for them."

The man shook his head. His hand opened, holding a single white feather.

"No, Zane. Not for you. For her." The man looked at him. "That night, over ten years ago. There were six children–"

"Wait, back home? You mean in Oallanakkhan?" Zane thought to himself. He knew everyone in that town. There were no other children.

"Wait, there were only five of us. Who is the sixth?"

The man looked at him with a growing sadness in his eyes.

"My daughter. Will you bring her back to me? Please?"

Zane nodded.

The man nodded in return, becoming very serious.

"There are rules that govern this world that we all must obey, Zane. You cannot tell anyone what you seek."

"Of course. I won't say a word."

"Good."

The man walked to him.

"One of you must stay here. It is the law, but this is different. Very different."

He placed a hand on his chin in thought.

"You destroyed the artifact you were sent to collect, I believe. That was the green heartstone. One of the five known pieces left of the great anvil of the world."

He placed a hand on Zane's shoulder. It was like ice, causing the joint to ache as it spread through his body. Zane was overcome by fear as he looked pleadingly to the man. The man smiled gently and Zane nodded, taking in a deep breath. He knew he was dying, but he felt calm now.

"Do you remember what your last thought was?"

"Yes. I thought of my promise." Zane felt his very being growing cold, frozen to the ground.

"Not your promise to me, correct?"

Sophie's voice carried in his memory.

"Will you stay with us now?"

"No, to Sophie. That I would never leave her."

The man nodded, and his cold blue eyes softened.

"She will never hurt again, never be alone, and you will always be with her."

Zane nodded, shaking. His lips were beginning to turn blue, even as they pulled back in a smile.

"Yes."

Zane felt the warmth of the man's smile as he looked at him. "And so you won't. I will keep your body here as the toll, but your spirit will be with her as one forever more."

Zane smiled through the burning pain, thinking about his life. For once, this was his choice.

And in one final moment, Zane Shieldheart was finally free.

BENEDICT GASPED DEEPLY, BRINGING AIR into his lungs with such force he rolled onto his side coughing. He was tangled in musty smelling sheets of coarse burlap. He frantically tore free of them, sputtering.

"Oh sweet Knight Lord, could it be? Is it you? Are you–"

Powerful arms pulled him free of the cart, dropping him on the ground with a thud. The midmorning sunlight tore through the leaves, blinding his eyes as he remembered the months they waited in the underworld. The tree sap was sweet smelling, mixed with the moss of the nearby stream. The man cradled Benedict across one knee, tears of joy streaming.

"Keldor?"

"Shh, calm down. Yes, it's me. Calm down, I'm right here. I'm right here, son, don't fret. I'm right here."

Benedict felt safe in his arms, and at peace, given the explosion a few moments ago with the dragon preparing to unleash its unholy breath on them all.

"How long has it been?"

"A week, Benedict. A long week. We thought you were all gone."

Benedict had been stunned a week?

"The day after the festival, we found you all in your rooms in some sort of deep dreamstate. Nonresponsive. We snuck you all out in this cart to avoid raising any suspicions."

"Wait. We? Who's we?"

"That would be me!" A halfling peered from behind Keldor with a big grin on her ruddy cheeks.

"Lorvana Birdsong, minstrel to the stars at your service!"

She took a deep energetic bow, but Benedict's head was still swimming with information.

"A week? How? We were gone for at least a month, captured by the dark elves."

"Dark elves?"

"Yes, they captured us. Keldor, the dark was menacing and we found our way to a city of iron with dark dwarves that had Zane enslaved and-"

Keldor became very quiet, his previously excited face pale.

"Benedict, I have to tell you something about your brother. "

"What? What, Keldor?" Benedict jumped up, the blood in his head rushing to his feet, sending his balance reeling.

He grabbed the edge of the cart to steady himself and looked in. To his relief, he saw his friends all beginning to stir. Cordelia, Sophie, Zorin, Vix and Skotmir. But-

"Where's Zane?"

"He took ill, my boy. One morning I heard him gasp slightly, and then he was gone."

"Gone?"

"Yes. We buried him by a tree at the Darkovnia country line on the way back to Bemil. His things are in that pack over there."

"Can I see them?" They both looked back at the cart where the voice had come from. Standing there was Sophie, one hand on the cart and the other on her forehead. Cordelia was getting out of the cart too.

"Sophie?" Cordelia weakly pleaded, trying to spare her friend's heart but knowing it was in vain.

Sophie ignored her friend, walking to the gear, steadfast in her resolution.

"Keldor, is it true? Zane is gone?" Cordelia began to well up.

Keldor took a deep breath. "Yes, lass, he's…"

"He's not gone." Sophie held the two orcish daggers of Zane's in her hands.

Deftly, she juggled them across her knuckles before letting them fly into the tree together with expert precision. A precision only Zane had ever demonstrated. Zorin stumbled to Sophie.

"What-" Zorin was awestruck.

"Zorin, do you remember the day we stole the entire tray of biscuits and fed the dogs behind old man Teller's farm?" Zorin was stunned

"We swore to never tell anyone. I-." He walked to Sophie, who smiled that crooked grin of Zane's. "It really is you."

"Yes, kind of. I can't really explain it. We are one person. Zane is always here with me. I can hear him, I feel his-" she paused, looking at Keldor. "His memories."

Sophie felt her arms, somewhat surprised that Zane's burns from so long ago were not there anymore.

"Of course. Keldor, you were a knight, weren't you?"

"I-"

"Don't lie to me! You were, weren't you?"

Keldor stood straight, slightly trembling, his beard pulled back in an uncharacteristic scowl.

"First of all, I wouldn't lie to you. There's no reason to. Yes, for what it's worth, I was a knight."

Benedict looked at him with compassion. Something terrible lay behind Keldor's kind eyes.

"I know you," Sophie began.

"Many knew of me! What does it matter?" Keldor walked away toward the grass where, in Zane's mind, the two coins had been placed.

"Served a Lord once. A kind and just lord, and I failed in my duties." Keldor was interrupted by a groan from the trees.

From behind a tree came a tall elven ranger with pale skin and a monkey on his shoulder. He stumbled past Keldor.

"Eralin!" Cordelia shouted, running to him.

"Jade is right behind me."

The name struck through Keldor's core.

"What? What did you just say?" his voice trembled out in a hoarse whisper of disbelief.

He knew someone with the nickname of Jade, but that was long ago. His heart was tightly gripped in his chest, half hoping for the impossible on a day where the impossible became reality.

He suddenly smelled elderflowers and honey.

He turned to see another elf scout. Her leather armor had thin silver work cascading in gentle knotwork around the Sword and Crown emblem at the center of her chest. His hand went to the tattered shroud at his own chest. Her fiery red hair was ablaze in the sunlight, illuminating her face and the cuff of a horse's head on one pointed ear. She looked at him with a blend of confusion and genuine recognition.

His face went white and his hands trembled. He reached toward her with tears streaming down his face.

"My love, is it really you?"

"I- I know you." Jade's voice had changed, but was more recognizable, familiar and deeply loved.

Benedict's eyes grew wide as Sophie threw her arms around an open mouthed Zorin. Cordelia covered her face, gasping as they realized who it was. Keldor fell to his knees, taking her hands to his damp cheeks.

"By the Knight's Shield, Elloveve!"

CHAPTER 10

THE SIX WINDS

Elloveve could smell the battlefield smoke from over two decades ago. The scorched grass, wood, and peat held a smell that hung in the air and clung to her memories.

They were all poised on the ridge astride six warhorses, overlooking a huge barbarian army in the green valley below. Their shouts and jeers were muffled at this distance by the gentle breeze. It was spring, she remembered.

This was her tribe, her family. All wearing armor or tunics emblazoned with the same Sword and Crown, the symbol of the Knights of the Glen.

She looked down at her leather tunic and the bow in her hand.

"I was a scout archer."

"You were one of the best."

She saw the jade bracelet on her left hand.

"You called me Jade, because of my bracelet."

Keldor nodded.

Elloveve closed her eyes and, in her memory, looked next to her at the young man in shining silver armor gilded with gold, a deep blue emblem on his chest matching his eyes.

"You were our Paladin, our beacon of the faith."

"Yes, I was."

She chuckled at something.

"What?"

"You were clean shaven back then!"

"Yes, I was that too," he said, stroking his bearded chin. She closed her eyes and welcomed the memory they shared.

There was a village in flames behind the raiders, and her keen nose filled with the iron and smoke of the slaughter below. She noticed the raven haired mage at her right turn away as they saw a few of the knights' bodies being paraded around. They were celebrating the slaughter they all came to atone for. The woman was wearing white robes, embroidered with flames at the cuff. A red and orange crown and sword, wreathed in flames, was depicted on her chest.

"She was an evoker. A fire mage."

"Yes, can you remember her name?"

She opened her eyes and thought of Cordelia, she looked so much like her. A smile crept across her face.

"Lora. Lorahana Shieldheart!"

Keldor smiled next to her, holding her hand in his. They were sitting next to the stream by themselves, the others giving them time to reunite. Keldor needed to help her remember her past, before everyone else tried sharing stories to jog her memory.

"Yes. She wasn't a Shieldheart yet, but she might as well have been. Do you see our brother next to her? He had a mustache. Can you tell me his name?"

She closed her eyes to focus.

On the other side of Lorahana was a strong man. His blonde hair hung to the shoulder and a long mustache was beginning to form on his upper lip, swooping down from the corners of his mouth to his chin. His armor was intricately carved and stamped with symbols of the order. He was a decorated warrior, for being so young. He drew his longsword at his side.

"They will pay on this day. I swear it."

His unmistakable booming voice rang out from his huge chest.

"Erebus. Erebus Shieldheart."

"Yes."

"My memory is hazy, I can't seem to remember the others."

"No, no I'm sure you can. Close your eyes, Elloveve. Hear them. Hear them, and remember."

"IT IS JUST US, THEN?" a knight stated plainly, turning her head to the black haired leader. Her dirty blonde hair hung gently to the shoulder, cut in a short style to ensure mobility in the heavy plate on her torso. It was a style all but Jade and Lorahana were wearing. The knight carried a polearm with a swooping blade at one end. "It was a glaive," Elloveve remembered. A glaive of the winds.

"Her name was Elona."

"Elona, you are correct." Keldor smiled gently, remembering the old friend. Her smile, eyes and honey blonde hair were so much like her son, Zane. "Who else do you see?"

Elloveve looked in her mind's memory toward a black haired man at the front who was surveying the battleground carefully. Spun obsidian black hair, like Benedict's in fact, was worn in a similar style along with a close cropped beard.

"Lucilius. Lucilius was his name."

She saw Lucilius turn to Elona to answer, the venom in his voice barely hidden behind his stoic stance.

"Yes, Bemil refuses to acknowledge this threat to our people. It is now up to us to defend Garnet Keep."

"Good, I like it that way. Now we do it our way.." she responded, gripping her glaive tightly with a smile.

"As do I, my sister." The raven haired mage touched the tattoo of the sword on her arm, a blade of pure orange flame leaping to her hand.

"I agree, less bureaucracy to deal with," Erebus stated. "Keldor, what say you, old friend?"

"Truly, the Knight Lord is with us this day," a young Keldor replied, smiling at Elloveve.

"May we ride like the wind!" Elloveve drew her bow and nocked an arrow. She felt the soft white and black hawk's feather fletching pass between her fingers as it gently snapped to the bowstring. Holding the arrow to the bow with one hand, she passed the oiled leather reins of her horse back into her right. She smiled at her preparation. She was ready.

"We shall." Lucilius smiled before gripping the reins tightly in his left hand, drawing a longsword with his right. Holding it aloft he cried, "To glory!"

As one force, the six winds rode not only into battle that day, but into songs and legends. They liberated that town and led the army to push back the bandits away from the former stronghold of Garnet Keep. This was the first of a series of battles, ending with the Battle of the Cheerless Swamp, where these bandit clans were believed to have scattered, leaving the land of Trull forever.

The soft babbling sound of the stream brought Elloveve's mind to the present. The smell of the raspberries along the bank and sweet birch sap mingled with the cooking fire back at camp.

"I remembered!"

Elloveve threw her arms around Keldor, who squeezed her tight in his arms. He was happy that she had remembered herself, though he was hesitant and worried about her remembering too much. A lump filled his chest as his own memories started to surface, unpleasant ones.

"Yes, yes you did, sweet Elloveve."

He groaned slightly, standing from sitting on the log for so long. The blood rushed to his armored legs and feet. His armor was blackened with soot and dirt, she thought. Nothing like her memory of him and his gleaming shine.

"Come, let's join the group. I'm sure they have tales to spin as well."

He smelled the air. "Not to mention, I am getting a bit hungry!" he said, smiling. Taking her hand, he led her back to the savory smell of the venison, carrots, parsnips and potatoes slow-cooking in the iron pot on the fire.

ZORIN WAS TAKING HIS TURN, talking about growing up in Port L' For. Elloveve laughed as she remembered their good times.

"So then she throws the spoon at me, knocking over the glass vase she was telling me to stay away from!"

Everyone was laughing. It was so good to see everyone together. Cordelia sat next to her, Elloveve's arms wrapped around her long lost friend.

Elloveve chuckled before a wave of memory hit her.

"Oh, wait." Everyone went silent.

"What is it?" Cordelia asked.

"I remember being on the roof, surrounded by fire." Sophie tensed, remembering the escape from Port L'For. Elloveve shook her head slightly and smiled at Sophie, clasping her hand in reassurance.

"But I remember you all escaped, and I was so relieved."

They all nodded and Benedict rose to put a hand of comfort on her shoulder when he saw a familiar glint of metal around Eralin's neck. He stopped and stared, wide eyed.

It was a dragon turtle.

It had the same exact design as the one adorning the sword of Lord Pallus, only this one had icey blue eyes.

"Where did you get that?" He stood, trembling.

"This? I've had it for as long as I can remember. Why?" Eralin clutched it as he coolly responded.

Keldor rose. "What is it, Benedict?" He paused. "This is an interesting design." He gestured for permission to examine it further. Eralin stood, his huge seven foot frame dwarfing even the tall Keldor, and passed it to him.

"Mithril silver. Impressive." He turned it and saw the forge mark, a reversed E and S entwined.

His eyes grew wide.

Benedict, noticing Keldor's reaction, pointed at it. "That's my father's mark."

Keldor stared at Benedict in shock. "Wait, your father had a mark like this?"

He gripped Benedict's shoulder tightly, not noticing the pressure of his grip. "Tell me, and tell me the truth! Was his mark like this, only reversed as if in a mirror?" Keldor was shaking his hands, gripping Benedict's tunic like a vice. If the young man didn't know better, he would have felt a bit threatened.

"Yes. Why?"

Keldor froze. His brow furrowed, his gentle eyes welling with tears.

"My-" He fell to his knees in racking sobs, twenty years of torment hitting him all at once. He quickly wiped a hand across his eyes. "I should have known you."

Benedict was stunned. Keldor rose and turned his back to Benedict, staring at Elloveve.

"Elloveve, do you remember that night?" Keldor began, as he looked down at his blackened gauntlets. Balling his hands into fists, he continued.

"For his expert leadership over the next months' campaign, Lucilius was named the Lord Protector of Garnet Keep. They soon settled behind the ancient granite walls.

"All six of us continued to work in harmony with each other. While Lucilius governed wisely and justly from the meeting halls, Elona the Fair helped to build the gardens and tend to the great tree in the center courtyard. Erebus set up a blacksmith shop with his now-wife, Lorahana, who was a wonderful seamstress.

"Elloveve, you were teaching the people how to hunt the forests and fish the lake behind the keep. I taught the word of the Knightlord and his righteous justice from the chapel.

"Soon, Lucilius and Elona married and had a first boy. He was blonde, and a thrill seeker. Rather reckless, as I remember, like his mother. A few years went by and Elloveve and I became fond of each other, but my vows would never allow me to love or take a wife. But I tell you all, I loved her. Lucilius and Elona had another son, dark haired like his father. Quiet, reserved. Never cried, really. Shortly thereafter, Lorahana gave Erebus the light of his life, a daughter.

"I became jealous. Angry. I was cursed with this feeling in my soul. It was a longing, like none I had felt before or since.

"One night I left my post and went to the stables to ponder and pray. I prayed for guidance, or deliverance. I cursed myself and all around me when I challenged the law of my order, saying that these feelings were natural, I shouldn't have to run from them. Why couldn't we be happy too?

"That night, a bandit raided the keep, sneaking past my abandoned post. Humans and orcs, likely remnants of those bandits we thought vanquished, came for vengeance. They set fire to the gardens and screams rang out in the night. People, terrified, ran from the keep that no longer protected them.

"The walls were ablaze. I saw Elona fighting them with her great glaive spinning. Before I could reach her, she dove into the building's fire, disappearing in the blaze. Lucilius was on the ground clutching his side, a mortal wound's blood pouring between his fingers.

'Keldor, my old friend-' Lucilius groaned. His eyes bored into mine with an unequaled compassion as if he could hear the cries of anguish that tore at my heart.

'I have failed you, my lord! I-' I gripped his hand, trembling. I was fearing what was to come and knowing I couldn't stop it. I was powerless as I watched my lord fade.

'Shh, not now, dear friend. Whatever you did, I forgive you. Now it's my turn to tell you, that which you told me many times, Keldor. May the Knight and Maiden watch you now.'

"A deep breath followed as he grew quiet. His eyes were bright, but now a growing emptiness was filling them. I couldn't accept that he was gone, I couldn't let him go. 'My Lord? Lucilius? Please- don't leave me,' I pleaded with him. Tears blurred my vision as I squeezed them shut, hoping for this nightmare to end. A nightmare I brought upon us all.

"I lost everything at that moment. My lord, my faith and my mind. I drew my sword and dove into the battle with a vengeance. I cut everything down I could find that wasn't one of our people.

"Their cries fueled my hatred and anger. After what seemed an eternity we were overrun and, even in my state, I knew it was time to flee. I lost my Elloveve, my friends and my home. I mounted my horse's back and rode into the night, down the high stone bridge and the mountain path, never to return to Garnet Keep again.

"My shame knew no bounds. I left the knighthood and spent the last twenty years as a mercenary and sword for hire. Until now."

Keldor rose and stood in front of the stunned group. Taking a powerful stride, he made his way to a wide eyed Benedict. His face was now resolute and filled with a renewed purpose. Drawing his great sword he again kneeled, but this time before the young man.

"I pledge to you Benedict, son of Lucilius and Steward of Garnet Keep, that you will regain your home and your birthright."

EPILOGUE

The sound of black and red boots echoed as the man ascended the cold, black stone steps. His hands unconsciously flexed his forearms, pulsing under the strain. He pulled his bright orange hair back from his dark face, red eyes glowing like embers.

"You called me?" He almost spat it out. He was no servant.

"Yes, make the troops ready, we will begin our march tomorrow. In two week's time we should reach the Celestine Tower in the center of the Great Glen valley." Lord Pallus stood, clasping his hand around the dragon turtle pommel of his great sword, its red eyes twinkling.

"Yes. I will do as you wish." The red haired man turned to walk away.

"One more thing," Lord Pallus sneered. "The blue dragons will lead the first sorties." Pallus took some delight in seeing the look of disappointment on his servant's face.

"Fine."

"We will be victorious! Won't we, Fury?"

Fury growled deeply as he turned on his heel to descend the stairs, the dragon's blood in his veins pulsing with anger. Anger which was barely contained by this magically human facade as he stepped on the mirrored black of the steps. Each step, he noticed, had a worn smooth spot for the foot that reflected the light. Black volcanic glass. He knew this stone well from his homeland far across the sea to the east, in the jagged mountains in the land of Bloodwood.

After stepping a few yards from the base of the stairs, Fury slammed an open palm against the iron plate that held an ornate handle. A shock rattled his elbow and shoulder that held a sweet painful reminder of the force of his blow. He felt the cold air and soft pine trees as the moon spilled her light on his body. He stepped away from the black stone of the fortress behind him, seeking a clearing.

Once clear of the walls of the Obsidian Fortress, he erupted into the full glory of his true form. Wings sprung out as he grew to an enormous size against the starry sky. Blood red scales and a mustard yellow underbelly topped by a familiar reptilian maw threatened as the guards outside took a step back in awe. Fury shook his scales clear of any dust as a deep rumble rolled from his throat.

Throwing his head back, the red dragon breathed white hot fire of unbridled rage into the cold night sky, and his army answered.

ACKNOWLEDGEMENTS

I have always loved Tabletop Role-Playing games since I was first exposed in the second grade. I was six or seven years old and my mother bought me the "Red Box" right in the middle of the "Satanic Panic". I remember some of the other moms talking to her, being worried for my safety. Instead of jumping on the hype train she took a moment and just asked the question.

"Have you ever watched it?"

None of them could provide an answer and grew very quiet. She smiled and told them something that will always ring in my ears. I was in another room at the time quietly playing something on the *Atari 2600*. For some reason I want to think I was trying to figure out *Empire Strikes Back* which was, like many of those games, not clear on what you were supposed to do.

"I see nothing wrong with Michael fighting demons with all that math."

I have never stopped smiling at this comment. Soon we were staying in during lunch at school to play our game. We became fascinated by the books and modules and being scared of the word Advanced we thought we could just use the Basic and Advanced rules wherever we want. So our ruleset was basic but we would borrow modules from the older brothers of our group.

As elementary school moved on I found *Teenage Mutant Ninja Turtles and Other Strangeness* but I had lost any chance of feeling like I belonged as I lost my friends along the way. I would sit in my room and make characters. Characters that only sprang to life in my head, a mutant boar and crocodile, driving a van with a gun turret on top Mad Max style. Or a sloth in a trenchcoat like Dick Tracy out solving crime behind the backs of the police.

Entering Junior High was, for many kids, a tough time. I retained my belief I was at the bottom of the barrel socially. As they say, the cruel can sense a victim. I had my hair set on fire, picked on, outcast from groups, last to get picked, laughed at and even was given the nickname of "Dumpster". That one looking back can make me laugh a little. My last name was modified to "Trashley" first and then "Dumpster".

I hung with the hoods and metalheads, though I was treated pretty awful until there was my time to shine. I grew up playing music in a musical family. I loved experimenting with all kinds of instruments and though I wasn't a "Band" kid I wanted to be a rockstar. So we were in the Guitar Lab class all strumming away on some basic chords when the teacher, Mr. Rulli, had each one of us do a little riff or solo. I was pleased when I shocked the room. All the sudden I was joining garage bands and building a dream.

In High School I was still playing in bands but more importantly I fell back into playing *Dungeons & Dragons, RIFTS, Vampire the Masquerade, Heroes Unlimited* and *Call of Cthulhu* with my best friends. Having some of the best times we were all music and drama lovers as well.

Fast forward through the river of time over two decades when for better or worse I realized I in many ways became a bully in my own way, shaped and molded by society but that doesn't absolve me of it, but that was the end of the music dream.

ACKNOWLEDGEMENTS

Over time I fell into the inky darkness of depression.

Brian Dowling, who plays Benedict Shieldheart, invited me to see the play *She Kills Monsters* with another good friend, Chad Patten. It resonated with me heavily to where I realized I hadn't played a roleplaying game in years and I really missed it. We soon built our group, our games and started weaving them all together and the rest is in the story presented to you in this book.

The players that made this possible by sharing their lives and stories with me are absolutely amazing and I will forever be grateful that we shared the same table many times. Storm S Cone (Sophie/Zane/Hazel/Zevitar Fallowspire), Joleen Fresquez (Cordelia Shieldheart/Sprig/Helena/ Isenatha), Colten Janssen (Skotmir Flintgrog/Yudoris/Reinold), Brian Dowling (Benedict Shieldheart/MyCroft/Arseris), Jordan Thompson (Elalin), Kara Danvers (Jade/Lorvana Birdsong), Sarah Jenkins (Sophie/Zane), Barret Giant (Vash Silverbrand/Saza), Corey Pfautsch (Ozmeros), Hayley Muñoz (Emerie), Laney Flannigan (Azaela), Becky Atchley (Una), JD Rose (Dabria/Kamron/Virion), Phil Brown (Vix), Daniel Nichols (Vix/Avicenna), Rori Christenson (Izzy), Chelsea Hunninghake (Gin), and of course Cody Miller (Zorin/Cypress) who I always drag into any of my projects.

As you have now likely found, our story is one that covers several different perspectives and that is the direct result of its birth during a roleplaying game. Like any art, theater and acting draws from one's soul and it often proves impossible to prevent the world around us from shaping it in some way. Our stories are no exception.

The story of Sophie and Zane is the story of someone seeking to find their true self within and finding how they can express it publicly and proudly. The story of Cordelia is one where someone who had been given so many bad experiences growing up can look back, face them and have the courage to walk away stronger. The story of Benedict is one that honor is not in one's appearance or a facade that we put on like the clothes we wear or a new haircut, but in one's actions towards others. Zorin faces many things in this story but one of the most important is that he finds the greatest power when he stops doubting himself. When Zorin finally stops following and starts realizing he can be followed.

This is just a sample of how those players interfaced with their characters and brought them to life. Being a part of their journey as well as my own has been the greatest honor and I will forever love these friends who brought me such joy.

I wrote the first audio episode partially as a joke because the story was getting so complex I needed to channel it somewhere for all of us to keep track of and just writing down the notes was too cumbersome. Posting it to social media just for kicks resulted in a few people outside our group suggesting we do a podcast. Colten encouraged me to get into reading audiobooks and doing more voice work and soon that lost creative outlet came back. Storm started drawing and painting the characters in the story and I started writing music again specifically for our show.

I will elaborate more in the future, but during this time and the story contained in this book, we had a flood of unexpected support from other creators who helped lend their voices to make this possible. A heartfelt thank you to these voice actors, who if you listen to the podcast as well you can hear their voices in the first two seasons:

Laura Jerdak (Lorahana Shieldheart), Jesse Jerdak (Erebus Shieldheart), Matthew Bianchi (Bosun, Purser, Jolith, other extras and Dekkion the Dark Cleric), Ben Corley (Lucilius Kettlebane, Guard, Navigator and others), Ian Wilkinson (Lord Pallus), Jesse Davis (Young Benedict Shieldheart), Gryffn Foote (Young Zorin),

Jessica Atchley (Elloveve Hawklight), Laura Atchley (Young Kartilaan), Arianna Atchley (Young Cordelia Shieldheart), Sabrina Patten (Young Sophie), Lesley Beckmann (Elona the Fair and Kiri), Adam Kidjoaka (Avar), Sam Weigel (Squire of Vindalas the Golden, Pike), Piper Cleaveland (Spindle, Squib, Beryl), Brad Zimmerman (Derry Goldleaf), Nikki Richardson (Fera Ironstone, Assassin), Chris Ponds (The Dragon Turtle), Cheyenne Bramwell (Librarian), Casey Kennedy (Kobold, minotaur), Scott C. Brown (Elias Silvertongue, Chalkos) Michael; J. Rigg (Duke of Ellington), Corbin Miller (Ellington Guard, Kegog the bartender), Aicilla Lewis (Shae Silverbrand), Bridgett Farruggia (Mistress Valya), Stephen Farruggia (Janick), Phill Usher (The Stranger), Steph Dewey (Greta the Ettin) Bhavneet Athwal (Trader), Brian Penaloza (Cultist leader) and Trevor Rupe (Dwarven guard).

I would also like to acknowledge our patreon supporters who have made this possible by supporting us along the way: Amelia Emberwing, Derek Kunz, Ryan Donnelly, Kenneth Hunt, Zachary Auld, Jane V Hunt, Michael Schofield, John Odell, Rori Christenson, Sondra Raby, Tony Folmar and Colin Holm.

We have played this game for almost a decade and over that time have had over six separate campaigns that weave between each other and this main storyline to build our universe. This couldn't have been possible without the help of Daniel Nichols, my partner with Good Ham Productions. He has pushed me so much further than I thought possible and helped weave our world of Avinol with his world in the *Chronicles of Eridul*. As these stories progress we hope you enjoy all the bridges that span our worlds we have built together.

Finally many, many thanks to Chelsey Hunninghake and Susan Thomas for the hours of tedious work reading, proofing and editing this book. Making sure what I wrote makes sense and was as good of a story as I hoped it could be.

The campaigns may have happened at different points in the timeline, with different characters but this book series aims to bring those stories together into one epic.

The podcast audio drama is a great story on its own, and also my new outlet into creating music again but this book contains so much more that couldn't be put in that show.

I'm happy to say the second book is in the works. My goal is soon you can join me again dear adventurers as we walk with honorable Benedict, strong Sophie, cunning Zorin and brave Cordelia in our world.

Most importantly however…remember the oath!

ABOUT THE AUTHOR

Born in Casper, Wyoming, Mike Atchley is a passionate actor, musician, artist, and author. He is most known as the narrator and producer of Dice Tower Theatre from Good Ham Productions and his voice has appeared in other audio works such as *Fate of Isen, Aethuran Dark Saga, Ninth World Journal, Chronicles of Eridul* and others.

His experience as an audio engineer on recordings, film and live performances has extended for over 30 years both DIY and as a professional. As a musician and foley artist he prefers to combine these elements as a creator of soundscape and underscoring and build an immersive audio experience. Mike believes in promoting the audio community both as a supporter and as a contributor; and share it with those who may have never experienced audio adventures.

A contributor to a live immersive theater experience called *"Avistrum,"* for many years he loves working with children and helping them to fall into the depths of their imagination.

Mike resides in Aurora, Colorado with his wife Jessica, daughter Arianna and their loving dog Freya. They love to enjoy games together as well as gardening. He loves berries, butterflies and smoking meats when not imagining himself as a pirate during the age of sail.

ABOUT THE PODCAST

This novel is the first in *The Chronicles of Avinol* series that follows and supplements the award winning audio fiction podcast "Dice Tower Theatre presents Dawn of Dragons". Set in a shared world with *The Chronicles of Eridul.*

Dice Tower Theatre presents Dawn of Dragons

"A clean, quality audio fantasy epic where swords and those behind them can change the fate of their world. A land where dragons speak, magic lives and wishes come true.

Young heroes bound in love and kinship are forced on a quest to discover the truth behind the magic of dragons, and seek those that stole it before their world itself is destroyed by the growing power of the Dark Army.

Originally created as a place to record the events of a collaborative roleplaying game, Dice Tower Theatre grew into a place where the players could discover themselves in a world where dragons speak, magic lives and wishes come true.

Raised by former knights in hiding, they have grown up taking on different skills, each one unique and valuable to each other. Not only bonded by use of magic or mastery of a sword, they are also tied to a great destiny - a destiny foretold in lost tomes they have yet to discover. Their world is cloaked in a great shadow that is spreading like a sickness that they seek to overcome.

When their home town of OallEnAkhan is destroyed by Lord Pallus (Zorin's father), young Cordelia - the fire mage, aspiring knight Benedict, bright-eyed mariner Zorin, and the deadly swordmaster Sophie fall under the tutelage of Elloveve Hawklight- a secretive yet legendary elven scout archer. Lord Pallus's ark army grows increasingly more powerful with the addition of a cruel dark cleric serving an evil queen of death along with her legions of dragons.

Finding themselves a decade older, escaping the ashes of yet another lost home, the group sets out to find passage across The Great Sea to the Ivory Library. Seeking knowledge within its infinite halls guarded by the ancient order of Stone Monks, Cordelia finds the answer. They must find the dragons of virtue and seek their help to turn the tide. All knowledge has its price though, and Cordelia must pay for it by recording her own story while reliving the worst night of her life all over again.

This is what takes place in just the first of several seasons of this clean, family-friendly, fantasy epic. Now, it has now grown to a production including over 80 voice actors, original scoring and sound design by the game master himself, resulting in several hours of quality entertainment. Many of the echoes of life's struggles came out organically at the table between the players as friends and were captured in the story. Those struggles come with lessons, and overall those lessons are to be a better person, both to those around them as well as themselves.

AWARDS

- 2023 Melbourne Webfest -
  WINNER *Best Sound Design in an Actual Play*

- 2023 Baltimore Web Fest -
  WINNER *Best Fantasy Audio Director - Mike Atchley*

- 2023 Baltimore Web Fest -
  WINNER *Best Fantasy Audio Fiction*

- 2023 Baltimore Web Fest -
  WINNER *Best Sound Design in an Audio Fiction*

- 2023 SENSEI Tokyo Film Fest -
  WINNER *Best Podcast*

- 2023 Film Revolution Montreal Fest -
  WINNER *Best Podcast*

- 2023 Cinesis Independent FilmFest -
  WINNER *Best Podcast*

- 2023 Climax Madrid FilmFest -
  WINNER *Best Podcast*

- 2023 Venus Community Awards (Turkey) -
  WINNER

- 2023 Nocturna Online Brooklyn Film Festival-
  WINNER *Best Podcast*

- 2022 NJ WebFest (USA) -
  WINNER: *Outstanding Fantasy* in Narrative Fiction Podcast

- 2022 LA WebFest (USA) -
  WINNER: *Best Sci-Fi Fantasy Podcast*

- 2022 Beyond the Curve WebFest (Paris,France) -
  WINNER *Best Audio Drama*

- 2022 4th Dimension Independent Film Festival (Bali) -
  WINNER *Best Audio Drama*

- 2022 Swedish International Film Festival -
  WINNER *Best Podcast*

- 2022 Asia Web Awards -
  WINNER *Best Podcast*

CONTACT:

Mike Atchley
DM@DiceTowerTheatre.com

- Twitter: @DiceTowrTheatre
- Instagram: @dicetowertheatre
- TikTok: @dicetowertheatre
- Facebook: @dicetowertheatre
- Website: https://goodhamproductions.com

JADE TEMPLE

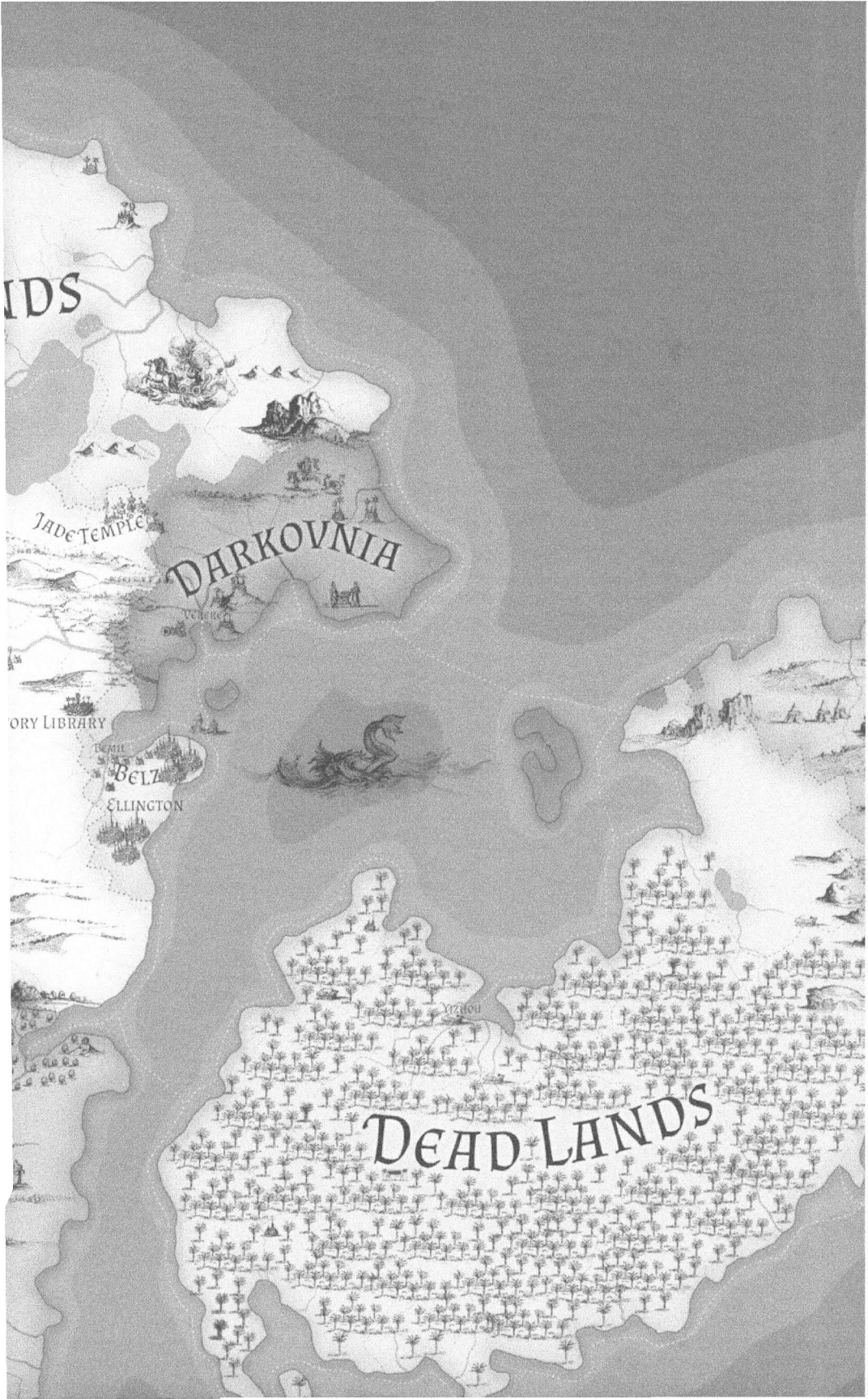

DARKOVNIA

ORY LIBRARY

BELZ
ELLINGTON

DEAD LANDS

Milton Keynes UK
Ingram Content Group UK Ltd.
UKHW030837021124
450589UK00006B/728